What the Small Gray Visitor Said

What the Small Gray Visitor Said

Stephanie C. Fox, J.D.

QueenBeeEdit
Bloomfield, Connecticut, U.S.A.

Library of Congress Cataloging-in-Publication Data
Name: Fox, Stephanie C., author.
Title: What the Small Gray Visitor Said / Stephanie C. Fox.
Description: Connecticut: QueenBeeEdit Books, [2020].
Identifiers: ISBN 978-1-7343743-0-8 (paperback)
Subjects: 1. Science fiction—Fiction. 2. Science fiction –
Alien Contact—Fiction. 3. Nature and the Environment—
Fiction.

www.queenbeeedit.com

Cover design by Stephanie C. Fox
Cover art by William J. Studenc
Printed in the United States of America

This book is dedicated to the virologists and other research scientists, for their efforts to find a cure for the coronavirus.

We should listen to scientists.

Table of Contents

Stranded

They were collecting plants in various spots around the crop field when they heard sounds from the south.

They were aliens who had ventured across the galaxy from the vicinity of the Owl Nebula by phasing out of their quadrant and into that of Earth's.

Now they were on a field in rural Connecticut, in the town of Simsbury, near its border with the town of Avon.

Two of them were males, and they were fairly close to the ship, which hovered twenty feet above the ground. Its lights weren't very bright; just a few whitish glows around the edge of the ovate-shaped craft. They were studying the soil.

The third, a female, was well south, near a narrow line of trees. It curved to the right, further south, diagonally toward the mountain. Another crop field extended into the triangular area in front of those trees. She would look at that next, she decided.

Right now, she was interested in the strawberry plants, and studying it with her scanner, a small, narrow, oval device that fit into the palm of her hand.

It was a nice night. They had waited until almost what the humans here thought of as 2 o'clock in the morning. The idea was that no one other than them would be out and about at this hour.

It was spring, and the trees were covered with leaves.

The female botanist was enjoying this excursion.

She liked to go out and collect new plants, especially if they were meant for food, so that she could then take them back to her laboratory on the ship, study them, and see what potential they possessed for adaptation aboard spacecraft and on her home planet.

They needed more plants like that on her planet.

The Earth's ecosystem was at the point that it had suffered terrible damage due to overuse of its resources for so long that, by the time technology caught up with that damage to the point of being able to remediate it, far too little would be recoverable.

As a result, their planet would not support the billions that it was forced to anymore. This had happened on the alien's planet, too, and then...there had been terrible times.

Now, scientists like this team worked to remediate their ecosystem by adapting species from other planets that had not – as yet – lost viable, healthy ecosystems of their own.

Planets such as Earth still had functioning pollinators such as bees and butterflies, and fruit-bearing plants such as raspberry bushes and strawberry plants.

The botanist wondered how much longer that would be true. Part of her job was to collect whatever food-producing plants she could while it was still true.

She wished she could look at flowering plants also, but they only had so much time, and it was always at night.

Back to work...

She had just uprooted a beautiful strawberry plant, and was about to slice a sample into her bag, when they heard the sounds of clumsy, large humans crashing through the trees, running across a grassy area, straight toward the crop field.

The others, who were much closer to the ship, ran to a spot directly under it, hit buttons on their signalling devices, and disappeared in a short flash, beamed up.

She wasn't going to make it over there in time.

The ship vanished, cloaked, and she felt it move away from the area at light speed, even though it was invisible.

She could sense whether or not her people were close.

They were gone now – far away.

They had had no choice but to leave.

The botanist hid behind one of the trees as two large, male humans in dark clothing rushed onto the field with bright flashlights, which they were holding clutched against their handguns.

With a gulp of horror, she remembered that in this country, humans were allowed to own all sorts of weapons, with or without a background check. It varied from state to state.

A moment later, however, she felt slightly calmer.

What the Small Gray Visitor Said

Her telepathy was heightened out of a sense of self-preservation. She realized that these men were off-duty police officers, and that they had seen her ship's lights from their shooting range.

The range was past the field, south through the trees, across a grassy area, and past another narrow thicket of trees.

What were they doing here at this hour?!

Oh…one of them had forgotten his wallet, and they had come back for it. Then they had seen the light from the alien ship and come to investigate.

She wondered what a wallet looked like up close.

She knew it was important, and that humans carried identity documents and money in them.

Life was complicated for humans.

No telepathy, and they used money.

She did her best to stay calm.

Humans, she knew, possessed a sort of low-level telepathy, and if she didn't stay calm, or if she stared too steadily at them, they would sense her presence.

The last thing she needed or wanted was to be found by police officers, no matter the circumstances.

She was dressed innocuously enough, in pale blue pants and a shirt, which were plain, and her flyaway, straight hair curved around her round head, framing her face with its huge eyes, small mouth, and long, thin nose.

But her head was a bit larger and rounder than a human head, and, slung over her bag was her gray environmental suit with its huge, dark, almond-shaped, eye-pieces, which were tinted to compensate for bright lights. Her huge eyes made it easier for her to see detail in the dark.

The suits had been inconvenient to wear, so they had taken them off and pushed them through their bag-straps, off to one side, available, but out of their way.

It wasn't necessary to wear them.

The scientists who had preceded them over the past century had worked to develop their species' immunity to the

3

pathogens of Earth's ecosystems. As the Earth's permafrost layer thawed, however, they would have to update their efforts.

It was all so that botanists could then work unimpeded to find, consider, and collect plants, which then might be used as food for their species.

The project was going well.

Liquid and gelatin forms of berries, apples, pears, and other such plant products were now regularly consumed on their home planet. Half a billion of her people existed, and they were fed in reasonable comfort, with sufficient nutrition, but there was always room for improvement.

Variety in any diet is not only desirable, but healthy.

Hence the reason for this risky excursion.

The alien botanist forced herself to breathe calmly and wait the humans out.

She would call her ship as soon as they decided that there was nothing here worthy of their time and attention, her colleagues would come back and beam her up, and she would be gone, with her strawberry plant.

At least, that was her hope.

The human men walked around the crop field for a couple of minutes, listening intently, staring into the distance. Fortunately, they didn't look in her direction.

After another minute or so, the men's posture changed.

Their shoulders dropped, they looked at each other, they holstered their weapons, and they actually laughed.

"There's nothing out here!" one of them said.

"We must have imagined it," his companion replied.

"Yeah…just as well. We'd get laughed at so bad back at the station if we came back with an alien sighting story."

His friend grinned. "That's all just conspiracy theory crap anyway."

"Uh-huh."

They walked back across the field, through the narrow line of trees about fifteen feet away from her, and on across the grassy area to the next thicket of trees, through that, and over to the car that was parked in the lot there.

What the Small Gray Visitor Said

She watched as they got into the car, put on their seat belts, turned on the ignition, turned on the lights, and drove away. The car turned right out of the lot, heading north. It was going to go right past the tree she was hiding behind!

She moved around to the other side of it and crouched behind the brush, watching until they were gone, off down road. The intersection at the northwest corner of the field offered two options – left or right. There was a place that went straight, but that led only to a huge sycamore tree.

She reminded herself not to stare as the vehicle went past her hiding place.

The car turned left and disappeared from view.

She breathed out and stood up again.

She wasn't very tall, but just the same, hiding had seemed like a wise move.

Now she stretched a bit, realizing that she had been holding her breath for much of the past several minutes.

She moved back to the edge of the field, pressed the button on her signalling device, and waited.

Nothing.

She couldn't sense the presence nearby of anyone other than sleeping humans in the distance.

Now what?!

She was stranded on an alien planet.

It was night, she was in a living ecosystem, with all sorts of toxic flora such as poison ivy, which even (most) humans lacked immunity to, dangerous, large, wild fauna such as coyotes, bobcats, bears, and even turkeys, which were really dinosaurs that had survived the impact of the asteroid that had caused this planet's 5th mass extinction event.

It was now in the midst of its 6th.

That was why she was stranded here, she reminded to herself: because scientists such as herself hoped to acquire as many important plants before it was too late.

This was not all for nothing.

They couldn't save the humans from their own short-sightedness any more than they had been able to save themselves from their own.

All they could do now was warn a random, few humans, as the occasion arose, and work to recover their own world's ecological health. They weren't even supposed to warn them officially. They were supposed to operate in secret.

Humans were dangerous, after all.

For the immediate future, however, the alien botanist had to figure out how she was going to survive until she could go back among her own people.

She couldn't sleep out here.

She couldn't even stay where she was.

She couldn't just stand out in plain sight, away from that line of trees, on the crop field, until another human drove by.

She had no intention of looking for other plants on that other section of the crop field. Not now that she was stuck here. Who knew what else could go wrong?!

She turned and walked back to the trees, and walked east, toward the mountain.

It was getting cooler, so she wanted to keep moving.

She could sense humans sleeping to her left, past the crop field, and mentally reviewed the land as she had seen it from above, when they were plotting where to land.

A horse farm was over there. She could sense not only humans sleeping but horses as well.

She decided not to go that way.

There was nothing beyond the horse farm but another road with fast-moving cars that went over and down from the mountain, and simply walking that way would mean going out into the open. She wasn't about to go where she would be easily seen.

Not yet, anyway.

Not while she still held out hope of being picked up.

She moved closer to the mountain, into the trees, with her scanner out.

She was scanning for toxic plants.

Fortunately, she didn't encounter any.

It had to be luck.

She had heard of luck often enough as a human concept by monitoring their communications and watching what they called movies and television shows.

It wasn't very scientific, but there was definitely something to the concept.

She walked around the perimeter of that other crop field, staying close to the trees, moving slightly farther south as she did so, heading for the wooded area.

As she approached the woods, she realized that it was not realistic to go up the mountain to hide.

Also, a neighborhood of human housing was just beyond what looked, from the ground, like a thick, wooded area. She could sense them, house-pets and all.

She couldn't go north, so she went south, just to keep moving and to avoid deciding what to do next.

She could manage without sleep for at least a full day's cycle, even if it meant hiding during the bright hours.

In her present predicament, however, she discounted – or perhaps forgot – that she had already been awake that long. It happened whenever she found her work intensely engaging. And that happened whenever she was anticipating an excursion to gather a plant that she had wanted for a while.

She had really wanted a strawberry plant.

She walked just inside the wooded area and kept moving, thinking, but not reaching any decision.

She glanced to her right and realized that she was passing the back of the property that included the police shooting range.

Its outside lights were on, but no one was there.

Good.

She kept walking, picking her way carefully through the edge of the woods.

She was about halfway through her life-cycle, which was roughly one hundred and eighty years. She was still quite strong and healthy; she should be okay until she could get back.

She told herself that she would get back before long.

Meanwhile, she found herself passing another grassy area, one with poles that had very small, numbered flags on them, which were stuck in the ground on areas with even shorter grass, areas that had odd, randomly ovate shapes.

The shapes reminded her of the shape of her ship just a little.

She pushed that thought from her mind and kept going.

As she walked, she realized that what she was walked past was a golf course. She had watched a movie with a plot that involved a golf course, and a game on it that had lasted for a couple of days.

At the edge of it, she noticed a tall, white structure that seemed to rise out of the ground in sections, ending in a round piece at the top. She was too distracted to think about that.

After the golf course, she came to more woods.

There were human houses through these woods, too, but fewer of them. They were a bit larger than the other ones, and more spread out.

She was getting tired, and decided that it was because she had been so anxious about being left behind and on her own. That had used up a lot of energy that she couldn't afford to lose, but there was nothing she could do about that.

Being a member of a technologically advanced species was not a guarantee that one would never, ever lose control of one's situation, after all.

She walked around this human settlement, taking note of the houses in it.

All were similar in architectural style.

McMansions, she thought they were called.

These were fairly attractive, if somewhat lacking in individuality.

On closer inspection, she began to notice that each family had added little touches here and there, details that made each house more easily distinguishable from the next by more than just its number.

What the Small Gray Visitor Said

At one point, as she cased the perimeter of an intersection, she saw a street sign: Tiger Lily Lane.

Too close to the street, she thought to herself, and moved back into the trees.

She walked back into the brush at the back yard of the nearest house, and moved toward the mountain. She didn't want to go near the main road. Nod Road, it was called, she remembered from her research before leaving the ship.

No, she wasn't going that way.

Cars still went by, even in the middle of the night.

She had seen and heard a few more of them while she was passing the golf course.

She noticed that the back yards she was skirting curved around to the southeast.

She looked around to the right, through the gardens, between the houses.

A circular area of asphalt ran up to the last house on the street, which was in the center. Number 14, it said.

Its exterior was made of a gray stone, complete with a chimney. Humans shouldn't be burning wood, she thought, but brush collected from the wooded areas was acceptable. Collecting it would prevent forest fires if the climate got too dry and hot.

What was the matter with her?! She was musing too much about sustainability when she ought to be figuring out what to do to survive until she could be picked up.

But nothing helpful occurred to her.

She went around to the back yard of house 14 and looked from the relative safety of the woods across the yard and at the house.

It was dark and quiet.

A cat slept in a round cushion on a high piece of furniture that was next to an upstairs window. It was a black cat, and she could see its side rise and fall, slowly and peacefully.

She envied it.

It was settled somewhere with no problems.

What the Small Gray Visitor Said

Down on the ground, she looked across the lawn again, and noticed that cultivated gardens stretched all around the perimeter and close to the house.

She longed to explore the plants, but dared not.

What if she made a noise that woke the humans up?!

What if this house had an alarm?

She would never be able to get back to the woods in time before they got up, turned on the lights, and saw her.

Police might be called, and this time, they would find her and see her and...

...that sort of thinking was counter-productive.

She wandered around the woods at the back edge of the yard, looking, but not going near the gardens.

The gardens that grew food were up against the house.

Of course they were; that was the logical place for the human residents to have put those plants.

She saw herbs in the early stages of growth, and thought she recognized them. There was lavender, which most humans didn't eat, even though it was edible.

Nasturtium flowers in hues of red, orange, paler orange, and bright and pastel yellows grew next to the lavender, with round leaves that grew like little lily pads in various shades of green, from dark to light. Both the flowers and the leaves of these plants were edible. The flowers had a peppery taste.

She used to go on excursions for spices in India when she was a botanist in training, but when she finished, she decided that the snakes in that part of the planet Earth were creatures that she never wanted to deal with again.

Cobras were just too terrifying. So were the speckled snakes, called a swamp adder.

It was silly, really, as this continent had its own poisonous snakes, copperheads and rattlesnakes, but she found they were more easily avoided. It wasn't so hot and dry in the northeastern part of the United States.

She looked around at the back of the house some more.

There were more herbs growing up against it, herbs that she didn't dare to inspect up close.

What the Small Gray Visitor Said

It was frustrating to have to hide out here, after walking so far, only to find such things in plain sight, just out of reach, and have to leave them untouched.

She could have taken some small clippings, just a bit here and there of each plant, leaving the humans most of each one and her theft barely noticeable, but it was just too risky, and she wasn't a fool.

She could look, though.

She saw rosemary, parsley, chervil, sage, and thyme.

Flowers grew near the woods, but they hadn't bloomed yet. They would soon, though. They could be ordered online.

The humans' internet was easy to access from the ship.

She had spent a lot of time doing that, whenever her experiments were set up and the ship was hiding out of sight, either behind the Earth's moon, or cloaked in plain sight of their International Space Station.

Once the Chinese space agency had sent a probe to the dark side of the moon, the policy had changed to more frequent use of the cloaking device.

The fiction writers of *Star Trek* had figured out what humans needed to invent. Humans itched to invent everything that they could imagine, and those who survived the collapse of the majority of their ecosystem would probably go on to benefit from it all. Her people had.

The others, the vast majority, would miss out.

She was getting tired, she realized.

Her mind was wandering.

She brushed up against something, a tall plant, and jumped away from it, startled and annoyed with herself for not paying attention to where she was moving.

Then she relaxed. This was a flowering plant, a tall shrub that wouldn't hurt her. At least she could examine this one without showing herself.

She took out her scanner, studied its properties, and filed the data in its tiny computer. She wished she could record its lovely, sweet scent, but only the molecular data was saved.

What the Small Gray Visitor Said

There was no rule against studying anything and everything that interested her. Scientific inquiry, as long as it didn't interfere with necessary scientific work, was encouraged.

She sat down on the ground under a large maple tree and tried to relax. She had been out on the ground for over three hours now, and it would be dawn soon.

She wanted to be in the shade when it got bright.

What was it that humans wore for that?

Oh yes. Sunglasses.

She didn't have any.

A sweet scent wafted over to her as she settled down, and she realized that it was that same plant. She inhaled it deeply.

She glanced up and took the time to really look at the source: a large honeysuckle bush was between her and the large, open yard. She sat facing the huge yard and the back of that house, with its garden full of tantalizing plants.

She was just too tired to even attempt to gather samples.

She would let herself take a nap against that tree.

Her environmental suit was next to her, just under the honeysuckle bush. Some beautiful, bearded iris bulbs were flowering in the section of garden just past the honeysuckle.

Her thoughts drifted, and she sensed that there were two people sleeping on the upper level of the house, close together.

She wondered why they would do that when there were other rooms in the house, then remembered human movies and television shows. They must be a mated couple, she realized.

Her thought processes were getting slow.

Her plan of staying up until she could have herself beamed back up to the ship wasn't working. She would have to wait longer, and find a way to manage, including sleep and food, until then.

She would only sleep for an hour, she told herself, until the bright light of daytime woke her up.

Her thoughts drifted again, to the female human.

What must it be like to be her?

She didn't realize how tired she was.

Night Lights

Something in the night woke me up.

I had been sleeping soundly until my dream changed.

In it, I was suddenly wandering around in the woods near our house at the foot of Avon Mountain, unable to find my way home. It agitated me because I knew that our house was just through the brush, past the honeysuckle, through the iris garden, and across the lawn...but I couldn't find it.

I kept wandering, getting more and more upset, until a light shone briefly in my face.

I sat bolt upright in bed, staring out the window.

The light was gone.

But I was sure it had been there, and that it had been the thing that had woken me up.

Kavi's eyes opened when I sat up, confused.

"Arielle, what's the matter?" he asked.

"I don't know. I thought I saw a light flash in the woods." I told him about the weird dream.

He sat up and stared into the woods. "It's dark now."

Our window faced north and overlooked the back yard, and after that, it was just trees for about an acre, followed by a cornfield, and then a horse farm.

Kavi added, "Of course, you did say it was a flash of light, not a beam."

He was always thoughtful about how he came across.

I loved that about him.

I flopped back onto my pillow, smiling up at him.

"Well, I guess it's not going to happen again. Might as well go back to sleep," I said.

Kavi smiled, put his arms around me, and said, "I'll make you forget all about that light and the dream."

That was exactly what he did.

We fell asleep again, and I dreamed of walking into our garden, and into the house.

But what had made that light shine in the woods?

It's Too Early for Hallowe'en

It was a lovely, sunny morning, and I was staying inside as usual, sitting at my computer, editing another book.

It was a Friday.

I really should go outside more, I thought to myself.

The trouble was, I had a persistent feeling that something unsettling was going on outside, and that if I went out for long, it could get me.

There is a saying: 'Just because you're paranoid, that doesn't mean that they're not out to get you.'

But in this case, those who might get me were microbes.

It was a plague that was keeping me inside.

A worldwide virus, yet to be fully understood by scientists, was causing my unsettled state of mind. It was a zoonotic one, which meant that it leapt across species – from one to another. It had leapt to humans from a wet market, which meant one that sold live animals. 6 out of every 10 diseases were zoonotic.

The coronavirus had no vaccine as yet, though my husband, a virologist and geneticist, was among those who were working on one. A vaccine would enable the immune system of anyone who had been given it to maintain long-term immunity to the disease.

He was also working on a stop-gap measure called an anti-body drug. That would enable medical personnel and others who had already been exposed to the virus to fight it off. The immune response it would provide would wear off in, perhaps, a month or so, but it would save them if infected, buying them time to have a vaccine later on, when one was ready.

There was also the idea of coming up with an antiviral remedy, much like antibiotics were used to fight bacteria that was harmful to humans and our pets. But that was the least desirable option, because it only helped some people.

I knew I had plenty of company in what was really a logical sense of caution – company that I could not have any direct contact with outside of my immediate family.

Oddly, it hadn't changed my life all that much.

What the Small Gray Visitor Said

I had always stayed by myself, shunning most of society.
People were dangerous anyway.

Humans are, after all, the top predator on our planet.

We are an invasive species that consume everything,
imagining that Nature exists solely for our own use.

Often, that means abuse as well.

No wonder a worldwide plague was keeping us humans all
in our homes, isolated from one another, working remotely,
social distancing, and waiting for the scientists to develop a
viable vaccine. And still there were plenty of idiots who said
that they would refuse to take it if and when it was ready!

It was settled law that they had to take it to preserve herd
immunity, in *Jacobson v. Massachusetts*, 197 U.S. 11 (1905). That
case had involved a vaccine for smallpox.

That was what I wrote books about and blogged about.
That, and overpopulation, which had led us to this point. We
were more than 8 billion humans now, living on a finite planet,
in a state of denial about the fact that it is finite.

That was what I did when I wasn't editing and publishing
for hire.

I had some of that work to do now.

Therefore, instead of going outside, I sat down with a cup
of coffee with milk in it. At least this brand recycled their pods!
I refused to use a brand that didn't – and whose discarded pods
could circle the planet several times over.

Exercise and sunshine would be great…but I had work to
do. Maybe later. The Hazen Park trail ran behind our house.
Of course, I wasn't keen on walking alone. Another damned
excuse for not going! Well, I could do some gardening outside,
at least.

And maybe when my husband came home, he would be
early enough that we could go hiking.

I had written and published several of my own books, on
topics such as human overpopulation, honeybee colony
collapse disorder, and travel to places such as Hawaii. My
website detailed all of this on its various pages. The About

What the Small Gray Visitor Said

Arielle N. Desrosiers, J.D. page of *QueenBeeBooks*, had it all – education, projects, and so on.

I clicked on a tab of my web browser and scrolled through it, absentmindedly making sure that it suggested someone who could work with any variety of writing, academic or recreational. It did. Damn…I looked like a pompous persona.

And here I was, sitting at home in a tee shirt that said, "There's no such thing as too many books." It showed a woman in a cloche hat and dress who reminded me of Agatha Christie, seated at a table piled high with books. The artwork on it was by one of my favorite artists, Edward Gorey.

Yes, I could write whatever caught my interest.

And I could edit anything, in any style or genre, academic or recreational.

That was all well and good.

Right now, I had a big editing job, checking a client's novel for formatting, grammar, spelling, etc.

This one was about a vampire.

It needed a major overhaul; the writer had a learning disability but loved what she was doing. That was fine. I was happy to help her, and I was getting paid for it.

We lived on Tiger Lily Lane in Avon, Connecticut, off of Nod Road and up Woodford Hills Drive, with Avon Mountain overlooking our property.

It was a lovely spot, secluded, and completely shielded from view by other houses in the backyard. We were at the end of a cul-de-sac, too, so there wasn't much chance of being gawked at by passersby from the sides or front, either.

I looked at this novel draft, checking the length.

214 pages.

214 pages of prose to basically rewrite.

I opened the scientific journal article that Kavi was working on and looked that over.

He was working on the genetic structure of the pandemic that was keeping everyone in a state of social isolation, and this article was a project that he had wrapped up just before it hit – unfinished business. It needed a final edit.

What the Small Gray Visitor Said

This was something that I would not get paid for, but I would be mentioned in the acknowledgements, with my name, degree, and editing business. It was only 8 pages.

That settled it. I would do this first.

It was always easier to do the short stuff first.

Why not? Then Kavi would have it back right away, and he and his colleagues could submit it to *Nature Biotechnology* and hope that its editors would publish it. A journal such as that one would be a great credit on his CV.

His faculty page looked even more impressive, I thought. Maybe that was because he didn't work completely on his own. It meant that he could go out and work all day, every day, with others, whereas I worked at home, on my own. But I loved it that way.

Kavi's page read: "Kavi Anil Ravendra, Ph.D., Ph.D., is a clinical research scientist at the UConn Health Center, at Jackson Laboratories. His Ph.D.s are in virology and genetics. He works with stem cells, developing tissue that can be grown to be whatever organ a patient may need replaced."

That placed him squarely on the political left, in favor of keeping women's reproductive rights as free and convenient as possible, because stem cells came from miscarriages and, more often, abortions. They could also be grown in a laboratory, and Kavi worked with both kinds.

I really ought to stop thinking and start editing, I thought to myself.

The beautiful day was very distracting, though.

The shades were up to the max, and light streamed in past the pretty curtains, which had a blackberry bramble pattern in blues, greens, and purples. I had gotten the kind of shades with no strings so that the cat wouldn't swat at them.

I sat at my computer at the back of the house, enjoying the sunlight coming in from the garden. Occasionally, I glanced up and admired the pastel blue and lavender iris beds, and anticipated the blossoms of pastel and raspberry pink peonies that would soon follow. I would have to get some kitchen twine and stakes for those, I reminded myself. It was late May – my favorite time of year.

I had just planted the herb garden the day before yesterday, with rosemary, basil, lavender, thyme, parsley, chervil, and nasturtiums in reds, bright and pale oranges, and yellow. The chives grew back each year.

Soon it would be time to set up the tomatoes – heirloom tomatoes. I never had much success growing them. Nonetheless, I had some, plus some yellow and orange ones. At least it got me outside, working in the sunshine.

After about an hour, I finished the edit of the journal article and e-mailed it to Kavi.

As I did that, the cat appeared, leaping onto the table in front of the window and settling into his basket. He was a black shorthair with a lithe, athletic build. He curled up into his fleecy-covered ring-pillow bed, put his paw on the tip of his tail, and stared at me with his huge eyes.

"What a good boy you are, Bagheera!" I said, reaching out to pet him. He purred, then turned over to look out the window. He wasn't allowed outside. Too many bobcats, lynxes, turkeys, foxes, hawks, and black bears – not worth the risk of losing him!

I glanced at my computer screen. Another e-mail.

It was from Kavi, thanking me for the edit. "I love you!"

I grinned and clicked to look at the vampire novel.

Bagheera suddenly sat up and stared out the window, tensing. He was perfectly still, his triangular face fixed with a steady gaze at a point in the woods just beyond the honeysuckle bush at the back left of our yard.

I reached out to pet him, and he jumped.

"What? I don't see anything."

He sat up and continued to stare.

No birds – not even the hummingbirds. They usually came right up to the house, though, to the feeder that hung from a hook over the windows at the back of the kitchen, where we had a table and four chairs.

What the Small Gray Visitor Said

I got up and washed my coffee mug, put it away, and looked at the cat again. No change. Something was fascinating him, that was for sure.

A bird suddenly flew out of the honeysuckle bush, chirping and squawking. It was a chickadee. What was out there? A bear? I didn't keep a seed feeder for just that reason.

The cat settled down at last, curled up, and was quiet, but he stayed facing the window. Well, that was the point of having his basket on the table next to my desk, I thought, and sat down again, forgetting all about the cat's interest in the area by the honeysuckle bush.

After another hour, I decided that I was wasting this beautiful day, saved and backed up my work, and went into the kitchen, twisting my long hair up into a curved, matte-gold clip.

I took out the old plastic jar that used to hold raspberry sorbet and pulled a length of twine out, snipping several short pieces off and shoving them into my pants pockets (I never wore anything – pants, shorts, skirts, or dresses – without pockets). I got some stakes out of the garage, too.

Then I went outside to look at my irises. I wandered around the garden, snapping off the wilting blossoms carefully so that they wouldn't stick to the ones that were just emerging. Next, I tied the stalks to stakes.

The garden was coming along beautifully, and thanks to catalogues such as Burpee's, which was conveniently online, I had not needed to shop in person to get the plants I wanted to grow this year – not one of them.

I already had the irises, all in beautiful pastels of pinks, blues, and lavenders. Soon the peonies would bloom, too, in a riotous shade of raspberry pink and a delicate hue of pastel pink. I was looking forward to it.

The Burpee catalog had supplied heirloom tomatoes, various herbs, some butter-and-sugar corn, cucumber squash, purple carrots, snap peas, a pumpkin plant, and a lot more.

The yard was a decent size. Kavi often said that he was glad it was over an acre because it ensured that I would go outside and get some exercise, aside from the yoga stretches we did together. He was right; I tended to forget to move around without a garden to tend.

When I got near the honeysuckle tree, I suddenly noticed something in the brush. It was a gray shape.

"Damn it!" I muttered, reaching out to pick it up. "Some slob is letting plastic litter blow all over the neighborhood!" Could it have come from some fair, the kind that sold plastic, inflatable toys to children? No...fairs had been stopped because of the pandemic. Also, I remembered that those had been in fluorescent hues of pink, green, and purple.

I had already grabbed it, however, so I stood up and looked at it...and stopped short, suddenly out of breath, even though I hadn't been running.

It was a small, gray suit.

It had a headpiece with dark, almond-shaped eyes.

And it didn't seem to have a way to open it.

It was seamless, but clearly meant to be worn, and by someone who was about four feet tall at most.

"You've got to be kidding me," I muttered to myself.

It wasn't just a small, gray suit – it was a Small Gray suit.

My gaze moved up, though I dreaded to find anything, whatever it might prove to be. I was still holding the Small Gray suit.

My eyes met those of a short, spare, blue-eyed woman who was crouched just behind the honeysuckle. Her huge eyes had a shape that matched the suit: like almonds. She seemed to have been reaching for something...which was probably the thing that I was now holding. I suddenly felt frozen, and as if I had had an iced rather than a hot coffee.

"Hello," I said. I wondered what she would do.

Was she about to shoot me with a phaser, grab the suit, and run back into the woods?

In spite of myself, I found her too fascinating to just drop the thing and run like hell for the house. Besides, she didn't seem to be armed, nor was she reaching for anything...and I was worried that I might have come into contact with a contaminant that might hurt Kavi and Bagheera after picking up this suit.

She didn't move. She didn't even look ready to pounce.

In fact, I now realized that she had been sitting on the ground, up against a tree trunk just behind the honeysuckle bush, and not ready for much of anything. She looked as though she had just woken up, and, judging from the expression on her face, was horrified that I had picked up her Small Gray suit.

I thought of it with capital letters…and I knew she knew.

Her face was narrow, with a pointed chin, and her thin, wispy yellow hair was swept close around her face, almost clinging to her cheeks. She had bangs, and her hair was parted slightly to one side.

Her skin looked papery and so pale as to be almost white, though I could see pores and faint lines around her mouth.

She was wearing the palest of blue clothing, a thin, form-hugging outfit that consisted of a long-sleeved shirt with a plain neckline and pants that came down to her ankles. Her feet were covered by a similar material that looked so thin that, at first, I thought she had been walking around the woods in her socks. But they were shoes. Her hands were bare. A small bag, made of a white material that was equally thin but likely strong and durable, was slung over her shoulder.

She wasn't human.

That much was clear.

But she was sentient.

We had that in common, at least.

She continued to regard me an unwavering gaze, assessing me while saying nothing and holding still.

I took a deep breath.

She did the same.

I didn't move. It occurred to me that she must be alone, and not in any position to attack me. No one who looked wide-eyed and unsettled could be.

She just stood there, looking up at me, and then she reached for her suit.

I was at least a foot and five inches taller than her.

I held it out to her.

A bird chirped, and I turned, started. Then I turned back to her. "So...where did you beam down from?" I finally said. "Or did you beam down? Are you going to say anything, or will you just communicate with me telepathically?"

Why was I joking?! It wasn't every lifetime that one got to meet an alien from who knew what planet – not ours! – and not seem to be at imminent risk of abduction.

The alien woman – I had decided that that was what she was – smiled slightly. "I can speak. I don't prefer it, but as you must use speech, I shall do so."

Her voice was clear and low, but easily audible.

What a relief – she wasn't planning to just project her thoughts into my mind.

I managed a small smile myself. "That's good."

I paused.

She said nothing further.

"How long have you been out here?" I asked.

"All night."

I suddenly remembered the odd light and sounds from the middle of the night.

"Oh! So that's what I noticed last night. You're stranded, aren't you?"

She looked displeased, but not with me; maybe with her situation. "Yes," she answered.

"You must be tired."

She looked sorry to admit it, but said, "I am. I thought I could just stay awake all night and call to be picked up, but I fell asleep, and they never answered. I now realize that I can't just stay awake until they come back...whenever that is."

"Come out here and sit down," I said, "and you can tell me...whatever you are willing to tell me. Maybe I can help you figure out how to get back."

She looked at me skeptically.

"Oh, I don't mean with technology or anything like that," I said, smiling. "Obviously, you have more advanced everything, but you are stranded, as you just admitted, and you have revealed yourself to me, so let's see what I can do."

Now she smiled a bit more than before. "All right."

I stepped back into the grass, feeling a bit relieved to do so, and wondering whether she would come with me.

I paused, and then said, "My name is Arielle."

She looked at me for a moment, thought it over, and then said...at least, it sounded like she said, "My name is Ileandra." That was the closest I could get to understanding her, anyway.

"Ileandra?" I repeated. "I hope I'm not messing up the pronunciation of your name too badly..."

"No, you're pronouncing it fairly well," she replied.

"So...extra-terrestrials are real, not fantasy, not a conspiracy theory, and not a substitute for religion," I said.

She did a great impression of Spock from *Star Trek* just then with one eyebrow, but said nothing.

No doubt, she and her people knew about all that.

I stepped back into the middle of the lawn and waited.

I was suddenly glad that our house wasn't close to the others, and that they were around a curve, so that the neighbors wouldn't see us and think that I was taking in a missing child. That would be the last thing I needed!

It was quiet except for the birds and insects, and we weren't talking loudly.

I wanted her come out to the middle of the lawn of my back yard before I invited her inside. What microbes could I have been exposed to? I wanted to deal with that first.

She did just that, and I wondered about telepathy again.

"Well...come sit on the lawn with me for a bit," I said.

The alien looked at it doubtfully.

"Don't worry," I said. "I don't put any insecticides on it. I weed it myself – well, I leave wildflowers with the grass – and I mow it with a push-reel lawn mower. It's not toxic."

Looking reassured, the alien sat down on the grass.

I sat down, too.

Next, I felt in my pockets. Right pocket: pocket watch, Kleenex...and cotton face mask. I pulled it out and looked at it stupidly. It had elastic ear-loops, a white cotton gauze interior layer, and a pretty cotton front that depicted whimsical bees and pink, blue, and purple flowers. I had made it, along with many others, in that room that I had stupidly wandered out of. I should have heeded my cat's warnings! What was the point of covering my face now?!

I stuffed the face mask back into my pocket and felt around in the other one, hoping that I had put my cell phone in there. It was a black, fold-in-half, flip-phone. Yes! It was on.

How convenient.

I took it out, opened it, and said, "I'm going to call my husband. He's a doctor, and I want to make sure that neither of us is contaminated with the plague that is going around my planet before we go inside. He'll know you're not human the instant he sees you, and I live with him, so if you're known to me, you're going to be known to him."

She was sitting across from me, perhaps four feet away (less than the recommended six feet!). She nodded.

"Don't zap me with anything."

"I don't have a gun."

Well, that was good news.

Fortunately, Kavi answered his cell phone right away.

"Hey, Honey, what's going on?" he asked.

"Kavi, you are not going to believe this…"

I explained what was going on, begging him to believe that I was perfectly sane. "You're a doctor; you'll know as soon as you see her!" I pleaded, feeling foolish yet certain of the situation simultaneously.

"Of course you're sane! You don't even drink much, and at this hour all you've had is coffee with milk in it and orange juice!" he replied. "I'll be right over to do a COVID test. Whoever she is, and wherever she's from, we'll check that."

I breathed a slight sigh of relief, thanked him, and ended the call.

We waited for about fifteen minutes. I spent the time talking nervously, pointing out the plants in my garden. My guest didn't say much, but she looked at everything with interest.

After about twenty minutes, I heard Kavi's car in the driveway. He must have grabbed what he needed in a big hurry.

His footsteps raced through the house and out the back door. Too close!

"Kavi, don't catch anything from me! Why aren't you wearing your mask?!"

He smiled, slowed down, and said, "I don't care. If you get terminally ill, I hope I do, too."

I looked at him wryly. "Let's not assume that we're doomed just yet."

Kavi was already kneeling on the grass, rooting through his medical supplies. He glanced up at Ileandra, nodded politely at her, then looked back at me. He smiled at me.

Yeah…he knew she was an alien.

"That's why I'm going to test you both for coronavirus and be done with it right now," he said. "Hold still."

With that, he brandished a very long cotton swab.

Damn…that thing was going to go all the way into my sinus passages. I took a deep breath and tried to hold still.

Ileandra watched with interest.

The swab went in…and in…and in…and out!

What a relief – Kavi was quick.

He bagged the sample.

Ileandra was next.

As he got the next swab ready, a strand of his thick, dark hair blew down to his upper eyelid and tickled him. He needed a haircut, but everything had been closed for over 2 months, and although things were just opening up now, he didn't have time. Rather than touch his face, he moved his entire arm up and across his eyes. It worked. He was comfortable again.

"I wish you would cut my hair," he told me, laying out the next container for the swab.

"You have great hair," I said. "What if I mess up and make it too short?! I don't want to make you look like you've been to a dog groomer."

He grinned and said, "Yeah…the Chris Cuomo look."

Then he turned to our guest.

"So, you're Ileandra?" he said. It was not a question. "I'm Kavi, I'm a doctor, and a geneticist. I should be wanting your DNA, but first things first: let's make sure it's safe for us to interact with you. Ready?" He brandished a fresh super-long cotton swab in front of her.

"Ready," she said. "My sinus passages are approximately two-thirds as deep as a human's," she told him.

I didn't blame her for sharing that.

Alien secrecy be damned. If I were her and a doctor were about to stick something in one of my orifices, I would share that much anatomical data, too.

"She's probably been inoculated against every pathogen on our planet prior to coming here," I said.

"Probably," Kavi agreed, "but let's be safe rather than sorry. I'm glad you called me. Plus, now I won't be shocked when I come home tonight."

Kavi stood up and packed everything up.

He had labeled each sample.

"Keep your phone on. I'm going back to the lab to do the assays on these samples. I'll call you with the results. If you're positive for COVID, I'll test myself, probably be positive, and come home. If no one is positive, I'll tell you so and you can just go inside. I'll work in my lab until it's time to come home if that's the case. I love you."

To the alien, he said, "Don't abduct my wife."

She looked startled at that, but said, "I won't."

With that, he went back to the garage.

I heard his car's engine start, and pull out to the road.

He drove off. I was going to be outside for at least an hour – a record for me!

Ileandra made an odd sound just then.

I looked at her.

"Did you just giggle?"

She looked down at the grass, then up at me. "Yes."

"You can definitely hear my thoughts."

What the Small Gray Visitor Said

It wasn't a question in my mind anymore.

"Yes."

We sat there, running out things to discuss for the moment. I didn't feel like checking the flowers just now.

A hummingbird came into the yard, emboldened by the fact that I was outside, alien or no alien. I could hear it before I saw it, due to the distinctive whir-beating of its wings.

It went for the red-and-clear plastic feeder and took a drink. At last – something else to talk about!

I asked my guest if she knew about hummingbirds.

"I know that they pollinate some plants," she replied.

Bees were in my garden, I noticed, doing that. There were honeybees – *apis mellifera* – and some huge, black, furry bumblebees.

We watched them, and I told Ileandra about my bee book, just for something to say.

She looked very interested at that, and said, "If we test negative, maybe you can show it to me."

I smiled.

Finally, after about forty minutes, my phone rang.

It was Kavi.

"You're negative!" he practically shouted.

"Both of us?"

"Both of you."

"Yay! Thank you, Kavi! I won't lose my senses of taste and smell in two weeks, have my alveoli die in my lungs, and fail to take in oxygen when I breathe. It will be great to go on without that happening."

He laughed. I knew anatomy from ninth grade, and hadn't forgotten it. Most people that he talked to needed a recap.

"Will you come home later?"

"Of course. We're lucky. Hopefully, we'll stay lucky."

"Yes, indeed," I said. "I love you."

"I love you too."

We rang off.

"Okay, let the visit begin!" I said, standing up.

I was stiff.

What the Small Gray Visitor Said

Ileandra got up, seeming a bit stiff herself.

Unlike me, she had slept outside after a tough night.

"Come on – come in and meet my cat and get comfortable," I said, backing up.

I continued to back toward the house, still holding the small gray environmental suit, until I was practically at the door. My surprise guest followed me.

"Oh!" I realized that I was still holding her suit. "Do you want this back? Are you okay without it?" I felt foolish asking her this, seeing as I had found her out and about without it on. I held it out to her.

"I can survive without it on." She took it back, and slung it over her arm. A moment later, she pushed it through the strap of her bag, letting it hang there.

She stood there, in the middle of the yard, watching me.

"Come on. You can't just stay out here. It's okay."

At last, she came out into the middle of the grass.

"Let me guess: you and your people are scientists who have sampled and studied our microbes, developed antibodies to them in your on-board laboratories, and can therefore breathe our air and move about without difficulty," I said.

Ileandra smiled at me like a pleased professor. "Yes."

Not very talkative, I thought, but she was the one who was stranded on an alien planet. She was probably scared. I would be!

As I led my guest inside, my mind raced with all sorts of possibilities, some exciting, some terrifying, and many downright unpleasant.

We went into the back of the house and I shut the door behind us, looking back at the woods suspiciously even though I knew that it was unlikely that anyone was actually in there looking at us.

At least I hadn't seen nor heard anything like a drone overhead while we were out there...

I mindlessly wandered over to the breakfast nook (Kavi and I ate every meal there, but called it by that name anyway) and sat down, motioning to Ileandra to take the other seat that faced the window.

Bagheera was crouched in his basket, staring at our visitor with wide, intent eyes, but he stayed put.

"That's my pet cat, Bagheera," I told my guest. "He's four years old, and not allowed outside, so if he tries to get you to open the door for him, just say 'no' to him and don't do it," I told her. "Bagheera, this is Ileandra. She's temporarily stuck here for some reason. I guess I'll find out what that is at some point."

I closed the back door, suddenly uncomfortable with the breeze coming in through the screen door.

"I locked the door," I told her, "though I suppose that if more of you showed up, that wouldn't stop you."

She settled carefully into the chair, which was a bit too high for her, looked at me steadily, and then said, "They won't show up unless and until I call them." She paused, and then said, "I have called them, but they can't come back for me right now. I don't know when they can." She seemed loath to admit that, but there it was.

I looked at her.

What the hell was I in for?!

After a moment, I spoke. "I realize that you and your people, and quite possibly other sentient species from various other planets, have likely been spying on us – us idiot Earthlings who toxify our planet and fight over resources while doing little to keep our numbers within the limits of our finite planet – but the movie E.T. the Extra-Terrestrial inevitably keeps coming to mind. I half-expect to experience some nightmarish version of NASA-meets-the-CDC in my own home as they detain you, me, my husband, and my cat, and then drag you off to live in miserable isolation!"

"I am not familiar with that movie." She looked a bit worried. "You seem unwilling to just call them and let them do that," she remarked.

"Well, yeah!"

I paused, then figured it didn't matter whether or not I told her this. "I have massive anxiety attacks over changes to my surroundings. I get nervous over moving, traveling, etc. I still travel – I'm not going to let anxiety stop me from living my life and doing things – but I'm not inclined to force someone else into a feeling that they've completely lost control over absolutely everything. I mean, being stranded on a planet that is not your own is bad enough. I'm not willing to make it worse. If it were me, I wouldn't want that."

"You are an unusual human," Ileandra said, staring steadily at me.

I breathed out and in deeply for the first time since I had spotted her, and laughed. "You're not the first person to say that to me."

She looked at me appraisingly.

"You are not neurotypical. I can see that."

I looked at her, startled. "What, can you see my brainstem?! Or are you scanning me under the table? …or did you read the entire DSM manual before getting stuck here?"

She put her hands on the table where I could see them.

No tricorder, or whatever passed for one with her.

She gave me another tiny smile.

"The last one," she replied. "I know what autism is, and Asperger's. That should have been left in the 5th edition."

I laughed. I couldn't help it; I liked her.

I hoped I wouldn't get abducted for my trouble.

"You certainly picked the right household."

She paused, taking that in. And then she actually smiled. "It was foolish of me to expect to be able to hide from all humans."

Ileandra picked up her gray suit, which I had tossed onto the sofa that was next to my desk. "How did you know that that is not a costume?" she wanted to know.

"It's too early for Hallowe'en." I told her.

30

I Don't Want to Deal with Area 51

My guest seemed relieved that I knew what she was.

I guessed she was glad to dispense with any need for deception, at least with me. It did make this easier...

"So...Ileandra...it's convenient that I know what you are, and that Kavi does also, but where does that leave you with everyone else?"

She thought that over.

"I don't know yet. I need to understand just how different I look from humans, and to figure out how I might blend in if I have to go out anywhere."

"Well, I have some ideas, and Kavi's a doctor. Maybe when he gets home, he can help us figure that out."

"What are his qualifications?" she wanted to know.

"Here: let's look him up on the internet. You can read all about him." I went to my computer, got onto Google's search engine, and typed in "Kavi Anil Ravendra, Ph.D. in genetics and in virology." The entries showed his LinkedIn profile, his professional page at the lab, and his ResearchGate profile page. I opened those up in separate tabs, put a pillow on my desk chair, and invited her to sit down and read it all.

She thanked me, settled in, and sat there for about five minutes. And then she was done, no doubt having memorized everything. I just watched from behind the kitchen island, absentmindedly scrubbing the gray granite countertops.

"I see how he will be able to help. Thank you," she said.

"You're welcome. I'm looking forward to finding out what he makes of this situation too," I commented.

Ileandra stared at me for a moment with a pleasantly intrigued expression in her eyes. Then she turned back to the computer. She clicked on something, read for about a minute, and turned back to me.

"Now I see why you are so welcoming."

"Oh?" I raised an eyebrow at that. "Why is that?"

"You like science fiction, you wrote some, your internet search history has things like *Star Trek*, I see books on your shelves with the work of Isaac Asimov, Frank Herbert, Arthur C. Clarke, Jean Lorrah, Janet Kagan, Diane Duane, A.C. Crispin, H.G. Wells, Jules Verne, and so on. I recognize that facial expression you just gave from watching Mr. Spock on human television broadcasts. And…I read your website. You are interested in real, provable facts, and can separate fact from fantasy with precision. You wrote your law thesis on outer space law – orbital debris. You care about your planet."

"All that in just a few minutes here – not bad!" I said.

"Yes. I'm a fast reader, and as you may have surmised, our species monitors human telecommunications."

I looked around the living room, which spanned the right half of the first floor, just off the kitchen. "Yes…I care about the planet and love science fiction, and I insist upon watching the line between science fiction and science fact. A lot of the gadgets shown in *Star Trek* gave engineers ideas for things that they went on to invent in real life."

"There is something familiar about your husband," Ileandra suddenly said.

I smiled. "Well, a lot of people – and I must say that I agree with them – have said that he looks a lot like the actor Manish Dayal."

"That's it!" she exclaimed. "I have seen him in some movies and a television show.

"The one in which he plays a doctor…*The Resident?*"

"Yes, that one. And *The Sorcerer's Apprentice*, and *The Hundred-Foot Journey*. The study of human foods and innovations with your diet and the cuisines of your many different cultures was fascinating – plus seeing personalities clash and then mesh."

I smiled. "I liked that one best of all, too. I have a copy of those movies on DVD. The TV show, no. I only watch it when friends or family want to. The subject matter doesn't lure me in as much."

"No…I don't care to follow that show, either. I just watched a couple of episodes, and that was it. There are so many things to keep track of as it is," Ileandra said.

What the Small Gray Visitor Said

"This is odd...I expected you to be a disturbing, invasive mind-reader of a telepath, rudely preempting my every comment, already knowing exactly whatever I might be about to say, and to have conducted complete surveillance on my entire life before approaching my house. But now I wonder...with billions of humans to watch, maybe you extra-terrestrials have other jobs to do." I grinned.

"That's exactly the case," she replied. "I can do that with my telepathy, but as you said, it's rude, I'm your guest...for however long or short a time that proves to be...and I should become accustomed to speech."

"So...you usually telepath all of your conversations?"

"Yes."

"Of course you do," I said, laughing a quiet, short laugh.

Yes, I do, she telepathed to me, by way of proving that.

Can I reply to you with telepathy? I thought back to her.

Yes.

"Wow," I said aloud.

"Why are you helping me?" Ileandra suddenly asked.

I thought about that for a moment, then decided I might as well admit it – to myself, as well as to her. "I don't want to deal with Area 51, or whatever secret hiding place the U.S. government keeps captured alien items, and, worse yet, any men in black. I don't want them dragging me off anywhere, and I don't want you to be forced to go with them. What if you can't go home again?! I would be terrified if that were me. I realize that there must be many species of extra-terrestrials, some who kidnap and study humans like lab rats without a thought for the terror they inflict upon those of us whom they abduct, but you don't seem to be one of those...a member of one those particular species."

"No, I am not one of them. We don't approve of what they do. You are sentient beings, even though you are still toxifying your planet – as a species, I mean, not you in particular. I noticed your recycle and compost bins," she added with a slight smile. Her smiles were all rather slight, I realized.

What the Small Gray Visitor Said

"So...what do you do when you're not stranded?" I asked. "I mean, you personally, and your particular species in general." I waited, wondering whether or not she would actually tell me.

Ileandra got up and moved over to the coffee table and sofas. We had a pair of them facing each other at the front of the house, with the television in between them, on the wall between the front windows, plus one more facing the bookcase that had my sewing things on top of it.

I came over to her and sat down on one.

She looked around, and then climbed up onto the one across from me. Her feet just barely touched the floor.

I waited.

"I'm a botanist. We all share many of what you call professions, but we do specialize, and I was out last night with a team of three, collecting samples of flora and fauna in the area. We were just north of here, in a field near a horse farm. I collected a few strawberries to study on board our ship, and handed them off to a colleague before we split up."

She opened her bag at this point, and showed me a carefully sectioned piece of a strawberry plant. Oddly, it didn't look sliced or torn; it was as if she had been able to heal the area that had been separated from the original plant.

"Should we put that in the fridge – er, refrigerator? It's looking just a bit wilted."

She looked up at me, surprised.

"Well, you aren't going to be able to put this in your on-ship lab for at least a few hours – until it gets dark, I'm guessing."

"I can save it in my bag without it breaking down," she told me. "At least, I can do that for the next 24 hours."

Intriguing...what technology enabled her to do that?

She had 'heard' me wondering about that.

She seemed to consider the matter for a moment.

Then she decided to tell me.

Or, rather, show me.

What the Small Gray Visitor Said

The alien produced a tool from her bag. It looked like a laser scalpel, but with a reverse button on it as well as a cutting beam. She showed me how it could both slice and seal plant tissue as she cut a piece of the strawberry – the fruit, not the other parts of the plant – and saved it.

"They won't miss one plant. What were you going to do, study its DNA and surface for neonicotinoid insecticides?"

She looked up at me, startled. "I'm impressed. That's exactly what I was planning to do."

"Don't be impressed. I'm a honeybee and pollinator activist who has written about this and done a decent amount of research about the topic."

She nodded the nod of someone who has just gotten new and useful information and understood the difference it made.

She took another tool out of her bag.

It looked like a container of some sort. There were other plants in many compartments. Except…they seemed to have shrunk.

"They are images of the plants I have sampled," the alien told me. Their molecular structures, and seeds, are stored in each compartment."

I almost burst out laughing. "Of course they are."

"None of the technology I have seems to surprise you," she remarked. She sounded very surprised at that.

"I've read a lot of science fiction, and I have a logical mind and a good imagination. Plus, I write it, so I'm just enjoying seeing that you really do have what I could have guessed at."

She looked at me, still surprised, but had nothing to add.

"So…how did you get stranded here?" I wanted to know.

She took a deep breath, seeming a bit disgusted, whether at herself, her situation, or someone or something else, I couldn't tell.

"We heard some humans moving around through the trees to the south of the field. Our ship was hovering above it, out in the open, fully visible. We had thought that no humans would be out and about in the middle of the night, but clearly, we were wrong."

"Clearly…" I was surprised that aliens had failed to be sufficiently stealthy, but I supposed anyone could screw up.

She looked at me, decided that that was all I intended to say, and went on, "We were just going to calmly pack up and leave when we heard shouts. My colleagues ran over to the beam-up point, just under the ship, but I was too far away, on the edge of the field, near the road…"

"They just beamed up and left you?!"

"Yes. I can't blame them."

"I blame them! They abandoned you!"

She stared at me. "They had to get our ship out of sight."

"But they didn't come back! I mean, you were obviously out there alone, all night, scared, and here you are still!"

"Yes, but there is more."

"Do tell. You might as well tell me the rest, now that you've started."

"Yes, I might as well…"

I waited.

Ileandra continued, "Two human men in dark blue clothing with yellow writing on it came running out into the field, and the ship was gone, invisible just in time. They stopped short, holding guns, and looked around."

"Did they say anything?"

"They spoke to each other about having seen the light cast by our ship, and wondered what it was. But it was gone…"

"Whereabouts were you at this point?"

"I was behind a tree, not very well hidden, near the road, but keeping it between myself and both the road and those men. They didn't see me, but it was close. Fortunately, there are a lot of wild plants growing around the trees there that shielded me from view."

"Hmm…plants that you might have collected in other circumstances."

She looked nonplussed by that, and then nodded in agreement. "I stopped collecting plants after that. I missed a lot of good opportunities last night thanks to my predicament."

36

What the Small Gray Visitor Said

"That sucks," I said. "I should tell you what I think happened: that piece of land next to the field is a police shooting range. Most likely, those cops were out there, not necessarily to practice, but to go into the small buildings that are on that piece of property. Maybe one of them forgot something and went to get it on the way home. "We'll have to check the news and see if there is anything about that – but don't count on it."

Ileandra looked chagrined. "Clearly, we did not choose our timing nor our location for this away team excursion well."

"No point in beating yourself up about it now," I said. "How long was it before those men left?"

"Perhaps five minutes, but it felt longer. I think they only stayed five minutes."

"Well, when you're under stress, everything feels like it's taking longer," I told her.

She looked at me.

"Oh, come on. Everyone has felt stress at some point"!

She smiled. "Yes. No life is without it."

"When they finally left, what did you do? How did you decide what to do next, and which direction to go in?"

"I had seen the layout of the area from our ship, so I knew what was here. I didn't want to go near the road – any road – so I made sure that they were gone, kept to the trees along the perimeter of that field, and went into the woods. I kept walking until I found a path in there, and then went south, because I had seen the houses in this area. I knew I could go deeper into the woods, and hoped to signal the ship from there."

"That area is Hazen Park. You found the hiking trail."

"Oh. I see. It wasn't something I was looking for before we landed. In the future, I shall pay more attention to such things before leaving on any missions."

I hoped she would be able to get back to her people and go on more of those. I didn't want to voice that thought, however, because I also felt anxious for her. What if she were really stuck here, and couldn't ever get back? That would be

awful for her. A moment later, horrified, I realized that
Ileandra might very well have picked up on it regardless…
…and she was looking at me when I glanced up at her.
Oops…

"Oops…" I said. "You sensed that wish, didn't you?"

"Yes. But I can't expect you to stop thinking. Thank you
for your concern for me. I'm glad I met you. I was going to try
to wait it out for another night out there, but you came into
your yard just as I was pausing to check my suit and relax, and
I just froze."

"So that was why you took the suit off?"

"No. I had taken it off when I started walking around last
night. It's difficult to work in it, and I didn't need it. We just
bring them in case we are going into a wet environment, or one
with insects that bite, or to study a volcano. Plus, I was walking
quite a distance."

"You got overheated in that thing?" I was curious. She had
put the suit down on the arm of the sofa next to her when she
sat down. It looked like a flattened, nonthreatening, caricature
of itself lying there, flopped over on its back. The face was
staring up at the ceiling a bit, and slanting toward the kitchen
bookcase at my recipe books. However, it could never be
mistaken for a souvenir at a fair.

"Yes. I forgot to turn on the environmental control, and
before I knew it, I had walked into a prickly plant. Taking it off
and carrying it seemed easier. At least I could tell if I was about
to walk into another problematic plant."

"I see." I was imagining the night she must have had, and
mentally comparing it to the very different one that I had had
with Kavi. I found that I preferred my terrestrial existence.

Ileandra laughed.

"What?"

"Naturally, you prefer your life here. I have no point of
reference of my own for what you and Kavi did when the light
and noise woke you last night. I was bred differently."

She had seen what I was thinking again! Damn…how was
I going to manage?! I didn't want her to know when I was

38

thinking about sex, using the bathroom, or worrying about her feelings and anxieties while trying to think of ways to keep her from being upset.

"I'll try not to focus on your thoughts," she suddenly said. "I apologize; it's such a regular part of my existence that I forget I'm telepathically reading others when I do it…and we don't have such a need for privacy and space."

I looked at her.

"Why is that? Is life quieter among your species? Cleaner? Do you not have sex and romance?"

"You are very perceptive," she replied. "Are you sure you are not at least a little bit telepathic yourself?"

I laughed. "I did hear laughter in the Trinity Church graveyard on Broadway in Manhattan once, where Alexander Hamilton and his wife Eliza are buried…among others. It's on the south side of the yard there. I asked who was laughing, and the gardener just looked annoyed and refused to reply. Months later, my mother and I were watching a documentary about that place on the History Channel, and we found out that that was a famous but anonymous ghost! No one knows who the ghost is or what the joke is."

Ileandra considered that for a moment.

"Yes, that is one of the signs. The dead do leave a molecular signature behind, sometimes. That is why we don't abduct humans or experiment on you. We don't want to be responsible for causing any of you to leave something behind. It's not right."

"Huh…well, thank you for that," I said. "Ghosts tend to be people with unfinished business, or so I have heard. I never thought I could sense any of them, but seeing that documentary made me reconsider that."

She nodded. "It's not a sign of insanity."

Damn. She had read my mind again.

Food, Glorious Food...Sort Of

I stood up and stretched.

Kavi's car appeared in the cul-de-sac, and the garage door went up.

"I just realized that I haven't eaten since breakfast. Now it's time for dinner. I'm hungry." I looked at our guest. "But what about you? What do you eat or drink?"

I thought of the movie *E.T. the Extra-Terrestrial* for perhaps the twentieth time since this morning. I sincerely hoped that Ileandra wouldn't establish a telepathic link with me that put me into a trance right after she drank all of the beer in our refrigerator.

And with that, for the first time since we had met each other, she laughed.

"Oh, you read my mind again, did you?!" I said with a grin. "So do I have anything like that to worry about, or not?"

"I don't think so," she said, recovering her composure. "I won't get drunk. Do you have a copy of that movie?"

"What movie?!" Kavi asked, coming in from the garage.

"She wants to watch *E.T.*," I told him. "She caught me worrying about that scene in which Elliott lets all the frogs out of the jars in his science class because E.T. drank all the beer and, well, you've seen that movie." Kavi and I were movie buffs as well as voracious readers.

Kavi found the movie in the bookcase by the television, and started to set it up. Then he paused. "Wait...shouldn't we turn on the news and check to see if anyone has the slightest clue that anything unusual happened last night?"

"Yes!" I said.

We did that, but the local news seemed fairly bland. There was a story about a golf course that some developer had tried to expand down the road from us, in Avon, another about a school field trip, and another about the University of Connecticut, which was offering free tuition to students whose families' income was below $50,000 per year. Not a word about a disturbance on Nod Road. Good – all good news! We put the movie on.

I looked at Kavi. "So...once you saw her, you knew I wasn't crazy, huh? She looks only vaguely like a human...as for the shape of her head, her small ears, large, almond-shaped eyes, and long nose...I mean, showing her to a doctor ought to confirm that she's an alien, right?"

"Right," he said. "Yeah...I knew as soon as I saw her. I was so curious I had to come right home – and make sure that you weren't infected with coronavirus from contact with a surprise visitor in our backyard, no matter who she might be."

"So...you had to see this for yourself. Fair enough."

He hugged me. "I know you have read all about aliens without drinking the proverbial Kool Aid. You kept an entertained, inquiring, yet skeptical mind about it all."

I had read everything I could find about aliens in my twenties, after college and before law school, which was a period of five years. I had just been having fun.

"We are really lucky to get to meet you, Ileandra," Kavi said. "But if we were to out you as an alien visitor, we would either be treated as lunatics, or conspiracy theorists gone insane, and either way, you could be taken away from here and not be able to get home again. So, we will have to hide you until you can get home."

Ileandra listened to this with wide eyes – no pun intended! "I do want to go home. I would like to try to make contact again when it is dark out, ideally around 2 o'clock in the morning, when few humans are out and about."

"That can be arranged." I added, "And if it doesn't work, you can come back here and keep trying until it does."

"What about dinner?" Kavi asked.

He was hungry. He had eaten a salad at the cafeteria for lunch, but as usual, was now craving spicy food, rice, fruit, and a chance to sit with me. He was raised in Philadelphia by Hindu parents who had immigrated from Mumbai, India in the 1960s. His father was an endocrinologist, and his mother was a historic preservationist at the art museum. Kavi had come home every day to delicious, homemade, spicy food made by his mother while he was growing up.

Yet he had married me, a woman with French and Irish ancestry who cooked French and Belgian recipes, Italian food, some Native American recipes, and lots of American favorites. I baked, too, and I did a lot of complex, gourmet desserts and dinners for the sheer fun of it.

It was only after we met that I added spicy Indian cuisine to my repertoire. His mother taught me some dishes, and so did Kavi, who had taken an interest in cooking as a teenager. I guess that was why he didn't expect me to just wait on him. Well, that and the fact that his mother had trained him not to expect that.

Kavi and I both shared household chores plus the fun of cooking. I did the baking on my own. But now we were at a loss. What were we going to offer our alien houseguest?

I looked at her. She was watching E.T. get stranded, and I paused to watch with her. I reminded myself that it was spectacularly unfair to feel like a cliché for being the adult host of an alien visitor while she was the one who was trapped here for an indefinite amount of time, out of her familiar environment and surroundings.

With that thought in mind, I found myself feeling terribly sorry for E.T. yet again. That movie always made me feel bad for E.T., an elderly alien botanist who got left on Earth by accident, and who was clearly terrified about it.

It wasn't cute, and it wasn't funny.

Ileandra turned and looked at me.

She knew what I was feeling.

We smiled at each other.

Then I broke the silence. "What can we give you?"

Kavi was making a lot of noise behind me, taking out the rice cooker, the sack of basmati rice, the saffron, plus some okra and a piece of salmon.

He looked up as he plunked a can of mango purée and a large container of plain yoghurt onto the counter.

What the Small Gray Visitor Said

Ileandra said, "I can drink smooth, fruit- and vegetable-based liquids. Nuts, and milks, if necessary, will do. I'm not used to eating anything solid."

Kavi and I looked at each other, and then at the blender. "We really should try more smoothies than always mango lassi," I commented. "Though I do love it."

He grinned. "I was just about to make one. But you're right; if we're going to be feeding Ileandra, we should vary it a lot more."

"What is a mango lassi?" our guest asked.

"You mean you can't just read our minds for that?" I teased her.

She smiled. "Well, I could, but it will get tiresome."

"It's mango purée, plain yoghurt, milk, and a little sugar – we don't like much of that in it – blended into a smooth texture. We like to drink it with dinner a few times a week. It's an Indian drink that Kavi grew up with. Restaurants offer it, too, but we want it so often that we just make it.

"That sounds good. I can have that," she told me.

"Great!" I turned to put on my apron and cook the salmon on the stove. Kavi had already started the saffron rice, and was busily chopping jalapeno peppers, fresh garlic, red onion, and tomato to go with the okra.

We got that going and worked on the mango lassi.

That was when I realized that dinner was going to take us a lot longer to eat and drink than it would for Ileandra. Oh well. She could just drink hers and watch us eat. We couldn't do anything about that. Maybe she was looking forward to observing us.

I smiled at that thought. This shouldn't all be an upsetting experience for her. It should be an adventure. The people of the starship *Enterprise* didn't seem miserable about most of their visits to other planets, even when they didn't know how they were going to get back to their ship.

Soon we were sitting at the table in the breakfast nook of the kitchen, enjoying our feast. Well, Kavi and I were enjoying it. Ileandra was enjoying her mango lassi.

"When was the last time you had something?" I asked. "And how often do you need it?" I wanted to know in case our expedition tonight was a failure, and she ended up spending more time with us.

"I can go for a full cycle of day and night if I have to, but I usually have something every twelve hours."

Oh! I felt terrible. "I should have figured out how to feed you hours ago..."

"No, no...I couldn't have drunk it anyway. We both needed to adjust to this situation. I probably couldn't have kept it down until now. I needed to know from all three of you – you, your husband, and even your cat – that it was okay for me to be in your house."

Bagheera was eating from his dish on the floor, a ground mixture of chicken from a can. He suddenly stopped eating and stared up at our guest, looking surprised.

I believed that cats understand human language, even though they can't speak it. How could it be otherwise, with us constantly speaking it around them?

"He can understand us," Ileandra confirmed.

She smiled at him.

He gave her a slitted-eyed cat smile.

"Looks like all three of us are happy to have you with us," Kavi and I said in unison, then laughed.

"Are you sure we aren't just a bit telepathic?" Kavi asked.

I laughed again. "Maybe a little. We do know each other quite well after living together for over two and a half decades," I reminded him.

Ileandra watched this, then added, "You do have some mild ability as a species," she told us, "but you discount it so vehemently that you don't develop it."

I wasn't surprised.

We finished watching *E.T.* after dinner was cleaned up.

Leaving a Note

With the movie finished, we suddenly realized that we could not just go out and try to get Ileandra back to her ship.

It wasn't even fully dark yet.

What were we going to do for the next few hours?!

I was excited to go outside.

I looked at our visitor.

She didn't look excited.

She looked…sleepy.

Of course! She had been up all night in the woods, hiding, then meeting me, my cat, my husband, and trying to decide whether or not she had found a safe place.

She must be exhausted.

"Come on," I said. "You need a long nap. I'll take you upstairs to the guest room – well, one of them, as we have two extra rooms – and you can sleep for a few hours. You do sleep. I can see that from your sudden lack of energy."

She shook herself slightly, trying to fully wake up.

"Just tell us what time you want to wake up and we'll wake you up so we can go out and find your ship on time. Or, at least, try to."

She looked at me.

After a long moment, she said, "I should be there at 2 a.m. if I'm going to try. They may not show up right away, but if they aren't there by 4 a.m., they won't be able to come tonight."

With that settled, I led her up the staircase, and brought her into the smaller of the two guest rooms because its windows faced the back yard. The bed in there was a double, and not too high for her to climb onto.

The cat had followed us. He jumped onto the bed and sat there staring at us.

"Get off the bed, Bagheera," I said. "Let her get in it."

I picked him up, pulled the quilt and sheets back, and stepped aside.

What the Small Gray Visitor Said

Ileandra took off her shoes, put her bag on the bedside table, and got between the sheets, pushing the pillow aside. I picked it up and moved it to the other half of the bed.

Then I walked over to the windows, drew the curtains shut, turned around, walked to the door, pulled it shut, and left her to sleep.

Bagheera was purring. I let him go and went into the bedroom I shared with Kavi, crossed into the bathroom, and washed my face. The cat watched me briefly, then left. I heard his rapid little footsteps going down the stairs.

I changed into something suitable for a walk in the woods, including sneakers and socks. I spent most of my time at home in black flip-flops with crisscrossed, woven straps – not suitable for walking and hiding in the brush.

Downstairs, Kavi was sitting with the cat, who was curled up next to him on the sofa.

With the alien asleep (I hoped!), I decided that it would be a good idea to leave some notice of our absence, in case we never came back to take care of Bagheera.

I told Kavi my idea.

"Yes – definitely do something. But what?"

"An e-mail to my mother, I think, asking her to come over tomorrow afternoon for a visit. Something casual. I don't want to tip her off about this situation, in case we just come back – which I think we'll do. That would be really silly. But if we don't, she would find Bagheera and take care of him."

"Perfect!"

He watched me write and send that, and then I joined him and the cat on the sofa.

We all sat together watching television for a while.

Hours passed. We were thinking about our guest, but we were also excited – too excited to talk about it. We didn't know what was going to happen, but who does in life?!

We watched a summer rerun of *The Good Doctor*, then the local news – again, nothing about anything happening on our main road. The news concluded with a segment that had been added since the coronavirus shut-down: "Moment of Calm".

46

What the Small Gray Visitor Said

It was a local news station, and I liked to watch that particular news team. Tonight, we were shown a view of Wethersfield Cove, with the water lapping at the shore and some Mallard ducks swimming near the edge.

Next, we watched *The Late Show with Stephen Colbert*. After that, we watched *The Late Late Show with James Corden*. Those two were my favorite late-night talk show hosts. Kavi was happy to watch with me if he wasn't tired.

I was fascinated to see those comedians doing their shows at home, complaining good-naturedly about not being able to go out for haircuts, missing live audiences, and so on. They did a great job nonetheless, each in their own way.

Colbert dressed casually and sat in his study, bantering with his wife, Evie, who also acted as his audio-visual crew. She had gotten the hang of the job after some initial stress with the unfamiliar, heavy, complex equipment.

I didn't feel sorry for her. She lived a comfortable, happy, fun life with her family. And now she was in the groove of handling that equipment, having fun.

Jon Batiste, a talented jazz musician who had gone to the Juilliard School, talked with Colbert from time to time, and clips of him were shown at home – calling his ensemble "Stay Homein'" instead of the in-studio moniker of "Stay Human". They would discuss current events, then Colbert would get back to video chats with his guests.

Corden took a completely different approach. He wore a wool suit and sat at a desk in the corner of his garage, which was set up to mimic the stage at the studio, and video-chatted with Reggie Watts and the other members of the band many times throughout the show.

All that time, we just sat, curled up together, petting Bagheera, who alternately purred, glanced up at the ceiling, obviously thinking about our guest (we all were!), and slept.

When *The Late Late Show* ended, we each had to use the bathroom. Kavi went to the half bathroom by the kitchen. I went upstairs.

While I was up there, I flossed and brushed my teeth.

That done, I was out of tasks that would justify any further delays in checking on our sleeping visitor.

She wasn't asleep.

I wasn't surprised.

She must be excited at the possibility of being able to get home, even if that just meant going back to her ship. It would mean being back with her own people, and that was what mattered. It's what we all needed.

She was sitting up on the edge of the bed.

"Did you sleep at all...or enough?" I asked her.

"Yes. I just woke up when I heard you coming up the stairs. I'm ready to get up."

With that, she hopped down to the floor, pulled her shoes back on, and slung her bag over her shoulder.

"Um...do you need to use the bathroom?"

She looked at me. "I suppose that would be a good idea."

I led her out into the hall to the guest bathroom, pulled a small wooden stool up to the sink, showed her the soap, towels, toilet paper, light switch, etc., and left. At least this bathroom also overlooked the back yard. The neighbors could see the front of the house from some angles, trees, lilac bushes, and other greenery notwithstanding.

Ileandra was out of the bathroom in five minutes.

I realized that I had been standing in the dark on the upstairs landing, staring out the huge window with the rounded top. Damn! Could people see in as we walked up and down the stairs? I pulled the filmy, lacy curtains across the glass. At least the details would be obscured.

The stairwell light was off anyway.

It was easier to look out without being backlit.

I did it late at night when I couldn't sleep, sitting on the window seat with the cat.

Suddenly, I needed to sit down right there, so I did.

I stared at the floral pattern on the cushion, wondering how to say what was on my mind.

Ileandra just stood in the hallway, watching me, letting me take my time to say it.

What the Small Gray Visitor Said

Finally, I looked up and said, "For whatever this is worth, I want to go with you into the woods to make sure that you either get back to your ship, or, if that doesn't work, can just come back here with us. If that's how this goes, we just figure something else out. But if they show up, I want to have told you, for the record, that you and they do NOT have permission to abduct us. We want to come back to our house no matter what, without being experimented on aboard your ship or elsewhere. No scoop-marks on our skin, no needles, no nothing."

"Understood." She was watching me steadily.

"Do you do any of that?"

"No."

"Do other aliens do that?"

"Yes."

"But not you."

"No."

"Well, isn't that lucky."

"Yes."

"Why is it that you don't do that?"

"It's unethical, and we are botanists. We abduct plants."

Now we both laughed.

Abducting plants. That was pretty funny.

Hiking in the Dark

At a quarter to 2 a.m., we set out.

Fortunately, the moon lit our way nicely.

The forest was beautiful, even at night, thanks to that.

I hoped we wouldn't have to deal with any bears.

They could be out at night.

An owl hooted in the distance.

That didn't faze me.

Snakes? I hated snakes. Well, it was cooler at this hour.

Snakes liked it warm.

What about coyotes, lynxes, bobcats...turkeys?

Turkeys wandered all around this area during the day, and I never concerned myself much with them.

No. It was silly to worry about encountering turkeys.

Foxes? No. They weren't scary.

Raccoons? I was just keeping my thoughts occupied!

A branch brushed against my pants, and I shoved it off, annoyed. I had put on sneakers and sweatpants for this – dark blue ones. I didn't like jeans. Kavi did; he was wearing jeans, sneakers, and a tee shirt with a light jacket.

Ileandra was wearing what she had arrived in.

A fox barked.

Fortunately, that one didn't startle me. I knew that sound.

I was annoyed at myself for being afraid out in the dark. I wasn't alone, whereas our visitor had no doubt had a terrifying night out here alone last night.

"What are those tall white things?" Ileandra asked as we walked along the trail. She was looking back the way we had come, to a spot that was off of the trail.

I looked in that direction.

"Oh! Those are on the edge of the golf course. They are wind turbines without rotors. Birds kept getting killed in rotors on wind turbines elsewhere, so these are an updated version. They're the best yet, because whenever a storm with higher-speed winds than normal weather patterns comes along, these things retract into the ground, so that all that's left is one huge disk."

"Didn't you see them from above, when you were still aboard your ship?" Kavi asked.

Ileandra was quiet for a moment, even as we kept walking toward the crop field. Then she spoke. "Yes! I did see them. But, of course, they looked entirely different from above, like white dots. And we weren't focusing on them."

"No, you wouldn't have been," Kavi conceded. "You were likely finalizing your excursion plans and checking your equipment to see that you had packed it all correctly."

She glanced at him sideways as we moved through the darkness. "It takes a scientist to know that. Have you done much field work?"

"Not since shortly after medical school." Kavi had done some time in Bangladesh after completing his residency, helping the Rohingya refugees there. A huge, temporary settlement sprawled near the border with India, on the side near their former home, Myanmar.

There was another pause, one in which we could sense that she had something else to say.

We waited it out, looking at her from time to time.

Finally, she said, "I know I'm not supposed to comment on your thoughts, but…"

"Too late!" we both said, grinning. "Now we know that you've got something on your mind. Don't keep us in suspense."

Her mouth dropped open a tiny bit, but she recovered and spoke. "Rohingya refugees. Your species has an overpopulation and resource-sharing problem, one that will not be solved peacefully."

Kavi and I exchanged glances.

"Don't tell us you're a time traveler from the future now," I said. "Even so, we have figured that out. It doesn't take a psychic or someone who has already found out from a trip to the future to do that. Of course, most humans haven't figured that out – or refuse to – which is why I keep writing about it."

She smiled wryly. "No, I'm not a time-traveler."

"She's probably just aware that the Myanmar government has allowed Chinese dam-builders into their nation's territory – territory occupied by the Rohingya. That is inconvenient to the Chinese, who want that land to themselves, so they are using terrorism to get it. The leader of Myanmar ought to have her Nobel Peace Prize revoked for putting up no resistance to all that."

Ileandra gave me a sharp look.

If she stayed with us, she would not be bored, I decided.

We had been chatting to pass the time and to make enough noise to deter the wildlife from coming near us.

Would bears possibly be out and about?

I didn't want to meet one up close and personal.

What about criminal humans?

Kavi seemed to sense my unease. He took my hand as we walked along.

How had Ileandra stayed calm and in control of her thoughts and actions last night?!

"I had to," was her unbidden answer as we moved through the starlit night.

She had heard my thoughts.

She had probably picked up on my emotions, too.

We walked on and on through the darkness, keeping to the trail. Hazen Trail wasn't that far, but it felt just the opposite in the dark, especially considering our reason for being out on it now.

We found it, and headed north along it, skirting the police shooting range.

Fortunately, no one was there tonight.

"Last night, they only came back because one of them had forgotten his wallet," I said.

I suddenly stopped walking.

How did I know that?!

Had Ileandra told me that? I didn't recall her doing so…

I looked at her.

She was staring at me, surprised.

What the Small Gray Visitor Said

"We may have a slight telepathic connection. Don't worry; it will go away when I leave. I'll make sure of it."

Kavi gaped at the two of us.

We had arrived at the back of the field where Ileandra had been working the night before.

No one was around.

I knew the lay of the land here, horse farm, road up and down the mountain, and all – just as the alien had scoped it out, before and during her night alone out here.

We had a clear view of Nod Road from here, unobstructed by much – just a few trees here and there on the edge. We stood well back from the road, at the perimeter, without emerging from the trees, looking at the agricultural field that our small gray visitor had been chased off from the night before.

"You were working right out in the open last night?!"

I had to ask.

Kavi looked incredulous.

He asked, "Weren't you concerned about being seen?"

"Yeah, what if a car had gone by?" I wondered.

Ileandra said, "We had waited until most humans were asleep for the night, and not out in their cars. This road is almost always empty at this hour."

She looked reluctant to admit more, but then went on. "We have researched the professions of the people who live both on this road and with routes that would take them to an emergency location such as a hospital, and found no firefighters, police, or medical personnel who might abruptly come rushing by at any hour."

"Okay…but someone could always have a medical emergency or a fire and change that. We humans have a saying about the 'best-laid plans' – they can always go awry."

Ileandra looked even more chagrined when I said that.

"We can only plan for and research so much, and then we have to make a decision, choose a spot, and get to work. Humans have settled so much of your planet that there aren't many isolated spots anymore."

"True."

We paused and glanced around.

"So…now what? Do you call them and just wait here until they phase into place, levitating above this field, or what?"

"How do you know that we phase in and out?"

I grinned. "Research, and logic."

Kavi shook his head and grinned.

"You'd better get on with it and phone home, E.T."

She took something out of her bag and did so.

We stood there, watching her fiddle with what looked like a hand-held digital device, much like an iPhone, but smaller. It fit into her small hands.

After a moment, she looked up at us. She looked upset.

"No answer?" I asked.

"There was an answer."

"And…?"

"They can't phase in right now."

"Why not? Did they go all the way home to your planet?"

"Yes…but that's not the problem."

"What is the problem? Are the astronauts in the International Space Station staring at the spots that they need to phase into before they come to this area? Are our orbiting telescopes pointed in their direction? What is it? Why should that matter if they can just phase in?"

I couldn't help being curious.

She looked trapped in more ways than one.

"Phasing in takes planning. Apparently, there are humans with plans around here that will take them down this road at random times for a while. They won't be able to come here until that stops."

Kavi and I looked at each other. What plans?

Flashing orange lights blinked in the distance, just up the road. There was a small area, by the river, across the street that was devoid of trees and other vegetation – perfect for a construction crew to put their gear.

Kavi smacked himself on the forehead.

"I should have remembered! That bridge by the giant sycamore tree is going to have work done this summer."

We both stared at him in shocked disbelief. It was mixed with disappointment. I felt it for Ileandra...and perhaps along with her.

"Ileandra," I asked, "was any of that stuff here last night?"

"No, it wasn't," she said, looking up the road in dismay. "It was quiet. If those police officers hadn't come back, I would be on my ship now, studying that strawberry plant, and perhaps a few other ones."

I felt sorry for her.

She was stuck here for a while.

And we didn't know for how long.

"Let's go home," Kavi said. "You can stay with us until we figure something out to get you back there."

I smiled at him. He was a good guy, and he understood how horrible this was for her. Perhaps he had too much empathy; that was why he preferred research to clinical medicine.

Then I looked at Ileandra. "I have a garden with strawberry plants. If the one you took from here isn't okay, we'll freeze one for you to keep until you can go home. You can save the one from here plus one of mine, plus some of everything else in my garden."

She looked up at me, pleased and surprised, and I knew that she had been close to crying. She felt better at that idea.

"Thank you," she said, trying to smile.

I could feel her emotions, just vaguely.

Damn...we did have a telepathic link.

"Come on," I said, and backed away from the field.

We turned around and went home the way we had come.

Alien Hotel

We came out of the woods after about forty-five minutes of careful trekking and retracing of our steps, emerging from the same honeysuckle bush that I had found our visitor behind that morning.

Keeping together and moving quietly, we slipped into the house through the back door, using our key.

We had gone out into the night telling no one.

I thought we were lucky to be returning.

Our cat did, too: he was sitting on the back of one of the sofas, craning his neck to see into the woods, waiting for us. I saw him there as we approached the house.

Once inside, we spoke out loud again, instead of in the hushed tones we had used the entire time we had been outside.

"Hi, Bagheera. We're back. Nice cat." I kissed and petted him, and suddenly scooped him up off the sofa, holding him close. I buried my face in his fur, cuddling him as I plopped myself onto the sofa. He smelled good: fresh air and warm cat.

Kavi locked the back door, and Ileandra came into the living room area to look at me and the cat.

I looked up at her.

"Welcome to our alien hotel," I said to her. "You can stay with us. We'll figure something out."

She looked uncertainly at Kavi.

"Yes, welcome to the alien hotel on Tiger Lily Lane."

I smiled, and the cat settled in on the sofa next to me, curling himself up at my hip. He purred some more.

"Don't worry. Well...I know you are worried. We don't know what's going to happen. But that happens to everyone all of the time. You can stay here. We'll figure things out."

Ileandra listened to me, then seemed to relax slightly.

She sat down on the sofa across from me.

After a moment, I reminded her, "It's summer – more and more plants will grow. You can go out in my garden and watch them grow. I'll bet you will have some fascinating data when you finally do get home from doing that. It'll be a rare professional opportunity for an alien botanist."

She looked up at me, startled, and smiled.

"Aha – I knew I could cheer you up with that. By the time you get to go home, you'll have so many more plant samples that it will be worth the wait. Your people will be pleased, too."

Ileandra looked worried.

I didn't blame her.

We had no idea when she would actually get to go home.

"You'd better give me that strawberry plant after all. I'll put it in a zip-lock bag and save it for you in the freezer. If you're here when some more plants bloom, sprout, or whatever, you can add them to the collection. There's room in both my freezer and your sampling box. I'll give you another bag to carry them in whenever it is that you go back."

The alien looked both pleased and bemused.

"Thank you," she said.

Kavi laughed. "Mixing stasis technologies will work." Then he yawned. "I'm glad it's the weekend. We can sleep in after that clandestine hike. Don't worry, Ileandra. We'll work out how to explain your presence here – or just concoct some elaborate way of being socially distant with everyone due to the pandemic we're in, so that that won't matter."

I laughed quietly. "This pandemic may make the logistics of hiding you here a lot easier. I'll make you some face masks so that if you decide to go out anywhere, you can hide most of your face. That's standard for everyone now anyway. Our governor mandated it."

Ileandra looked at my sewing table in the darkness.

We hadn't turned on any lights since coming home.

"Can you see well in the dark?" Kavi asked.

"Yes. I can see better in the dark than in bright light."

"That figures," I said. "You have huge eyes, and your ship has you in artificial light, doesn't it? You must be used to it."

She looked at me. "Yes."

What the Small Gray Visitor Said

Yes to what, I wondered? Was her species adapted and evolved to low levels of light, or did she just spend most of her time aboard that ship?

"Both," she said, having read my thoughts again.

My eyes snapped back to her face.

A moment later, I had another thought.

"You must be a head-ties kind of person, not an ear-loops kind of person. I mean for a face mask. Your ears are small. We don't want to draw attention to that feature with ear-loops. I'll make two face masks for you tomorrow, even if you aren't going out anywhere just yet. Better to be prepared either way, and have options."

Kavi said, "She'll need something else to wear, too."

"Let's worry about it tomorrow," I said. "It's almost 4:30 in the morning. I want to go to sleep."

"Me too."

"Come on," I said to our visitor. "Let's go back upstairs."

Masking and Un-Masking

"How are you going to take an alien out in public with you?"

"The face masks ought to help. The rest will be counting on people to not be any too observant, which most aren't."

Kavi and I were lying in bed, waking up from an extended night of sleeping off our failed attempted to get Ileandra beamed back up. 'Where was Scotty when we needed him?!' I thought to myself.

Kavi stretched, rolled over, and threw his arm over me, snuggling up close.

Neither of us wanted to get up yet.

I hoped our guest felt the same way, because if she didn't, I couldn't quite wake up yet anyway, so she would just have to wait a bit longer before I figured out her next meal.

Or ours.

I shifted a little, and Kavi lifted his arm so that I could get comfortable.

I thought about what he had asked, then said, "The Thrifty Shopper will help me, even though I can't tell her where Ileandra is actually from. I'll have to say that she lost her luggage."

"That's a good idea. Wait, what? The Thrifty What...?"

I grinned. "The Thrifty Shopper, a.k.a. my mother. She loves thrift and consignment shops. It'll be recreation to her to find outfits that look good and fit our visitor."

Kavi lifted his head up from the pillow, propping himself up on his elbows. "That's brilliant. And you hate shopping for clothes anyway."

"Yeah, I do. Stupid fashion industry. I just want a steady, continuous supply of pretty, comfortable, loose, natural fabrics with floral prints and deep-enough-to-be-useful pockets. And it doesn't care." That pretty much summed up why I hated shopping.

"I know." He smiled, settled back into his pillow, and closed his eyes.

What the Small Gray Visitor Said

"Yeah…I just like to gripe about it." I closed mine too.

It was Saturday, and I didn't care who might want what of us. I just wanted – and needed – more sleep. And Kavi was here to get it with me. That was what weekends were for, as far as I was concerned. If we didn't have them, I would have just worked all of the time, and forgotten to eat and sleep and play on a regular, healthy schedule.

I would have slept enough, though.

I loved sleep.

Once I was up, I tended to stay up, but Kavi got me to bed and to sleep fairly regularly. He was good for me.

We slept until half past twelve o'clock, at which point we felt slept out and able to wake up comfortably.

We also felt a mess.

We had walked and walked, out to the supposed rendezvous point and back, to no avail.

No spaceship.

No aliens.

Just a stranded alien botanist who looked like she felt as miserable as anyone who was without definite hope of being able to go home was likely to look.

I was glad that we had insisted that she come back with us. She probably was too, dejected though she had looked.

I had seen her into her room, given her my shortest nightgown to wear, and gone to bed myself.

Kavi had already gotten into his pajama bottoms and was snoring away when I had joined him.

Now I got up, used the bathroom, and brushed my teeth.

Kavi went in there and did the same while I was making our bed. This was our standard routine: I would get the bed looking like something out of a magazine while he was in there, and then we would both be in there, using our huge, 2-person, 2-shower-head, marble-tiled, glass-doored shower stall, both at the same time.

The bed looked good in under 5 minutes.

What the Small Gray Visitor Said

It was just a quick job of pulling the sheet and blanket straight with the pink-rose-patterned quilt and then arranging the pillows at the top of the bed. Done.

I glanced up at the bathroom door.

Kavi was grinning at me in the doorway.

I followed him in there and we got into the shower.

But we couldn't spend a lot of time in it.

We had a guest to attend to, and we hadn't forgotten her.

"Do you think she slept at all?" I asked him, rinsing the conditioner out of my hair.

He was shaving under the water, and he looked at me. "Yeah, I do. Alien or not, she looked exhausted, both physically and emotionally. Anyone runs out of energy after a while. Don't try to tell me that an alien has found a way to survive without food, water, sleep, or a safe place to relax."

"That's what I was thinking," I said, "but it feels better to hear a doctor say it."

I shut off the water, stepped out of the stall, and dried myself off. Then I picked up my hairbrush and started working on my wet hair. At least I was clean.

"You left me to squeegee the shower again," Kavi said through the door, which I had left ajar so that we could keep talking to each other. But he was grinning at me.

He didn't actually mind having to do that.

I made our bed and did most of the cleaning, after all.

It didn't hurt him to have to deal with the garbage and recycling and squeegeeing. Besides, I had to take care of our guest. We were both girls; he couldn't do that. Well, he could, but I should be the one to do that.

I grinned back, blow-dried my hair, put on lavender lotion, and did my makeup – just a little, including purple eyeliner.

Then I went out to the bedroom to get dressed.

Kavi appeared as I was heading out into the hallway to check on Ileandra.

"I'll meet you downstairs," I called to him, and walked across the hall.

"Okay."

Ileandra's door was closed.

I hoped she was still there.

I knocked.

"Come in," said a voice in my head.

My heart seemed to leap into my mouth.

Yes – she was still in there.

I would have to see if I could get her to talk out loud more. That had startled me.

But it was also kind of cool to feel it in my head – like living a *Star Trek* episode. I should be so lucky…as long as I could leave it and come home!

I opened the door and went in.

She was sitting up on her bed.

Last night, I had pulled the covers back from the top of the bed for her and encouraged her to climb in between them after realizing that she had napped on top of them.

Today, she was sitting up against the headboard with her feet tucked up to her chin, and the covers were thrown back.

But it looked as though she had slept between them.

"How did you sleep?" I asked.

"I slept between the covers, like you showed me, but they were heavier than what I'm used to. So, I folded the quilt down at the end of the bed."

Sure enough, it was neatly folded, separated from the sheet and blanket, in a perfect, flat layer at the foot of the bed. And the sheet and blanket were laid about halfway down, just as neatly and just as flat.

I tried not to laugh, and pulled the blanket out of the covers to lighten them. Then I remade the bed.

"I meant did you get enough rest?"

She looked at me. She did look better than the day before.

"Yes, I think so."

"Oh, good. I was worried that you would be too upset about not getting beamed up to relax and really sleep. But maybe you just ran out of energy and couldn't think about that and stay awake any longer."

She looked at me. "Are you sure you're not a telepath?"
"That's a joke, right?" I said.
She considered that. "I supposed it could be."
"Do you want to take a bath or shower or something? I could find you something to wear during the day – this nightgown isn't for daytime – and then we can see about food and figure out what to do next."
"A bath or a shower?" She looked confused.
"Yes – there is a guest bathroom across the hall. It has shampoo, conditioner, soap, lotion, towels, dental floss, a toothbrush, toothpaste, and so on." I thought for a moment. "Do you have teeth to clean? Do you need those things?"
I had just realized that she hadn't smiled once since arriving – though she hadn't had much reason to do so.
She smiled at me now, time deliberately showing me her teeth. "Yes, I have teeth. I don't eat solid food, but cleaning them is necessary. We do it with sonics on our ship."
"Huh. Just like in *Star Trek*," I said to myself. I was talking to myself on purpose, out loud, as if to substitute that for telepathy and thus willingly share my thoughts with her.
She picked up on that.
"So – you clean your teeth with those other things, plus a lot of water. I know this from monitoring your television commercials," she said.
"Want to try it?" I asked. "There's no point in letting your teeth rot just because you can't clean them with minimal resource use."
She smiled and got off the bed. "Yes, I want to try it."
She seemed to be trying out each smile, determined to interact with me on my terms to some extent. Perhaps so as not to freak me out...I appreciated it, but kept it in mind that she must still be even more freaked out.
She hadn't expected to be here, and to be stuck here.
We went across the hall and into the bathroom, and I took out the dental supplies.
She was too short for the sink.

What the Small Gray Visitor Said

I got the little step-stool that I kept for my little niece and nephews' visits and pushed it up to the vanity cabinet for her.

"Thank you," she said, not asking why I had it, and got up on it.

She probably read the images of those kids from my mind, and saw that they were Kavi's relatives and my in-laws.

She looked at herself in the mirror.

I looked, too.

Her hair was a bit more fly-away than it had been yesterday, and her face was a bit puffy.

But she looked like she didn't need more sleep.

That was something.

I turned on the faucet taps for her, and directed her to put the toothbrush under it for a moment. Then I opened the tube of toothpaste and squeezed a little bit onto the brush.

She stood there, holding the brush, watching me, and I was reminded of my nephew waiting while his mother did it.

But this was different.

I wasn't a mother. I wasn't maternal. I was a friend to her. I liked this.

I wouldn't have liked parenthood, but I liked helping her.

I looked up at her.

She was watching me. She put the brush in her mouth and cleaned her teeth after realizing that she had 'listened' again.

"That's all there is to that," I said, capping the tube. "Just leaning over the sink and brush all of your teeth, on all sides, and don't swallow any toothpaste. Spit it out, rinse your mouth, rinse off the toothbrush, and put it in this cup."

I pointed to the porcelain cup near the wall.

She did all that, glancing around at the walls, floor, and fixtures of the bathroom with interest.

The walls were painted an eggshell blue, the floor was tiled with large, white-and-gray marble squares, and the fixtures were white. The vanity cabinet was also white. The lights were too bright for her, I realized, and shut them off. It was sunny out anyway.

What the Small Gray Visitor Said

"Here – this is the night-light. If you need to see in here, it provides enough light." I switched the scallop-shell-covered device on. Then I switched it off, because I was just showing it to her.

Ileandra nodded, finished with her teeth, and put the toothbrush in the cup.

I passed her a towel, and she dried her face off.

"How about a shower?" I suggested. "I'll show you how to work it, so you don't get a shock from it being too hot or cold, and get the towels ready for you. While you're in there, I'll find something for you to wear."

I was planning to wash her other outfit, which was a bit dirty from our middle-of-the-night hike.

She seemed okay with that plan, except for one thing.

"I have a kit with me that I can mend the hole that I tore in my pants with," she said.

A branch had ripped an inch-long gash on her upper right pant leg. She wasn't scratched, though.

I nodded, opened the shower door – glass like the one in our bathroom, and went in. I lifted the shower head off of its bracket, turned the lever on the mechanism that made the water run from the other, built-in shower head above that was too high for her to reach, and showed her how to turn the water on and off and to control temperature. Then I pointed out the soap, the shampoo, and the conditioner.

She took off her nightgown, nodded, and stepped over to take the handle of the movable shower head from me.

No shrinking modesty from her, I thought.

She heard that and glanced up at me.

"Was I supposed to wait for you to leave?"

"Some people would. It's considered rude to stare at a naked person, unless you are married to them, or you are their doctor," I told her.

But I had already seen her.

She looked like a thin, small, blonde woman with minimal secondary sex characteristics – though she did have them.

What the Small Gray Visitor Said

She also looked like the aliens that I had read about in alien abduction stories when I was in my twenties. It had been fun then, in a removed sort of way. That had been because I hadn't felt connected to what I was reading about then – just fascinated to think that there could actually be aliens.

Of course, considering how big the Milky Way Galaxy is, and how many stars it has in it, and how many other planets must orbit those other stars, the idea that Earth was the only one with sentient life forms on it had always seemed absurd and laughable to me.

It was just a matter of time before we would be able to prove that, I had always thought, and I recalled all this as I went back to my bedroom to root through my clothes and find something for Ileandra to wear.

I had very little that looked like it would work well, but I managed to come up with a few small tee shirts and some old shorts that I hadn't bothered to get rid of. Thought I wasn't fat, I wasn't thin either, unfortunately. At least it was evenly distributed, and I still looked good.

I had gained a slight bit of weight over the years, sitting still to write, edit, and publish, only moving when Kavi or my mother got me up and about, and I tended to forget to go through my clothes.

Hence, the supply of "outgrown" shorts and tee shirts.

They were one size too small for me.

I was glad it was only one size too small!

But I wondered if even that would be too big on her.

Thinking of how planets in other solar systems were just now being spotted – astronomers could see wobbles of movement as they passed in front of their suns through telescopes in places like the Atacama Desert in Chile, atop Mauna Kea on the Big Island of Hawaii, and better yet, from telescopes in high orbit – I went back out into the hall.

The water was being turned off as I approached the guest bathroom.

What the Small Gray Visitor Said

Ileandra stepped out of the shower, wet, and took the big bath towel that I had left just outside the door.

She stood there, rubbing herself dry, and considering her hair. It was a rumpled, wispy, wet mess, but it was clean.

I stood in the doorway, holding some black cotton shorts and a tee shirt that said 'Cape Canaveral – Kennedy Space Center' and grinned.

"Here," I said, opening a drawer and picking up a brush that I kept in there for guests (never used!). "Try this."

She looked at it, took it from me, and ran it over her hair.

A few strokes, and she looked almost like herself, though still wet. She rubbed the ends of the towel across her hair a few more times, brushed it again, and gave up. "It will dry."

I showed her the clothes.

"I think those will just fit," she said, putting them on.

"The shorts at least have a drawstring to make them stay on," I said. "Here is another pair, and some other tee shirts."

The other pair was white, and the tee shirts all had slogans on them, except for one, which depicted plumeria flowers. I had gotten it in Hawaii 10 years earlier, when Kavi and I had gone there.

Ileandra looked at that one with interest.

"Plumeria." She said that in a flat tone.

"Have you been to Hawaii?"

"Yes. It was 10 years ago."

"Which island?"

"The Big Island, and Kauai. We had to avoid the human military, but we managed to get some plumeria flowers, and some pineapples."

I laughed. "Good for you. We got some orchids, some plumerias, and some pineapples, but it was a bit easier. They were in lei – no 's' in the Hawaiian language – and from a farm in central O'ahu. We also saw a coffee plantation on the Big Island. The coffee plants have flowers that are related to gardenias."

"You know that?" Ileandra asked.

"Yes. I wrote a history book and travelogue about it, and I paid close attention to the lecture at the coffee plantation in Kona. I'll show you the book as long as you're going to be here with us for a while."

I hoped that wasn't a sore point with her.

I wasn't interested in upsetting her.

She looked up at me.

"I will have to keep trying to leave."

"We'll help you. Don't worry about that."

She looked at me. "I believe you. You have been very good to me – better than I ever expected any humans to be."

"We're not all bad." I grinned.

She gave me another smile.

"Your teeth look good," I said, smiling back.

She looked amused.

I thought for a moment.

"Do you have to actually hike out into the woods just to call your people to come and get you?"

She thought about that. She seemed to be considering whether or not it was advisable to answer me.

After a moment, she decided to go ahead and do so.

"Not anymore. Not unless they are actually coming to get me. They answered last night. They cannot get close to the Earth for several weeks because of your satellites and space stations, nor can they phase to the crop field because of the construction project. But they will be able to get here and take me with them eventually. I just won't know when until they are almost here and about to arrive."

I thought about that.

We were going to have to keep her with us for the summer, it seemed.

"Will you be okay with us? Can we keep you healthy enough with our food?"

She looked steadily up at me.

"We'll find out. I think I have a good chance of that with you and your husband. You are willing and able to make smoothies, as you call them, and to let me stay with you, so yes, I think it will be fine in the end."

I breathed a slight sigh of relief.

The responsibility of this had been worrying me.

Now I smiled.

"Good. Now let's go downstairs and make you a one of those. I have recipe books for them. We can vary them a lot."

She smiled.

"Let me just get my shoes."

She walked across the hall to her room and put them on.

I picked up her dirty clothes, followed her into her room, and put the shorts and tee shirts down on the chair by the window.

"I'll wash this outfit and give it back to you right away," I said. "I have more dirty clothes waiting downstairs to wash, so don't worry about the water use – I'll get a lot of laundry done along with yours."

She listened to this little speech, looking mildly dismayed about all the water use.

"I don't have a sonic cleaner for anything here," I went on, "so you'll have to live with the luxury of water this summer," added.

She let the matter drop without a word.

But I understood her.

Downstairs, with the laundry churning in the machine, Kavi and I put together a smoothie that she could ingest without difficulty: strawberries, blueberries, yoghurt, cinnamon, milk, wheat germ. We ran the blender and poured some for her.

Then we stood there like idiots, watching her try it.

She took a sip, then took another, long, deep gulp of it.

Success!

The coffee was ready, so I poured some and put milk in it for myself.

Kavi was making pancakes with cardamom mixed in.

I got out the maple syrup.

What the Small Gray Visitor Said

He had poured 3 glasses of orange juice.

Ileandra went over to the table and sat with her smoothie at the same spot as the night before. She knew that we had our usual spots and that we wanted to keep them! Of course she did…she was a telepath, I reminded myself, laughing inwardly as I flipped the pancakes over.

A car rolled up the driveway.

Kavi and I looked at each other, and then at our guest.

Ileandra looked like she wanted to bolt.

"It's okay, Ileandra," Kavi said in a soothing tone. "It's just Arielle's mother. She drops by unannounced a lot to visit. Arielle's parents live near us."

Ileandra looked at me, alarmed.

I looked back at her.

"We have to introduce you sooner or later," I said. "If we spend your entire stay with us hiding from everyone we know, we will just call negative attention to ourselves."

She gave me a steady, calm look. "You're right."

"She's not really unannounced," I said, and told her about the e-mail I had sent out last night, on the off chance that we didn't make it back. "She was going to visit. I just didn't tell her anything to tip her off about you."

Kavi nodded, and, after a moment, so did the alien.

She couldn't have actually expected me to leave no note.

"We're going to say that you are visiting us from New Zealand, that you read my books, and that you wanted to meet me. I knew you were coming, but forgot to tell my mother because I had a big edit to do."

I had been working for a week on one, and then another, and hadn't called all week. This might work.

Kavi was watching me think this over.

I guess I looked reasonably confident in my plan, because he nodded and went to let my mother in.

While he was going to the door, I was suddenly reminded of a Mark Twain quote: 'If you tell the truth, you don't have to remember anything.'

And I was about to lie to my mother. I never did that.

What the Small Gray Visitor Said

Damn. I had no training as a spy, either.

Well...full disclosure could come when our guest went home. Or when my mother figured it all out.

She was smart.

She was also a retired nurse.

She had worked as a licensed R.N., as a visiting nurse.

My father would be easier to deal with.

He was a retired city and regional planner who now liked to putter around with his drills and carpentry tools, making cutting boards and doing other small projects. And when he wasn't doing that, he liked to go on long drives with his camera to photograph landscapes and tinker with the color filters and lenses he had.

Kavi and my mother came into the kitchen.

"Do you want a pancake?" Kavi asked her. "Or coffee?"

"Pancakes at two o'clock in the afternoon? No thank you. I'll have some coffee, though." She got a cup and poured some, adding milk.

Then she noticed Ileandra sitting at the table.

"Who is this?" she asked, smiling politely.

"This is Ileandra. We're having mid-afternoon pancakes because we picked her up at the airport last night. We were up late."

"It's nice to meet you," my mother said, going over to shake her hand.

Just in time, Ileandra put hers out and let my mother take it. She had seen a few human commercials or movies that showed handshakes, I hoped and guessed.

"Where are you visiting from?" my mother asked.

"New Zealand."

"You must be tired!"

"A little."

Kavi and I looked at each other.

This was going well – better than expected.

But Ileandra had to be nervous.

"How long are you staying here for?"

"She has an open-ended ticket," Kavi answered for her.

"Really?" my mother sounded surprised. "You can do that, and the immigration people don't mind?"

"Oh yeah, New Zealand is a friendly country," I said.

My mother looked at me, not buying it for a second.

I hadn't really expected her to.

"Noelle, she's just visiting," Kavi quipped.

My mother looked at him. "During a pandemic," she replied. "Uh-huh."

Kavi looked at me.

I thought, 'We might as well get this over with.'

"So, what's the real story?" my mother wanted to know. "Nursing school teaches enough human anatomy for me to see that she's not from New Zealand. And international travel hasn't yet resumed in most places."

It was just as well to get this over with now, and see how it went over.

"I know," I said with a sigh. I really didn't want to lie to my own mother anyway. She was trustworthy. "International travel won't last anyway once the next wave of coronavirus hits, I'll bet."

I was stalling a bit.

My mother just stood there, arched an eyebrow at me, and waited.

Ileandra appeared to be fascinated by this exchange.

"There is a real story, and a cover story," I said.

Ileandra was quick to offer the cover story I had created. "Your daughter is clever," she added. "I will read her books."

My mother looked amused at this. "You mean to say that you intend to pose as a fan of her books?!"

Ileandra paused for a fraction of a second, then said, "Yes." She smiled a slight smile at my mother.

My mother turned to look at me, still with her eyebrow arched. "Wow. I knew you had fans through Facebook, but this is something else!" I told her every time someone said something nice about my books.

One woman had said that she had 're-read' one of them...twice. Perhaps this story would work and people other than my mother would accept it without too many awkward questions. Perhaps…

"Are those your old clothes that she is wearing?"

"Yes. They 'lost' her luggage."

"That's terrible! I hope you got a receipt and filed a report and a complaint with the airline." My mother quipped.

"We did before we left the airport, and we will check online for more to do this afternoon. But I doubt that will produce much of a result – probably just money, if that," I said, trying to sound as disgusted as I could about the dismal service that Ileandra had endured in this phony story.

"When do you think you can catch another 'flight'?"

Ileandra looked rather morose at that. "I don't know. I keep trying to arrange it, but I've lost contact," she said, dropping the cover story with the last part of her response."

"So E.T. is having trouble phoning home?" my mother couldn't resist asking.

Ileandra looked at me for a moment, entertained to realize that most humans seemed to know that line from the movie – and then said, "Yes."

"They phased out of our area, and can't just phase back until they know that they will be unobserved. She's stuck here until who knows when," I said.

The alien nodded. "Your daughter knows all about us."

"Well, for all I knew it was just so much conspiracy theory, but it was fun, and I wasn't willing to just dismiss people who sincerely thought that they had met aliens. Also, one of them described a constellation map that an alien drew for her – a woman named Betty Hill. Later, an astronomer named Marjorie Fish figured out that it was the Owl Nebula. Once I knew it was a real place in the known universe, I felt less like a silly Aspie pursuing an eclectic hobby and more like a researcher. Of course, I kept it all separate from my studies in law school of outer space law."

Kavi and my mother grinned.

"Arielle knows how to study what she's interested in while keeping it in perspective," Kavi remarked.

What the Small Gray Visitor Said

My mother turned to me and said, "As long as you don't
let anyone get a really good look at her – sticking to online
chats with face-time and having her wear hats and face masks
will help – you should be able to keep her here unnoticed."
"So you will remember this cover story and use it?"
"Of course. I just hope it works. It's plausible enough."
Kavi looked at me and smiled, pleased and impressed.
What could I say?
All that fiction-writing was paying off.
And we weren't going out anyway.
We were socially distanced from everyone but family
now, and only went out for groceries, personal care items,
fuel, and postal services.
My mother decided to eat some pancakes after all.
We had a nice time sitting together, with Ileandra licking
the syrup and eating a few crumbs of pancake. She was
curious about our food.

But that wasn't all that she was curious about.
I had a sewing table in the corner, next to my desk.
I could turn to the right, facing the side yard, and pick up
a piece of fabric to sew whenever I wanted to take a break
from writing and editing, without getting up.
"What are you working on at this other table?" she asked.
Ever since governors all over the country – well, the ones
who listened to scientists, at least – had decreed that no one
go out in public without a mask over their nose and mouth,
for fear of carelessly spreading virus microbes from person to
person, I had found a new vocation: sewing all-cotton face
masks. It was even making me some money.
"Masks. Face masks made out of all-cotton fabrics," I
told her. "We have to wear them when we go out in public,
so that we don't share our microbes with other people. If we
all do it, hopefully we won't get coronavirus, the plague that
is killing people all over the planet right now. No doubt you
know about from following our new reports."
She looked up at me. "Yes, we have been following it."

She looked back at my materials. It was a neat pile of fabrics, all cut to the shape and size I needed.

"You will have to wear these until there is a vaccine," she commented, looking at everything without touching it.

"I know. The record for developing a vaccine on Earth is for mumps, and that took 4 years. But that was decades ago, and medical technology has advanced a bit, so the hope is that the virologists can go faster," I said. "And unlike the 1918 influenza pandemic, we know that it is a virus, not a bacterial infection."

The alien looked up at me, and I thought, dejectedly, that she likely knew exactly what the problem was, how the microbe was spread, and what would be involved in fighting it successfully, plus at what human and financial cost...but was barred from telling us the answers.

But I had a few answers, thanks to online research.

"I visited the website for the Center for Disease Control when I was designing my masks. 2 layers of soft, all-cotton fabric are required. When we talk, microbes spray away from us to a distance of at least six feet, so that has to be held back. Combined with social distancing – which means staying at least six feet away from each other when we go out away from our families for any reason, and avoiding large gatherings, we have a decent chance of not catching it."

Kavi laughed. "You are stealing my lines," he said. "But that's okay. I love it that you know enough science to talk about this intelligently and calmly." He turned to Ileandra. "We're hoping to figure it out in 18 months, but there are no guarantees."

"Kavi is working on it at his lab," I told her. "But you knew that already, didn't you?"

She looked up at me, startled. "You must have some telepathic ability!"

I grinned. "No. I'm just logical."

Kavi and my mother burst out laughing.

"Lawyers are very logical thinkers," he said.

My mother had to add her few cents to the discussion. "She also writes science fiction and works in details from reality, so figuring you out is part of her skill set."

Ileandra took this in, then nodded, and commented, "You seem to have a lot of skill sets." She was looking at the sewing table again. Several completed masks were on top.

"May I pick one up and look at it?"

"Yes, of course. I said I'd make some that fit you."

"Good," my mother said. "Wearing a face mask will make it tougher to recognize her for what she is."

"Arielle created her own design," Kavi said. "It's close to medical-grade, and comfortable. It has the added advantage of not chafing on the bridge of one's nose."

I smiled. "If it's not comfortable, people won't wear it. And it has the added advantage of not being paper, which people wear once or twice, throw away, and far too often pollute the ecosystem with. The guidelines are online at https://www.cdc.gov/coronavirus/2019-ncov/prevent-getting-sick/diy-cloth-face-coverings.html, I said."

"It's a nice little side business for you," my mother said.

"I keep telling her she should do bumper stickers for your face with those, but she won't make them political!" Kavi said. He had been joking with me about that for a while. "You could make some money with those."

I said, "No – I get political enough with my blog and books. This is about listening to science. Science is not political. No...I'm going to stick with these politically neutral but beautiful patterns for now."

Kavi laughed, then said, "Okay." To my mother, he said, "Just wait. She'll find the perfect fabric for making a mask into a political message – a message that she agrees with."

Maybe later, I thought.

I had made whole face wardrobes of them for my family and friends, determined to do something to protect them rather than simply worry about the possibility of them getting sick. After that, I had decided to keep going.

What the Small Gray Visitor Said

It was oddly soothing to pull the needle in and out of the fabric, and I had amassed a decent pile of beautiful, as-seen-in-nature, patterns of the stuff, plus some elastic cord for the ear-loops, or some cotton twill tape for head-ties, plus a pile of white cotton gauze for the interior layer.

Ileandra looked through my pile of fabrics.

"They almost all depict plants…flowers…fruits…no, here is one of outer space…is that what this is?"

She held up one that was a brilliant, beautiful, sapphire blue, textured with a bit of darker blue, and finished with many tiny, random, white dots.

"Yes, that's exactly what that is," I said. "It reminds me on the viewscreen aboard the Starship *Enterprise* in *Star Trek*. That's what seemed so cool about it. It took me a while to find that one. It's wonderfully soft fabric."

"That's my favorite one," Kavi said, pulling the mask I had made for him out of it from his pocket with a grin.

I grinned back. I had married a man who loved *Star Trek*.

I turned back to the alien. "Of course, I understand if you don't pick that one."

She nodded went back to her perusal. "…and feathers…you have two of honeybees, which comes as no surprise…and…" She held up one pattern, puzzled. "Why would you want a pattern that depicts bolls of cotton?"

I laughed. "Because it's a joke made beautiful," I told her. "The fabric is all-cotton, and this one depicts the cotton that it is made from. That is the best material to make washable, reusable face masks from, so why not point it out?"

Understanding spread over the alien botanist's face.

"That makes perfect sense. Quite logical." She grinned.

Well, I knew I didn't have a Vulcan extra-terrestrial in my house, I thought to myself, all behavior to the contrary.

She "heard" that and a laugh actually escaped her.

We were suddenly laughing like two silly girls.

I guessed that people were not all that different, no matter how their planets were doing, or which one they were from…

The Thrifty Shopper

My mother was the epitome of chic on a budget. She bought high-end clothing at thrift and consignment shops, liked whatever was in fashion, didn't mind a lack of pockets in most items, and wore a bit more makeup than I did. She also liked her hair shorter than mine, framing her face elegantly. She switched earrings frequently, wearing all sorts, plus necklaces.

I wouldn't wear a necklace except, on special occasions, a string of pearls. No watch on my wrist ever – only pocket watches. And my earrings were usually the pierced Mikimoto pearl studs that Kavi had given me. No dangly ones, and certainly not hoops. I wasn't much fun to shop for, I thought, at least not for my mother. I was more of a challenge…

With our late breakfast over, my mother was ready to move on. She gave me a hug, and handed me a bag.

"You've been thrift-shopping!" I said.

She had found me a dress. It was a beautiful Laura Ashley cotton one with deep pockets from the 1980s – my favorite! It had a gorgeous flower pattern of pink, blue, and pale-yellow irises, with green leaves. Wow – challenge met!

"Thank you! It's perfect!" I said, hugging her again.

"I'll have to look around some more in the thrift shops and see what I can find for you," my mother went on, looking Ileandra up and down, assessing her size. "What size are you? Small? Extra-small? I can always take it back if something doesn't fit…"

Ileandra's mouth dropped open.

"I don't want to be any trouble," she said, "but thank you."

"Nonsense! I love doing this!" my mother said.

"We know," Kavi and I said.

She had stopped buying much for Kavi.

I liked to do that, mostly at L.L. Bean, but once in a while she got lucky and found something that looked good on him. Mostly, she shopped for herself and for me.

She was probably getting bored with looking around just for us, and saw Ileandra as a new project.

We smiled and started cleaning up the kitchen.

"Your accent seems more American than Down Under," my mother remarked after a moment. Good point...

But Ileandra saved me from having to explain this.

"I can say that I went to school in upstate New York – high school – and then to college in Montreal."

"Oh, I see. Yes, an accent can change a lot if you travel and then stay for a while. When I was in England, I found myself unconsciously picking up Britishisms in my speech."

I interjected, "James Corden, the British comedian who does *The Late Late Show* on CBS, did something funny during the quarantine. On his first night doing the show in his garage, he said, "Welcome to *The Late Late Show*, the only late-night television show that can be ruined by someone accidentally opening a garage door." And he said the word "garage" with an American accent. A moment later, his musician, Reggie Watts, pointed it out: "James, you just said 'gaRAJ' instead of 'GAIRaj'!" And James said, "Yes, I know – I'm very disappointed in myself."

Kavi laughed. "I remember that. That was hilarious!"

My mother looked like she had been patiently waiting for me to stop telling anecdotes. This happened a lot, but it was me, an Aspie enjoying something, so she usually just let me do it, as she just had. Then she turned back to our guest.

"Which ones of my daughter's books will you say that you like best?"

Ileandra looked panicked for a second, so I said, "She studied botany in college, so she can start off with my bee book, since that deals with plants and pollinators, then move on to the dystopian series about overpopulation and ecosystems collapse. She can tell the truth with this part of the cover story. Maybe she'll enjoy the travelogue about Hawaii. She's been to the Big Island and to Kauai."

Ileandra just nodded.

I hoped my mother wouldn't probe further.

Ileandra needed some time to actually read the books.

But we were in luck; my mother was ready to go.

"I have to go if I'm going to check the Avon thrift shop, and then I'm going home to meet your father. I'll drop by when I head back with whatever I find."

And she left.

Kavi was stunned. "That went well!" he said to me.

"And she's going to buy some clothes that fit Ileandra!"

"Lucky you – both of you." He looked at our guest. "She hates shopping for clothes."

Ileandra looked at me. "Interesting." And then, "I did not know about thrift shops. They sound like places for used clothing. Is that correct?"

"Yes," I told her. "It is. You are getting an education in human culture already."

She smiled slightly. "That is an excellent sharing of resources. But why don't people just keep their clothing?"

"They outgrow it, they change shape and size as they age, or they are wealthy and like to buy and wear other outfits. Whatever the origin, the only clothing that those shops accept is in a good state of repair and clean. If it's a consignment shop, the original owner gets some of the money when the clothes are sold, whenever that happens."

Ileandra listened to this, and nodded.

Then she said, "I had better read those books you wrote."

I got them for her, and she went over to the sofa and got to work on them.

Wow. She may not be a fan, I thought, but she was studying for the part like her life depended on it.

I supposed that, in a way, it did.

She was studying for her role.

A little while later, she got up for more of that smoothie.

She had finished half of the batch and read the bee book plus the first one of my dystopian novels. There were 3 of them in the series.

"Just how fast of a reader are you?" I asked

She looked up at me, startled.

"I guess faster than a human, or you wouldn't have asked that question."

"Yeah…I hope you are letting yourself enjoy it, though."

She looked at me again.

Then she looked at the books.

"They are very good. I have seen bad writing, and I don't…enjoy that. Yes, I think I enjoyed this novel, though it is the first one I have ever read. I have nothing to compare it with, so I can't be certain."

I shook my head and flopped on the other sofa, watching her delve into the next novel.

It wasn't at all surprising that she hadn't been reading novels, I told myself. She was an alien botanist from another culture. She had been focusing on her work with plants, probably almost to the exclusion of all else.

Then I picked up a book that I had been reading, one about Elizabethan history, and read for a while.

Ileandra finished the next novel, polished off her smoothie, and moved on.

Was she going to finish reading all of the books I had written before my mother came back?!

Yes – that was exactly what she did.

And my mother had found enough clothes for Ileandra to go out to almost any place, as long as it wasn't a formal dinner party.

We didn't have any plans involving one of those, so that didn't matter.

Now the only problem was persuading Ileandra to go out somewhere.

One thing at a time.

After my mother left, I went into the kitchen. "I'm going to bake a cake," I announced.

"Who knows," I said. "Maybe you will be here long enough for Kavi's birthday. But that's later in June. I just like to bake, so this is just a cake – no occasion."

What the Small Gray Visitor Said

Ileandra got up from the sofa and came over to me.

"I have never seen a human's birthday celebration except in a movie or television show, and only by accident. I wasn't focusing on that."

I looked at her. "And now that you're able to watch one in person, you're suddenly much more interested in it, it seems." I grinned. Okay, so I liked a cake-viewing audience.

"What will you make?"

"I will make a recipe that I created years ago just for Kavi, which combines his favorites. It's a 2-layer, round cake with frosting, which is standard for birthday cakes, made with plenty of butter and sugar, some eggs, a little milk, real vanilla extract, flour, baking powder, salt…but here is where it gets distinctive: instead of kosher salt, which many bakers favor due to its intensity, I use Himalayan pink salt. Also, he loves cardamom, so a teaspoon of that goes into the mixture. But it doesn't stop there. Rosewater goes into it as well, along with coarsely ground pistachios and almonds, and flaked coconut. For the frosting, I do a buttercream with more rosewater and coconut, and I use coconut milk in that. To garnish it, I sprinkle on a few more pistachio nuts, just because the green is pretty, and a few pink rose petals."

"You really make wide use of the things that grow on your planet in this cake," she said, sounding impressed.

"Why not? Life should include lots of great tastes."

I turned the oven on and got to work laying out the equipment, greasing and flouring the pans, and measuring the ingredients. Soon the cake was mixed, and I poured it into the pans. We licked the wire whip on the mixer, and shared what was left in the bowl.

"I'm surprised that you are able to eat small licks of almost everything we make without a problem," I told her.

"It's safe as long as I don't make a meal of it."

"So, if you make most of your intake smoothies made of fruits and vegetables, you'll be okay until you can get home?"

"Yes."

"That's good."

What the Small Gray Visitor Said

I cleaned everything up and got going on the frosting.
"You keep your kitchen very neat."
I looked at her. "What do you mean?"
"Some of the human movies I've seen have shown the cook or chef or baker piling up all tools and pans and equipment, dirty and in the sink, to clean all at once at the end of the project."
"Oh...I see. Yes, lots of people work that way, but I find it depressing to have all that waiting for me at the end. I like to clean as I go along instead. It's better when I have company, too. It means that at no time will I have to just stop visiting and spend a long interval working on a boring mess."
With that, I finished mixing the frosting, detached the bowl from the KitchenAid mixer, stuck the large pink spoonula in it, and washed the measuring spoons.
That was it; I had washed the measuring cups after I had put in each ingredient. I stared at the counter for a moment. "Yeah...I guess I am the OCD baker."
"OCD?"
"Obsessive Compulsive Disorder. But it's not a real problem with me. I don't have to retrace every step I take and touch things that I pass by or double-step over every crack in the ground. There are people who have the urge to do such things, and they do them. All I do is clean my own habitat so that it's almost always reset to beginning mode. That's okay."
She nodded.
I could be talking to a guest from anywhere, not necessarily outer space.

A little while later, the cake was complete, on a beautiful glass platter that depicted purple wisteria, and with a huge Tupperware cover over it, having been duly photographed and posted on Facebook and Instagram.
No sense wasting any cake art!
"Why do you photograph it?" Ileandra asks.
"It's good for social media, blog posts, and fun to share with people. It's also fun to get comments such as, 'It looks

too beautiful to cut' because I can tell people who say that that it's okay, because it's been photographed. Besides, it won't stay beautiful if it doesn't get eaten."

She grinned.

"You humans make food an experience rather than merely a sustenance."

"Damn right!" I said, and grinned back.

Clinical Inquiries

I was measuring Ileandra's face for her face masks.

They would have, as discussed previously, head-ties rather than ear-loops to draw attention away from her very small ears.

What did a telepath need ears for, except to keep track of her surroundings, I wondered? Then it occurred to me: even with telepathy, there was still a reason for hearing the physical world.

Ileandra "heard" those thoughts and smiled sardonically.

I looked at her.

"Eavesdropper!" I said to her. "You ought to read a few of my *Star Trek* novels if you're looking for something to do. The Vulcans are telepaths, and they talk about the ethics of telepathy often. It's not polite to listen in on other people's thoughts."

I had a collection of *Star Trek* novels. They were old favorites. Old favorite books were like old friends to me.

"I'm sorry. I can't help it. I'm not doing it deliberately."

"I know. It just seemed worth mentioning."

"Agreed. I shall try not to pay attention to what you are thinking."

I grinned. It was never going to work. I was sure of it.

"What patterns are you going to choose, Ileandra?"

It was Sunday, so we still had Kavi home with us for the weekend. I liked having him around all day for a couple of days a week. Because he was a scientist, with a laboratory to go to and experiments to do, he still left the house on most days.

But he was home more than he used to be, due to social distancing requirements that even extended to the lab. This was to enable sharing the space without the scientists actually being present at the lab together.

I liked it. More Kavi, but still plenty of time on my own.

Ileandra looked at Kavi, and then at me.

"What should I choose?"

I laughed. "Whatever you want! That's the fun of it."

With that, I laid out an array of completed masks for her to consider.

Rosebuds…feathers…shells…bees…butterflies…cats…

I put the measuring tape down, then picked it up again, feeling distracted. It was a long, pink, rubber tape, with 60 inches delineated on one side and 150 centimeters on the other. I started coiling it up.

The measurements of the alien's face were a bit smaller than that of most children – narrower around the lower part of her face than a human's. Yes, it definitely needed a mask if she was going to stay.

I tried to distract myself, knowing that she was able to 'hear' my thoughts. I deliberately thought, those measurements had been sent to me on the Nextdoor app and on Facebook, which was how I had been getting a lot of my customers.

Well, that and my aunt in Newport, Rhode Island.

Aunt Eloise was a retired artist who had graduated from the Rhode Island School of Design, and she was having a great time – vicariously – with my mask-making enterprise.

As a result of her suggestions, I had a lovely collection of patterns to work with in my pile of fabric, all neatly cut into rectangles to sew into masks, sitting atop a cloud of white cotton gauze, which was cut into identically sized pieces.

Ileandra liked the pink-and-white rose garden. The blossoms were mostly wide open, with green leaves around them, and a few buds here and there.

"Okay, that's one. I'm going to make at least two, so pick out something else."

She seemed hesitant, so Kavi said, "It's better to have multiple masks so that they can be washed regularly. I only wear the disposable paper ones at work, in my lab. Otherwise, when I go out elsewhere, such as to a grocery store, I wear a cloth one made by my wife. I have the feathers one, an outer space one, gold bees on dark blue, and several others."

The alien nodded and turned back to the pile of cloth.

She picked up a bee patterned one with a few flowers of different colors strewn here and there.

"Another light color. Good choice," I said, and started cutting the two fabrics and their cotton gauze layers. I cut white cotton twill tape for the rose mask and black for the bee mask.

Ileandra saw the black and started to speak, then stopped. I glanced up at her.

"Don't worry about the black head-ties. It's not too much on you. Now if you had chosen the raspberry-pink rose buds on black, that might have called attention to your pale coloring and your different shape, but a few head-ties won't do that."

Reassured, she nodded and settled down on the other end of the sofa that Kavi was sitting on to watch me sew.

Bagheera was in his basket, in his bed, on his fleecy blanket, curled up in the sunshine. He had stopped staring at our visitor as of yesterday, lost interest in how different she was, and accepted her as part of his world. He was staring out the window at the hummingbird that hovered by the feeder.

"Funny how unconcerned that cat is by our guest," Kavi said, watching him and grinning.

I glanced at him. "Cats know what's worth worrying about and what's not."

Then I reached up behind me and petted the cat. "Good boy, Bagheera."

He purred.

While I sewed, Ileandra talked to Kavi.

Well...she interviewed Kavi.

"Dr. Ravendra, you are a geneticist and a virologist?"

Kavi looked at her and cracked up.

"Call me Kavi. And yes, I am those things."

He waited.

What was he, on the witness stand, being cross-examined?! I tried not to laugh.

I had known him since I was in law school, and I had told him about a guest lecturer I had invited to speak there once. This guest lecturer had talked about being an expert witness. The only response an expert witness should give in court is one that answers the question asked, and nothing more.

What the Small Gray Visitor Said

Kavi had found that advice useful over the course of his career. He had even had to use it once, when asked to testify in a case ten years ago.

Now he was clearly remembering that experience. Perhaps he was being careful not to say too much about his work. Or, perhaps he had another reason to conceal things.

Ileandra was curious about something.

"What did you do with that sample you took from me?"

"Aha…now we are getting to it." Kavi smiled. "You want to know if I did anything more than test it for coronavirus."

"Yes.

"Okay, I did. But first I tested both yours and Arielle's for coronavirus. Safety first!"

"I see. Admirable. What else did you test it for?"

"I tested it to see if your DNA looked familiar in any way. That meant putting in into the DNA code reader."

I had seen that machine twenty years earlier. It was fascinating to know that the human genome could be mapped.

Apparently, Kavi had tried to map the alien genome.

Why not? I would if I were him.

Ileandra looked a bit dejected about this.

But what else could she expect after being taken in by a human whose spouse was a curious scientist?!

She heard me…

So be it, I thought to myself.

She looked back at Kavi.

"What did you find?"

"I found your genome, of course. It would take some detailed study to get familiar with it, but I could see that it wasn't the same as a human's DNA. But that wasn't my main concern. What I was looking for was something else."

The alien looked like she was wondering what else a human scientist with Kavi's qualifications could possibly want from an extra-terrestrial's DNA sample.

Kavi laughed slightly. "I was trying to understand whether or not you had been immunized against any and all pathogens you might possibly encounter on our planet. It would make sense that you would be, so that you would be able to go about your business, collecting and studying our plants."

I looked up from my sewing. "I had wondered about that, too. In H. G. Wells' *The War of the Worlds*, the aliens had no immunity to Earth's pathogens, and so they died while they were invading our planet. But for you to not only collect but also work with our planet's plants, you would have to open the containers with plant microbes on your ship and expose them to the contained environment on it. That would suggest that you would need to have prepared your immune system first."

Ileandra looked impressed in spite of herself.

Kavi smiled. "If you were hoping to pass your time here among clueless humans, you're out of luck. But we are a better bet than most, as you have probably realized by now. We may be capable of logical reasoning and have advanced powers of deduction, as Arielle just demonstrated, but we will hide you."

Ileandra nodded and smiled.

"Thank you. Thank you very much. It's fine."

I settled in to the task of sewing the masks.

After about an hour, they were done.

Ileandra tried them on, and they fit.

"I wonder if you can take them home with you," I said.

She looked up at me, surprised.

"I can. Thank you very much for these."

"You're welcome."

I smiled, imagining aliens looking over my handiwork.

We had a pleasant morning and afternoon once those masks were finished as I showed Ileandra around the house and, of course, the garden.

She was interested in it all, but most particularly the garden.

"How can we store samples of plants for you?" I asked her. "Do we just freeze them? I mean, if you're here for eight or ten weeks, plants will finish their growing season, and others will come along. Remember, I am hoping to send you back with some of everything."

She looked up at me like a kid in a candy store.

I grinned. I sincerely hoped that the prospect of acquiring a plethora of plants that she might not otherwise have access to was a cheerful one – one that would take her mind off of her predicament.

Apparently, it lifted her mood a little bit, at least.

I could even feel it.

It made me wish I could feel such certainly to share with Kavi, but he smiled and hugged and kissed me often enough that I always felt that he was sharing his emotions with me.

I caught the alien staring at me as I thought this.

Damn!

I would have to focus on something else.

"The iris and peony flowers are out, and they're my favorites. They're not useful as food, so I don't know if they will interest you, but I love them, so I make room for them."

"They are beautiful, and their scents are wonderful."

Polite interest? Maybe not…she was leaning over to take a whiff of a pastel pink peony, followed by a bearded lavender Dutch iris with variegated leaves.

Perhaps I had found another fan of those!

The bees and hummingbirds were here, too.

She was fascinated.

I wondered about her planet's ecosystem.

"We don't have such creatures on our planet," she told me. She looked sad about it.

"Will you tell me about it while you're here? I would love to know about the plants and food and so on."

Ileandra considered that.

"Or will you get into trouble if you tell me?" I asked.

She looked at me.

"No, I won't get into trouble."

I waited, carefully snapping off a wet, shriveled-up iris blossom from the stem of a tall, bearded blue one so that the adjacent blossom would be undisturbed by it.

"It will be all right. But my planet is not all right."

I stopped fussing with the flowers and looked at her.

"That's why you sample our planet's plants, then, isn't it?"

"Yes. Our ecosystem has collapsed."

I was horrified, but not surprised.

Still, it was a sickening, startling feeling to know that.

Obviously, there were many details that I wanted to draw out of her while she was here, if I could.

For lunch, Kavi and I concocted another smoothie for the alien. "We're going to have to vary them a lot," Kavi said.

"I know." I looked at her.

Ileandra was looking around the kitchen, studying the appliances and inspecting the bins for garbage, compost, and recycling.

"Somehow, I think that she will get plenty of nutrients this way…maybe even more variety and benefit from whatever diet she has among her own people."

Kavi looked at me, surprised. "What makes you say that?"

"She told me that her planet's ecosystem has collapsed."

He stared at me, appalled, glanced at her, and then put a carrot, a tomato, and a large sprig of dill into the blender. He seemed to be thinking that over has he ground it together.

I made us some grilled cheddar cheese sandwiches on my homemade whole wheat bread with avocado, tomato, and a little jalapeno pepper…more in Kavi's sandwich than in mine.

Then I asked her a question that had been burning in my mind. "How old are you, Ileandra?"

She smiled. "I'm the same age as you and Kavi."

"You're fifty years old?" She looked… "I can't decide how old you look, one way or another. Sometimes I think you look young, but you carry yourself like an older person. And you are a scientist. You would have had to have spent time preparing and qualifying…"

She smiled again. "I did, just as you do for your professions. I should clarify: I'm roughly halfway through my life cycle."

Well, that was nice. Something we had in common with aliens. "Your life cycle is longer than ours, though, isn't it?" I had to ask.

What the Small Gray Visitor Said

"Yes."

"How much longer?"

"Twice as long."

Kavi and I looked at each other.

The alien could live as long as 180 years to 2 centuries.

After lunch, I decided to do something that I had been putting off doing: go on the internet, find a hair-cutting tutorial, and see if I could do an acceptable job on Kavi's hair.

It was bothering him, and I sometimes worried that cops would bother him if he weren't well-groomed. He was Indian, and cops weren't entirely trustworthy, unfortunately. They ought to be required to go to college and have psychological profile tests before being hired, but they weren't in the United States. That meant that there were always some angry, trigger-happy, rough cops on any force. There were racists to avoid.

That was why I was doing this.

That, and, well, Kavi looked really handsome with a good haircut. I might as well be honest about that!

Kavi was as American as the next person, born and raised here, well-educated, and a lovely, sweet guy, but that didn't matter until a cop got to know him. And it was always the first impression that tended to determine the outcome of any police road stop.

What if his car had a tail-light that wasn't working?!

I was sick of worrying about things that I could probably fix, so I sat at the computer, trying to eliminate at least one reason to worry.

It was crazy, but I didn't care.

After about forty minutes, I was finished.

Kavi didn't notice what I was doing, because he was going through his e-mail. That was just as well.

Also, I wore headphones. Only I heard the video.

But Ileandra knew.

She knew why I was doing this, too.

What the Small Gray Visitor Said

As soon as I realized that, I looked steadily at her and thought, as hard as I could, 'Don't tell Kavi any of what you have found out by reading my mind!'

She nodded and kept quiet.

I turned around, got scissors, a comb, a spray bottle, and a towel. Then I filled the bottle at the kitchen sink.

"Kavi, are you almost done with that e-mail?"

He looked up at me, confused. "Yeah, just a few more. Why?"

"I'm going to cut your hair. I just watched a tutorial."

His mouth dropped open.

"Do you trust me not to make a mess of it?"

He grinned. "I trust you."

Wow. That was easy!

A few more minutes and he was done.

I pulled a kitchen chair out onto the patio, brought the tools with me, and he sat down.

My plan was to let the wind, not the alien, take the clippings.

Damn...I think she knew that, too!

Oh, well...somehow, I knew she wasn't interested in taking them anyway. Good...maybe I would be on the receiving end of some telepathy, too!

I sprayed my husband's hair all over, combed it, took a deep breath, and started cutting. Long on the top, short on the back and sides. Trim around the ears and hairline.

It took me about half an hour.

When it dried, we would know how it had come out.

But Kavi took the towel off without the slightest concern, rubbed his hair dry, and combed it back.

"Thank you! That feels great – much better!"

He kissed me.

"Maybe you shouldn't kiss me until you look in the mirror."

He grinned, said, "Okay, I'll do that now," and went into the half-bathroom by the kitchen.

Ileandra and I waited for the verdict.

What the Small Gray Visitor Said

He came back.

"I like it – you got the hang of this. But then, you're a quick study with any independent work."

He did look pretty good – close to what the barber had been doing for him before the coronavirus pandemic had locked down everything that wasn't deemed "essential".

Ileandra asked, "What about your hair?"

I took the clip out of it and it fell. It came well past my shoulders, and I liked it like that. I wore it up most of the time though, in a waved, gold-matte clip, swept up to the side and around into a twist.

"My mother will trim it to just reach my shoulders if she sees how long it's gotten," I told the alien.

"Don't tell her!" Kavi said, running his finger through a tendril of it from my head to its end. "I love it like this."

I grinned. "Me too." And I put my hair back in its clip.

Early in the evening, I was thinking about dinner and what I might cook that would include enough sauce for Ileandra to make a meal out of, when a car rolled into the driveway.

It was my parents and uncle!

Kavi and I looked at each other.

"What do we do?" I asked. "My mother probably told Daddy and Uncle Louis everything!"

Ileandra stood in the living room, having jumped up from the sofa, looking like she wanted to run from the room.

I wouldn't have blamed her if she had run upstairs.

But she didn't.

"Your mother met me. It's absurd to think that she wouldn't tell her husband and brother," the alien said.

Kavi just looked at us both and shrugged his shoulders.

"No sense worrying about a done deed," he said, and opened the side door.

In walked my parents, carrying pizza boxes from my favorite pizza parlor, Luna Pizza, with my uncle right behind them. He was carrying an insulated blue bag, one that I knew was for beer.

What the Small Gray Visitor Said

Sure enough, he had brought Corona light beer – 12 bottles. Kavi took one look, smiled, and got some limes out of the fridge. He got one of the wooden cutting boards that my father had made and sliced wedges for the beer.

Ileandra stood still in the living room, wide-eyed.

She hadn't even bothered to put on her face mask.

There was no point in doing that.

Obviously, she was in the small circle of family members who were allowed to meet without masks...and my mother had told her husband and brother about the alien visitor.

We did this with no one else.

My uncle lived in the old family house, five minutes up the road from my parents, in West Hartford. They were all just over the mountain from us.

I should have realized that my family would invite themselves over in short order once I had taken in a stranded alien botanist.

My mother must have been determined to show my father and uncle that she wasn't crazy, imagining anything, exaggerating, or otherwise confused.

She had a penchant for not bothering to choose her words precisely, especially when she was in a hurry to say something, and that usually led Uncle Louis and me to correct her and tease her. My father would join in on occasion.

No wonder she had brought them here to see what she had no doubt at least alluded to.

"So, who's this guest you've taken in?" Uncle Louis asked.

He stood in the kitchen, looking right at her.

She looked back at him.

He towered over her.

Uncle Louis, like me, had a loud voice. He wore a plain, short-sleeved, buttoned shirt, cargo pants, and sneakers. His beard was short, and his hair, which was bald on top, had been cut, as usual, with a kit, which meant that he sometimes missed a spot or two.

He was a technical genius who could fix anything.

He could fix computers, toasters – you name it.

He was also a political liberal like me who kept track of the news in detail. We liked to discuss current events.

Ileandra glanced from me and Kavi back to my uncle.

"Uncle Louis, this is Ileandra. She's a botanist. Ileandra, this is my uncle, Louis Halloran."

She looked at him again and said, "It's nice to meet you."

I moved on to say, "And this is my father, Edward Desrosiers."

My mother had cut my father's thick hair very short – without a kit – during the pandemic lockdown. It looked okay, but not great. Nevertheless, at least he had a full head of hair.

My father, a retired city and regional planner, walked up the back of the sofa and stared down at her. He too, towered over Ileandra. Both men were just under six feet tall.

They towered over me, for that matter. I was a bit shorter than both of my parents, having grown to a height of five feet, four and a half inches. My mother had been five feet, seven inches tall at full height. She had shrunk an inch, but I was still shorter. Oh, well.

Kavi and my mother were now the same height.

And here was Ileandra, at four feet, yet clearly an adult.

"Wow," my father said. "You weren't kidding, Noelle."

My mother looked...vindicated.

I wondered how much mockery she had endured.

I didn't blame her for getting fed up and telling them to come over here and see Ileandra for themselves.

However...

"Benjamin Franklin made a comment about secrecy," I spoke up to say. "Something about how if two people know a secret, and only one is alive, the secret can be kept – otherwise, it can't. This secret is spreading and spreading."

My parents and uncle turned to look at me.

"Who would believe us?!" my father wanted to know.

"Yeah, who would?"! Uncle Louis echoed.

"We don't want to be locked up in a mental institution," my mother said. "Or worse...what did you call them, the men in suits?"

What the Small Gray Visitor Said

"They're the Men in Black, Mommy," I told her. "There are a few comedy movies about them, too, though they may be a conspiracy theory that is sold as entertainment."

"Or not," Kavi said. "Now that we've actually met an alien..."

"Oh, so now you have confirmed it!" Uncle Louis said, grinning. "Does she eat pizza?"

Unbelievable...

"No," I said, "but we've got that covered." I mixed up a carrot smoothie for Ileandra while we drank some of the beer.

The pizzas were a horrible sausage one for Daddy and Uncle Louis (which my mother had some of, since she liked everything), and spinach, garlic, eggplant, and basil one for me and Kavi (also shared by my mother).

Ileandra had taken one of the beer bottles and tasted it.

Too late, I remembered that scene in *E.T.* in which he drank beer and Elliott felt the effects.

"This is made from wheat products?" she asked.

"It's barley malt," I said. "Have some lime juice in it; it tastes even better that way." I squeezed some into her bottle.

She tried it. "Yes, it is even better..."

She was getting loopy.

I had only had half of a bottle, which usually did nothing to me, but I felt loopy, too.

Great...good thing I was in the for the night!

I quickly poured out the carrot smoothie and put it on the table for her in a mug with a large handle.

My mother and Kavi were laying out the pizzas.

I got napkins, plates, and forks and knives.

And then I quickly ate a slice of pizza to see if I would feel less loopy.

I never figured it out, because Ileandra drank her liquified carrots at the same time.

Someone that small had to be susceptible to the effects of even a mild alcoholic drink, especially with nothing else in her system.

And I was feeling what she was feeling.

What the Small Gray Visitor Said

At least my thoughts and actions were still my own.

This wasn't a movie, I reminded myself.

I ate some more pizza, got a large glass of water to go with my beer, and felt okay.

Ileandra seemed to be making a concerted effort not to get drunk. She let my uncle finish her beer.

As we sat there eating pizza and ingesting a carrot smoothie, my parents and uncle interrogated us about our small gray visitor.

"How long will you be here, Ileandra?" my mother asked.

Ileandra looked very uncomfortable. "I don't know."

Everyone glanced around the table at one another.

"Why don't you know?" my father asked.

I helped her out at this point by recounting the tale of our hike through the dark the night before last.

My mother was horrified. "You could have been killed – or abducted by aliens, apparently!"

Ileandra spoke up. "We would not have killed nor abducted them!"

My mother looked at her.

"You wouldn't? Good. But a bear might have gotten them."

Ileandra hadn't thought of that.

I had, but I didn't mention it.

"The bears were asleep," Kavi said.

We all laughed, except my mother.

"You still haven't answered the question," my father said.

Ileandra looked at him, and answered it. "I have been signalling and signalling to be picked up, but the ship has phased out of the area, back home, and can't come back until the construction crew finishes its work and removes itself and its equipment from that area across Nod Road from the agricultural field."

My father's face lit up with comprehension. "Oh. I see. Yeah…they are doing some structural work on the underside of that bridge, plus on the road, pavement and all, that connects to it. It will tie things up, mostly at night, for the next few months. All summer, in fact."

"When did they put all of that stuff in place?" Kavi asked. "Ileandra said it wasn't there the night she got stranded here."

"They brought it on Friday," my father said. "I visited Holloway & Associates and they told me about the project. They surveyed the traffic before it started." That was the engineering and surveying firm that my father had worked at until he retired.

Kavi and I looked at each other and then at Ileandra, stunned. She really was stuck here all summer!

Uncle Louis put in, "I served some papers about that," and he took another bite of pizza. "But I had no idea it would affect anyone I knew at the time."

I said, "How could you have?! Ileandra wasn't even here yet."

Feeling dejected on her behalf, I cleared the table and got some pistachio-rosewater ice cream out of the freezer. I had made it a few days ago.

I microwaved it to soften it up enough to scoop, and served it.

Ileandra was able to eat it!

The sweet treat seemed to cheer her up slightly.

I was glad.

I didn't envy her this situation, stranded indefinitely on an alien planet.

No...no matter how well educated she was about this planet, she was still far from home without a guaranteed way back there.

My parents and uncle seemed to realize that and suddenly became a lot more solicitous of her, speaking very kindly to her for the rest of the visit.

Kavi and I ate in silence, shocked by it all.

It was still a lot to get used to.

The Prime Directive

After my family left, I had another question for Ileandra. I just couldn't fathom that she wouldn't have a problem once she got back among her people about having revealed herself to us, even though it seemed unavoidable. "Will you be in any trouble when you get picked up?"

"Trouble?"

"Yes – what I mean is, there is something in *Star Trek* called the Prime Directive of Non-Interference in the cultures that they encounter when they visit other planets. Usually, that is complied with by maintaining secrecy. You can't do that with us. We know about you now. And we are learning more about you all the time."

The alien looked at us both.

"Yes, you are. It is too late for complete and total secrecy. This is the best I can do. I will not be in trouble."

I considered that. "Good. In *Star Trek*, they can't always maintain total secrecy either. And you are physically different enough from us that if you stayed here permanently, you would be noticed, so you have to go home – alive."

"Yes, I must take as much evidence of my presence here back with me. I cannot leave you any of my tools, nor a scrap of clothing."

"I know. It's already bad enough that Kavi had to take a little of your DNA just to reassure us that you did not expose us to anything – particularly the coronavirus pathogen we are currently avoiding without fully understanding it. And we don't want to be harangued by any government agents over your visit. We're going to be very careful."

Kavi looked alarmed at all this, but I was hashing it out in front of him just to make sure that he thought of all the angles. Despite the fact that he was a genius in his field, he could, like so many geniuses, become myopic about his view of a situation, seeing the fascinating scientific discoveries in front of him to the exclusion of the other facets of it all around him.

He saw me observing him and nodded. He got it.

What the Small Gray Visitor Said

We sat in the living room after dinner, all of us – the cat, Kavi, Ileandra, and I – and looked for something to watch on television. It was late, and we had gotten into the habit of staying up late in the hope of helping her get home, but thus far, to no avail.

Most evenings, we couldn't try to meet the ship.

It rained, or it was too overcast, or the police shooting club was meeting for practice. One night, the golf club had a wedding in its clubhouse, with lots of people, cars, music, and noise until late.

Ileandra seemed resigned to her fate, unconcerned even.

"I will get back eventually, even if we can't know when that will be, and I appreciate your hospitality and understanding. I'm sorry to be imposing on you this long."

Kavi and I had laughed at that eloquent speech.

"We are not sorry to have you here," we told her.

Indeed, this was the dream of a lifetime, clandestinely experienced though it had to be.

She appreciated that, too.

"Hey," I said, "how about this show? It's on ufology. You can see all of the wrong information, interpretations, and other hilarity associated with this field."

She looked at me, intrigued. "Why not? It would be good to understand human encounters with us from their perspective – not just from yours, I mean. You are educated, cautious people. Everyone who has a close encounter isn't like you, and they are all different."

"That we are," Kavi remarked.

Ileandra looked mortified. "I'm sorry. I shouldn't talk about you so clinically."

He laughed. "I'm a clinician too. I can take it."

I was shaking with laughter listening to them.

But then the show topped them both.

Abductees were talking about the aliens lacked genitals or belly buttons.

What the Small Gray Visitor Said

"That's because you were looking at them while they were wearing their environmental suits, you fool!" I said to the TV. Ileandra laughed so hard that she almost fell off the sofa.

I gaped at her.

"I didn't think anything could make you laugh like that!"

She took a deep breath, shifted into place on the sofa, and smiled. "I may be a space traveler and a scientist, but that doesn't mean that everything that ever happens is bland and without impact. As your species often says in such situations, everyone is 'human'."

"We need a different word to describe that. What are we all? Sentient?"

"Yes, that will do."

We sat there and watched the story of *Roswell: The U.F.O. Cover-Up* until it was over, and then went to bed.

We found ourselves watching a lot of ufology and science fiction – much more than usual.

Usually, I watched historical novels made for television – and read the novels – plus history, documentary, medical drama, anything that showcased Asperger's in a positive manner, a select few sitcoms, and police procedurals that included courtroom scenes.

Now it was *Star Trek, Dune, I, Robot, Star Wars, Brave New World, Logan's Run, Z.P.G. – Zero Population Growth, Fire in the Sky, Close Encounters of the Third Kind,* and more *Star Trek.* That last one is repeated because it has so much material to offer.

"I guess you really can't operate according to any Prime Directive of noninterference," I commented a few evenings later. "We now know far too much."

Ileandra just said, "Yes, you do."

I sincerely hoped that she wouldn't get into any trouble for having spent time here, no matter how careful we were.

The next day, Ileandra and I were in the living room and kitchen area again, looking at the computer. I told her that I

102

not only wrote about human overpopulation, but I also administrated a group about that on Facebook.

Therefore…she was looking at my Facebook account.

Against my better judgment, out of a desire to let her do a little anthropological field work, I had let her do it.

She had found the Overpopulation Discussion Group that I administrated, and was looking at the rather lengthy set of rules that I had pinned to the top of the feed:

Group Rules:

If you ask to join this group, ANSWER THE QUESTION as to WHY you wish to join. Don't just leave it blank, and have a profile not filled out, or rigged so that nothing about you can be revealed, and then expect to be added to the group.

Important Rule: Do NOT invite everyone you know to join. Ask them if they are interested first, and never, ever, attempt to add them all at once. They must be checked out by the administrator, and expecting us to just do all that at once say, in the middle of the night or in the middle of a busy schedule, is not reasonable, nor it is fair. Thank you.

If you invite people to join this group, tell them in a note that they MUST write an answer to the questions as to WHY they wish to join. Too many applicants say nothing, and have little to nothing filled out/ visible on their profiles.

Do NOT invite 20 or more of your friends to this group all at once. That means that the administrators must then vet them - a laborious process of checking their Likes lists, what groups they are in, photographs, and posts. That's a lot to ask someone to do all at once. And we want to check everyone carefully rather than just hitting "Approve".

What the Small Gray Visitor Said

Do NOT suggest nor direct people to donate money. You don't know the state of their finances, nor is it any of your business to know it.

No suggesting that women should have more controls on their ability to not reproduce than men. It's odd to find a reason to include this rule, but at least one has been provided.

No abusive language or name-calling.

No accusations that assume that people in this group are not doing things to mitigate the impact of human existence, such as refusing straws.

No bashing of other people's points of view or ideas.

No anti-autism.

No fascism. No nationalism.

No immigrant/migrant hating.

No holding it against anyone for not being vegan.

No fights over loving cats and/or dogs as pets.

No advertisements! No porn.

Such posts and writers shall be deleted from the group.

Internet trolls will be deleted, blocked, banned, and otherwise removed.

Please keep the comments that you post under posts relevant to the post. This means do not attempt to draw attention to a separate issue than that of a given post by putting comments, articles, etc. under it that are about something else! Thank you.

What the Small Gray Visitor Said

This group is about objections to the generation of more humans. Our planet has far too many. Humans moving from one place to another is not what causes more of our species to exist. This group is not meant as an anti-immigration forum. Unless and until we see so many all at once and unregulated as to mirror a dystopian horror movie about human overpopulation, hysteria about immigration comes off as bigotry rather than reasonable fear of a security breach.

When many from one culture migrate, they must not expect women to change their culture of dressing and living (i.e. Muslims moving to Europe and objecting to bikinis, short skirts, or women riding bicycles). Unless that barrier is breached, anti-immigrant posts are more about bigotry than about human overpopulation.

If you believe that any one group of humans ought to out-reproduce another, this is not the group for you.

She looked up at me when she had read it all. "How did you come up with such a detailed, comprehensive list of rules? It seems to plan for almost every contingency."

I laughed and said, "I try."

I was busy making smoothies and baking chocolate-chip almond cookies, so I didn't need to be sitting at my computer for a while.

"It wasn't done all at once. Those rules evolved slowly, over time, as issues came up in chats, comments, and other discussions. Some people got thrown out of the group over those things, and others didn't. If they can possibly learn from the rules or agree to abide by them, I keep them in the group, hoping that they can learn more. Not everyone researches human overpopulation and ecosystems collapse as much as I do, after all, but they do see the link of all that to climate change."

"Your media seem to be seeing that at last, too."

"Yes. I'm glad, but it is still too little, and likely far too late. We have a huge proportion of our species that just doesn't want it to be so, and therefore denies, ignores, gaslights, and outright lies about it."

"Why would they do that? I've seen it, but why?"

I looked at my alien guest, trying to keep a straight face.

"They want to consume resources in as large and varied amounts as they predecessors did, and to have descendants who display and repeat their genetic phenotypes in perpetuity, and to live out their lives seeing that, and to die believing that that will continue indefinitely. They feel entitled to it, and become enraged by the mere idea that such a thing might not be feasible."

Ileandra looked horrified.

I poured out our blackberry-blueberry smoothies.

She took hers absentmindedly and sipped at it.

"This is delicious."

I smiled and sat down on the sofa.

She took one more gulp of her drink and paused.

"What's the matter? Prime Directive weighing on you?"

She looked up at me, startled.

"How did you know that?"

"Oh, come on. I'm a *Star Trek* fan."

She smiled. "Oh, right. That makes sense, then."

I continued, "You don't need to worry about convincing me. I'm the proverbial choir, already in agreement, as you can see. And the rest of the human species…well…I'll just have fun shocking them into understanding the situation."

"Won't that cause anger and conflict?"

"We'll have that no matter what, so I might as well have a little fun poking, jabbing, and stirring the others into consciousness. There's nothing I enjoy quite like shocking parochial-minded conservatives out of their self-constructed comfort zones."

She nodded.

"How do you keep track of your species' numbers?"

"I use a website. Here: https://www.worldometers.com."

What the Small Gray Visitor Said

We looked at the latest count of humans on the planet Earth, at least, according to this site: 7.74 billion.

"That's not accurate. It's 8.4 billion," Ileandra said.

"Why am I not surprised?!" I said in disgust, and sat back on the sofa with my drink.

She looked at me as if to say that I was no fool.

Then she started rummaging around on my desk.

I didn't mind.

It had pens, pencils, and a ruler in a large, blue plastic cup that was left over from my college days. The ruler was one of those fun ones, made of wood, with measurements on one side and facts on the other side. This one had a list of famous authors in the order in which they had been born. Some were still alive. On top of it was a little finger puppet of Virginia Woolf, made by the Unemployed Philosopher's Guild (online at www.unemployedphilosophersguild.com).

"What is this?" she asked, pointing at it.

I explained what a finger puppet is.

"And you have it because she is another author?"

"Well, that, and I like her message in her lecture series, *A Room of One's Own*."

"What is the message?"

"It's that women must have money and a room of their own if we are to write fiction." I paused, then added, "Actually, it doesn't matter what we're writing. But she wrote fiction, so of course she made it about that."

"So, humans need quiet and solitude to work?"

"We tend to do our best work without too many distractions, but we don't always have our own space. Kavi works in a lab with other physicians and scientists around him. He has his own office, though."

"That's how we work too – in a shared laboratory. We don't use an office. We just keep entering data wherever we happen to be working."

"Why am I not surprised?" I said, more to myself than to her. I grinned. "You're not as different from us as you might think. Or maybe you aren't thinking such a thing. I don't know; you're the telepath."

She smiled. "I go back and forth like that about that, too." We paused, temporarily distracted by our own thoughts.

Then Ileandra took one of the pencils out of the cup and looked at it. It was white, and it said, in black, block-capital letters, "I'VE BEEN ABDUCTED BY ALIENS." She read it out loud in a surprised tone.

"Oh, that's a joke. It doesn't actually mean that anyone has been abducted. It was sold as part of a set labelled "INTROVERTS". It's meant to have an excuse for being left to one's own devices, to be asocial. I just liked that one best."

She was staring at me with the first truly incredulous look that I had seen on her face since we had met. "Of all the excuses to use..." She actually trailed off, at a loss for words.

"Yeah, it's a funny coincidence, that's all. It's more like I have abducted you for now, keeping you in my house. Except, I'll let you leave as soon as your friends come to pick you up."

Ileandra put the pencil back in the cup.

She looked unhappy.

"They are going to pick you up eventually, aren't they?"

She looked up at me. "Yes, but I don't know when. They most likely went all the way back home with the plants they had. I suspect it was because we had collected forty or so new ones, and it was time to process them – and because they didn't have a convenient way to pick me up without being seen by humans."

"What – back to the Owl Nebula?"

"Yes." She seemed resigned to me knowing where home was. It was probably because there was no way I could go there, and because there was no one among my species to tell without getting myself locked up in a psychiatric ward and drugged senseless.

"Well...I guess you're going to have the ultimate field study experience until they come back," I told her. "Want to go out in disguise and see how we humans live?"

What the Small Gray Visitor Said

She looked at me as though I had suddenly figured out how to build a warp drive engine or something. "Go out? Among other humans?"

"Yes."

"Where will we go?"

"Well...there's an ice cream place, a bookstore, grocery stores, and a farm stand. And I have a Zoom call online coming up with some friends who are authors. You could participate. You have face masks now. We'll just say that you're out in some public space, and that people keep walking too close to you to take the mask off."

"Will that actually work?" Ileandra looked worried.

"Yes, but I can do most of the talking. It'll probably be good practice for you, to test how well you do at passing for human. You make pretty good conversation with me. My friend is as knowledgeable as I am about what interests her, so we could find plenty to talk about."

"Okay...I'll try it if I can be made to look like someone who could be human."

"You're closer to that than you think. A lot of it is about people's assumptions. People assume the wrong things all the time. I think that's how spies stay alive long enough to have careers and gather information on their adversaries."

"But you're not a spy! This is quite a risk you're planning to have me take. And it's a risk to you, too. We could both end up...unmasked, literally and figuratively."

"We'll be here the whole time – at home."

"Okay..."

I hoped we would be able to go out somewhere.

The mere idea of showing her my world on its own terms rather than having her just observe us from a hiding place – a ship with an invisibility cloak, or whatever her species used to watch us – was really enticing to me.

But I could see her point of view.

What really had me wondering about problems was the Prime Directive. I just couldn't believe that she would have no trouble later over that, when she finally got home...

What the Small Gray Visitor Said

"Are you really not worried about violating a Prime Directive and influencing our culture just by talking to us? Isn't that against the rules or laws of your species?"

She looked up from the cup of pencils, which she had been rummaging through while holding it in her lap.

"Yes. Although…"

"What? We could use a little influence?"

She grinned. "Yes, you could."

"Okay. I'll start preparing Kavi's laptop so that you can use it on our café chat."

Ileandra looked pleased.

I was actually a bit excited about this adventure, and about other ones in which she would actually leave the house, dangerous or not. Maybe it was pointless to try to conceal her presence. Maybe it was wiser to explain it instead.

And if she wasn't concerned about the Prime Directive, well…on her own head be it.

Ileandra seemed to be eavesdropping on my thoughts, because she said, "As long as I'm not spotted for what I am, a little discussion about resource scarcity and ecosystems abuse and collapse could do some good."

I laughed. "You'll do fine. I do that often. I can't stop mentioning human overpopulation and ecosystems collapse."

"What should we say about how we know each other?"

I glanced up at my computer screen. The Facebook group on human overpopulation was still on it.

I grinned. "We're going to say that one of my readers – one of my superfans, who has enjoyed my novels on that topic – came to visit me. That can be backed up. I actually have fans. People around here won't check that. They'll easily believe it."

Ileandra looked impressed. "That's actually a good idea."

I grinned. "Well, I do write fiction."

Café Chats

I loved spring.

Not only did the iris and peony blossoms come out, but it was also nice and warm without being so hot that I couldn't enjoy open windows and fresh air while inside.

A little longer and the air conditioning would be on.

But not yet. It was still June.

Thus, conditions were ideal for a video chat with my author friends.

Thanks to the pandemic, we had gone from meeting at the Barnes & Noble café in Canton, just a few miles up the road, to video chats.

It made me glad that I already had Kavi before this happened, so that I wouldn't be thinking that I wished I had someone, but couldn't go out and meet people until who knew when…because although scientists guessimated that it would take twelve to eighteen months to create a vaccine for the coronavirus, that was just a guess. No one knew when we would have one, or if it would be possible to come up with one. Also, once a vaccine was found, it would have to be manufactured in quantities sufficient for everyone on the planet – which would mean more waiting.

No…we were in for a long stretch of social distancing.

The video chat call would start in an hour.

I had set up my desktop computer, and was busy setting up Kavi's for Ileandra to use. I had invited her to the chat.

I had elected not to use my own laptop for this.

One with a different account was required.

This would make it possible to manipulate the signature on the account. We were going with my idea of saying that Ileandra was outside in a public place, and therefore needed to wear her mask.

In reality, she would be sitting in my back yard.

We had already gone out there and set up the lawn furniture, pulling it out of the back of the garage in a hurry. Table, chairs, cushions, etc. One thunderstorm warning and it

111

would go right back in, but that wasn't likely for a few more days. I had checked the weather report.

We had also fussed with the position of the laptop. The background behind her would have to be as nondescript as possible to make the story about her location plausible.

I was going to lie to my friends about our alien visitor.

What else could I do, though?!

Ileandra had her rose face mask in her hand. She was over by the bookcase under the window, next to my desk, looking at my published books.

"You have an academic background, but you write both inside and outside of it," she remarked.

"Yes. I like to write in many genres."

"Why?"

I thought about that.

"Well, academic books are slow, laborious reads that require greater concentration and a willingness – a desire, really – to commit their contents to memory. At least, that's how it is for humans. And most humans aren't like me, as you and I discussed the day we met. Most humans have short attention spans, and limited interest in learning new things. That's why our planet is so polluted – instant gratification leads to appalling carelessness. Fiction can cause a reader to learn things without really trying, because they're having fun reading, so they take in facts as part of following a story. It's just easier for most people. So…I make that work for my stories, which are always about something important – something to do with law, politics, science, ecosystems, overpopulation, finance and the distribution of resources – and I make sure to include beauty and fun, so that people will like learning it all."

She looked both pleased and demoralized.

I wondered why, until she spoke again.

"It's not good that humans like you are so few."

"Don't I know it," I replied.

"But you were telling me about why you write in different genres, rather than just the academic one."

"Right. Tangents…Aspies and academics do go off on them…which does get me back on track. Far fewer humans read academic books than other genres, particularly fiction, which is the fun stuff."

"Oh…I think I see where you are going with this."

"Yes. I want to reach those other people – the ones who don't like to study – with the data I learn from reading academic books. To do that – to influence voters and make people think about what matters, I have to present that in terms that they can relate to on their terms. So, I write fiction in the hope of saving the Earth's ecosystems by inducing other humans to care more about that."

"You can do this with fiction? You write imaginary stories with that data? How does this work to achieve what you are describing?"

"It builds the data into a story full of events that tie it to – the data to – the characters and their problems. The emotional impact of the effect of all that on people's lives is what lures readers in, making them unconsciously learn the facts that I hope to influence them to care about. It works without them focusing on it. It has to be that way, because if they feel it happening, they will lose emotional engagement with the story, and cease to care as much."

"Fascinating."

Cool…I had a Vulcan of sorts in my house!

I continued, "Enjoying the story, or feeling a sense of empathy with the characters, is what makes the reader absorb the ideas I want to convey, and why they matter."

"I see," she said. "When they remember, they may learn and change. You are trying to change things by changing your readers with your books."

"Yes, I'm trying, anyway."

"And fiction does this better than academic writing."

"Well, more academic writing is just preaching to a choir – that's a metaphor for trying to convince people who already agree with the person making the argument. Academics already agree that saving our ecosystem and not overpopulating the

Earth is crucial to saving and preserving it. But they are educated, thoughtful people who don't feel forced to take in science, facts, data, and whatever else to understand the world. I don't need to reach them. I need to reach everyone else."

"You give your planet hope just by continuing to do this. Never stop," Ileandra said.

I grinned. "I won't. I can't, anyway. It's addictive."

"Good."

We paused, wondering what to talk about next.

I got up and washed our coffee mugs and put them away, changed Bagheera's water, washed his food dish, and stretched.

"Let's get ready. The café chat starts in half an hour."

The alien suddenly looked terribly nervous.

I needed to reassure her.

Then I had an idea. "Have you heard of the great American humorist and author who lived in Connecticut in the late 19th century, Mark Twain, also known as Samuel Langhorne Clemens?"

She thought for a moment. "Yes. It was part of our research for this area."

"Good. I used to give tours in his house, and have read many of his novels. His quotations are terrific. Here is my favorite: 'If you tell the truth, you don't have to remember anything.'"

She looked worried. "We can't tell them that I am an alien visitor from another solar system!"

"We're not going to tell people everything. But think this over: you are our friend. You are a writer of botanical works. You would like to use your talents to write a story about plants and their importance, and the importance of protecting them. All of that is true. We are just going to tell people that much. Any more information is none of their business, and they won't inquire too deeply because we won't linger long enough for that. No one, therefore, will be able to induce a moment of anxiety in us, which is what leads to lies and being discovered as trying to hide anything."

She regarded me with a thoughtful gaze, then nodded.

What the Small Gray Visitor Said

"That actually sounds logical. Okay. I'm ready."

"Have you seen the ads for these schools?! 'Private, Christian, affordable, non-profit.' No good! Just add religion, and unless it's divinity school, it has been changed from education to indoctrination." I paused for air, having expended it in my diatribe, then added, "Future voters' minds will be tainted by that, which is just what the radical Christian right, Bible-beating gazillionaires want."

We were online, doing the video chat, visiting with my author friend, Elise, and Ileandra had psyched her out – literally, though of course we couldn't tell Elise that – enough to feel comfortable talking about life, politics, and resources around her.

I had introduced Ileandra as a friend who liked my books, a fan from Facebook who I had agreed to accept a visit from. We were going with the cover story that she had just moved here from New Zealand, and had met me when she bought some face masks from me.

I delivered them to people in zip-lock bags by ringing doorbells and leaving the bags, then stepping back several feet to chat. Elise hadn't been surprised when I introduced Ileandra Again, so far, so good.

Another friend, Nainsi, was going to join us soon.

Meanwhile, we chatted with Elise.

Elise was a graduate of Mount Holyoke College who had grown up in Amherst, Massachusetts and Boston. She had been writing all her life, and only recently published a few short books of poetry. I was trying to persuade her to do them up properly, with beautiful cover art and neatly-formatted front matter (the pages at the beginning of any book that included the title-author-publisher information, the copyright data, dedication, and table of contents, to name a few important items). The effort was coming along…slowly.

Elise had practically lived in the café due to its proximity to her home, and to her need to get out of the house. Her kids were all adults, in medical, business, and art school, and she had turned them into readers by bringing them to libraries and bookstores as they were growing up, while she wrote.

She was back there now, but outside, on the sidewalk. The store had moved the tables out there. Customers had to buy their tea or coffee and go out immediately – no lingering indoors. It was the same with book shopping – staying many feet apart, buying, and leaving.

I thought Elise was clever – she had done the right thing by both her children and herself. Too many women lost themselves in motherhood, ignoring their own intellectual needs and ambitions. Not Elise!

Elise exuded her own, unique sense of flair and panache as a well-known activist in our state. She was divorced, and determined to advocate for mother's rights and that of children to a safe, toxin-free environment with a high-quality education, so she was enjoying my tirade.

She wore black leggings, a long, wildly-patterned, short-sleeved shirt that depicted ferns on black, and she kept her hair loose, with bangs that didn't cover her eyes, and rimless, oval glasses. Her usual Barnes & Noble travel mug sat next to her laptop, and I noticed the steam of Earl Grey tea emanating from it – her favorite.

"You've got your favorite drink, I see," I commented.

Elise glanced at her tea mug. "Yes, I purchased some at the café before we started this chat."

I grinned, and said to Ileandra, "Elise never buys anything. She always 'purchases' it." With that, I took a sip of my latte. I had made it just before the chat, trying to simulate the mood of going out to the café to enjoy one. It helped.

Ileandra looked confused. "But those words both mean the same thing," she said.

"We know," I replied. "It's just a personality quirk of Elise's. I like to tease her about it. When she writes, her characters never buy anything. They always purchase it."

"Oh. I see." The alien was smiling behind her mask.

We got back into the political discussion.

There was a bit more to it.

What the Small Gray Visitor Said

"Funneling tax money from public schools to charter schools will just enable religion to be mixed into education, and science to fall by the wayside," I summed up, and sipped the coconut latte I had made.

I was disgusted by our current government's Secretary of Education, who seemed determined to not do her job, but instead to use it as a platform for her own parochial, isolationist, and ultimately destructive agenda.

Ileandra nodded. "It definitely will. I've seen it happen before, in history, over and over again."

Hmm…she must have finished reading all of my history and political science books, I thought to myself.

I had an extensive collection of political science and history books, because I couldn't bear to part with a book once I had read it. I had wanted to understand what drove World Wars and other major human conflicts, and how they were whipped up, and those books had answered those questions.

The answers were that overshoot, i.e. overpopulation within an ecological region, led to resource scarcity. When the general population couldn't understand what had led to their situation, political factions sprung up to take advantage of the situation, driving people's anxiety and fear with scapegoating, victim-blaming, isolationism, and nationalism. And so on…

Elise said, "I wonder what you make of Islam and the Catholic Church, then," grinning back.

Ileandra sat there in her face mask, settled in as one of the faces on the screen. The app divided the screen into multiple boxes with our faces, just like the ones I watched on my favorite late-night talk shows when guests connected to the talk show hosts. She looked back at me like someone watching a tennis match, her eyes going from Elise to me and back again.

She was having a good time, though. She was also enjoying her strawberry banana smoothie. The Starbucks café at the bookstore did a decent job on them, so to capture the mood, I had whipped one up for her before the chat began.

"The Catholic Church and Islam are two massive cults. They control the legal systems of far too many nations,

117

contaminating their laws with anti-abortion, anti-birth control, fascist dictates. They are the driving force behind many solvable problems, and a big reason for human overpopulation," I said.

Elise nodded in agreement.

Ileandra stared at me. "Are you sure you're not a telepath?" she asked.

I looked up from my latte, exasperated with her.

"You have got to stop suggesting that every time it turns out that we agree on some major point. Sometimes, the explanation behind two people voicing the same opinion is rather boring: they just happen to agree."

Elise burst out laughing. "Haven't you heard the expression 'preaching to the choir', Ileandra?" she asked.

"Yes," my alien friend said. She was trying not to laugh.

And she had stopped staring at me in amazement. Finally.

With that, Elise took out her jigsaw puzzle board.

She had a huge, folding one that opened its halves out onto two tables, which we pulled together. One half had a large board sunken into it, which we lifted out and placed on the top half of the case. Underneath that was revealed a 5-section area for puzzle pieces.

We had previously turned them right-side-up, sorted them all, and started putting the puzzle together. It had 1,000 pieces, and it depicted a gorgeous scene of Venice at sunset, with a view of the Grand Canal.

And now she was left to finish it without me.

I was glad I had started another one on my own, though I missed the chance to do the rest of this one with my friend.

"Won't Kavi be home for dinner soon?" Elise asked at one point.

"No," I said. "He's got a video conference tonight with the scientists at the Health Center, and then he is running a late experiment. He timed it for tonight, so that he could check on it after the lectures. He figured that since he had to be out late anyway, tonight was the ideal night to do it. We've got plenty of time to chat."

What the Small Gray Visitor Said

It was true. Sometimes experiments ran late. We would cook late and eat late...though I did have some mushroom velouté soup simmering on the stove. I mentioned that now.

"I see. Makes sense," Elise said, locking another piece of the pinkish clouds into place.

Nainsi joined us just then, and the app automatically made room for her in the screen. She had long red hair, which she wore with bangs and a barrette that held some of it back from her face. She wore strappy brown-leather sandals, jeans, and a gorgeous heathered green tee shirt that depicted Tara, an ancient site in Ireland. Over that, she had on an oatmeal-hued, cable-stitched, cotton cardigan. I thought she looked great, and said so.

She smiled happily, showed us her cup of hot tea with milk, and introduced herself to Ileandra. She didn't find it odd at all that Ileandra was wearing a mask.

The only logistical problem was that Ileandra couldn't take a drink of her smoothie without turning away from the screen, which she did from time to time. She also ducked out of sight to sip it, so my friends never saw her whole face.

Nainsi told us about an Irish ghost story she was writing, and we talked about the ghost story novels we could remember reading. My list wasn't long, but at least I had read some of those! I had enjoyed them, too. Nainsi hadn't published anything yet, but she was determined to learn about it. She had been writing for years, but had been busy raising her kids. Now she was ready to focus on her writing and become an author.

Next, the conversation turned to science fiction, which was a genre I had actually published in. It was one of my favorites, so at least I knew of more books about that.

"Didn't you do your law thesis on outer space?" Elise asked, prodding me into non-fiction territory.

"Yes, I did. It was about orbital debris, both in space and when it falls back to Earth, and a United Nations treaty."

"What is that treaty called, and what year was it made?" Ileandra asked.

"It was made in 1971, and it is called the Convention on International Liability for Damage Caused by Space Objects," I replied. "It is administrated in Vienna, Austria, in the U.N. Office for Outer Space Affairs. I'd love to visit it someday."

"What need is there for such a treaty?" Elise asked. "I always thought that outer space issues were existential – not an actual threat to us, and nothing that we really need, but rather something that we just want to be involved in. I mean, aliens aren't coming for us – that's the stuff of science fiction – so what's the point of spending all that money in orbit?"

Ileandra and I looked at her in mild disbelief. I was used to people saying this. It came from ignorance, though, not malice.

Ileandra glanced at me, wondering what I would say next.

I had plenty to say.

I smiled. "Actually, there are plenty of very real threats posed by outer space that can affect us on Earth. And we have plenty of things in orbit that we use in our everyday lives. Your cell phone works because of the hundreds of satellites up there. Those have to be maintained."

Nainsi looked at me, startled, then took a sip of her latte. "Well, yes, I'll give you that, but what else? Why do we need a treaty about it?"

"We have lots of treaties, but the one I studied was for a seminar on international environmental law. Satellites are powered by spent plutonium and spent uranium, which have half-lives of 4,000-5,000 years. If something goes wrong with them, and the satellites spiral back to Earth, they can spread radiation world-wide in the upper atmosphere, or worse, pieces of them won't burn up in the upper atmosphere. Instead, they can fall back to Earth. Never touch fallen space junk; call the people in the radiation suits with lead boxes to come and collect it."

Elise and Nainsi looked at me wide-eyed, then nodded.

Elise had a different set of questions.

I didn't mind; I was having fun with this.

"But what causes this stuff to fall back to Earth, and what else can threaten us from outer space?"

What the Small Gray Visitor Said

"Software issues could cause a satellite to fail, or the debris in orbit could smash a hole in one. There are naturally-occurring bits of orbital debris, such as pebbles, and even tools lost on space-walks by astronauts, plus jettisoned parts of the Mercury, Apollo, and Soyuz space programs up there. They move at the speed and with the destructive impact of a 22-calibur bullet."

"Wow," Nainsi said.

I continued, "To answer the other part of your question, I have another one for you: do you know what a Near Earth Object is?"

"No. What is that?"

"It could be a comet, an asteroid, or a meteorite. The time to plan how to bump one that is going to hit the Earth out of our way is not when we first notice it, as Neil deGrasse Tyson says, but six or seven orbits before the one in which we would take aim at it."

Elise and Nainsi had both heard of him, at least.

"But have any of those things actually hit the Earth?!" Elise asked in disbelief.

"Yes, they have," I told her. "There is an impact crater in Arizona that has been in movies: *Starman* and *Thor*. They put Thor's hammer right in the center of it. And a few years ago, a meteorite hit in Russia. The concussive blast it caused threw debris around a small city, and one woman ended up paralyzed."

They looked appalled.

"I guess it's not so existential." Elise looked alarmed.

"Nope, it's real. That's why I enjoyed that paper so much; I got to learn about the real-life effects of outer space on human-made law. The time to figure out how to handle a situation is not when it hits you, literally or figuratively. It's always better to do that in advance."

They nodded, impressed at last with the effect that outer space issues have on life on Earth.

Satisfied that I had educated more people outside of academia, I added, "That is why I love to write science fiction:

it educates people in a way that is fun, and brings issues that they might never otherwise notice into their worlds."

Elise grinned, and Nainsi smiled.

We ended up spending about four hours together, drinking lattes and smoothies, and chatting about our current writing projects.

Nainsi also ordered two masks – both of my rose patterns.

She said, "I love your advertising line of, 'Buy a mask for a friend or family member. It's like saying to them, "I want you to live."' That is terrific!"

"Thank you," I said, feeling really pleased.

If I had known Nainsi better, I would have just given her one. I had given Elise a few.

However, my mother and Uncle Louis had told me to stop it and make money with them. Oh well...

We had gotten through this virtual café chat without a hitch, which was a relief.

But it occurred to me that I would have to make a point of keeping up with my friends despite having Ileandra with me.

If she had to stay indefinitely, I would definitely need to watch my habits – to keep them as normal as possible.

This evening's entertainment was the start of that.

We might as well build her into our lives and routines, I thought. If that meant that her eventual departure came as a shock and we missed her terribly later, so be it.

After all, we had no idea when she would be able to get back yet...or if she would be able to get back.

She hadn't had an answer from her communicator since arriving, and it had been two weeks now. It was almost officially summer.

Kavi and I hoped that we were keeping her healthy, but she was starting to look frail.

We were getting a bit worried about her.

Caffeinated Telepathy

Ileandra was watching the news.

It was just after breakfast.

Kavi had left for the day, and I had plans to make masks out of some new fabric patterns that had arrived, to photograph them for my website, and post them.

If that went well, I hoped to also get an edit of a scientific journal article done for a colleague of his in Belgium who was hoping to publish later this week. It was ten pages; not much.

I decided to have another cup of coffee, checked that there was plenty of half-and-half cream (there was), and measured out some Mocha Java blend coffee into the filter.

As I did so, Ileandra looked up.

"That smells fascinating," she said from the sofa. "I can smell it from all the way over here."

I looked up and gave her a slight smile. "That's no surprise. Coffee has a pretty intense, strong scent to it."

"Could I have a cup of it?"

I turned to look at her. Why not? "Okay," I said, and measured out another 2-tablespoon scoop. I put enough water into the machine for two servings' worth of coffee.

"What variety of coffee is it?" she asked.

"Mocha Java," I told her. "From a place in western Yemen, in the mountains by the Red Sea. Most of that country is barren desert. They're the one Arabian Peninsula nation without any oil to sell, but they have great coffee in one spot."

"I've studied that plant, and got some once," Ileandra told me. "But we didn't know what to do with it once we had it."

I was surprised. "Oh, come on. You must have known about coffee. Haven't you seen any of our ads for it on television?"

"Well, yes, but we don't eat or drink in the quantities that humans need to, and it wasn't a fruit or a vegetable, so we just put it aside. But I was curious to know more about it."

"I see. Well, today is your lucky day."

What the Small Gray Visitor Said

It was a weekday, and she had the television tuned in to various news channels. It had been partly background sound for me, and partly of interest, depending upon what was being covered.

I laid out some fabric on the kitchen table, measured it, folded it where I wanted to cut it, and did so until I had lots of 11-by-9-inch pieces. I neatly stacked them up on the sewing table next to the rest of the supplies, then went back to the coffee machine.

I poured out a mug for each of us, added cream, and brought the cups over to the sofas.

Ileandra took hers with both hands, staring into the mug with great anticipation.

I tried not to laugh.

She inhaled the aroma deeply, then took a sip.

"It's good!"

I grinned. "Yes, it is. I can't start my work without a cup."

I ran through my e-mail quickly and decided to start in on the edit.

Ileandra turned her attention back to the television.

She watched CNN, MSNBC, C-SPAN, and the local and national news on CBS.

It was all COVID, all the time.

When that proved to be pure repetitiousness, she switched to the National Geographic channel.

Meanwhile, the edit took me an hour and a half.

That felt quick, but I checked it over and decided that the job was done. It was.

Therefore, I prepared the bill, included the PayPal fee after using the calculator site to determine how much more that would be on top of my own fee, and contacted the client.

I paused at this point to make some smoothies and watch a story about sloths with Ileandra.

We saw a post-doctoral graduate assistant to a microbiologist tromp through the tropical rainforest of Costa Rica to find a sloth, snip a bit of its fur off to save in a vial in his pocket, and then put that sloth back onto the tree that it had been climbing. The creature, smiling contentedly, calmly resumed its search for eucalyptus leaves.

The point of all that was to further the search for new strains of antibiotics. Microbes were rapidly evolving to resist the ones that we had, and scientists weren't waiting around for the next infectious disaster to wipe us out.

"I doubt they can come up with a new strain of antibiotic in time," I said. "There used to be more than twenty pharmaceutical companies in the United States. It was good that they were competing with each other, but that was sixty years ago. Since then, despite antitrust laws, they've been allowed to merge repeatedly. Now there are just four, and they're huge."

"And Kavi is among those who are working on a vaccine for the coronavirus," the alien interjected. "It will be good when it is formulated, and enough made for all humans to achieve herd immunity without contracting the virus and possibly dying from it."

"Yeah, well, there are plenty of anti-vaxxer idiots – selfish people, really – who say that they will refuse to take it, that it goes against their individual rights, blah, blah, blah. They disdain education, research, and data, and prefer emotionalism and religious nonsense to logic and proven facts."

Ileandra looked appalled. "How can that be allowed?!"

"It isn't really allowed. It is actually settled law, and has been for over a century, that an individual does not have the right to endanger the wider human community by refusing a vaccine – that people must all take it. It's from a smallpox case that was adjudicated first in Boston, and then was affirmed by the United States Supreme Court. It's *Jacobson v. Massachusetts*, 197 U.S. 11 (1905). The upshot of the ruling is that individual liberty is not absolute and is subject to the police power of the state – as well it should be for the sake of public health."

"And yet people still attempt to resist the logic of it?!"

"Yes, they do. The anti-vaxxers of today push for religious exemptions. The funny thing is that, when their kids grow to the age of legal adulthood, which is 18 years, they get vaccinated against the diseases that their parents fought against. It's kind of hilarious, and yet it's not."

"All that effort to avoid life-saving measures..."

"Indeed. And we have them, so it's just insane."

The next show was about the progress of the past century. We watched it for about twenty minutes in silence. Then its narrator extolled the benefits of scientific progress, and talked about population growth as if it were a good thing, and as if it could go on indefinitely. I sighed in disgust.

At this point, Ileandra turned to me and said, "So much effort is being expended to keep everything going as it has been during the economic age of excess that your people had in your planet's mid- to late twentieth century. Yet your numbers continue to increase exponentially. You cannot possibly hope to sustain things as they have been."

I looked at her wryly as I drank another gulp of blackberry-banana smoothie. "Oh, I know it. And you know I know it. It's one of the reasons why Kavi and I don't have kids. I mean, what a selfish thing that would be to do to the hypothetical kids! And...this smoothie is made with a variety of banana, called Cavendish, which is vulnerable to parasitic crop failure. Just wait and watch: if anything happens to it, most humans will be loath to try any other variety, even though this planet has many other ones. People don't like change, and many don't like to try anything new."

She looked into her glass, considering that.

"Can you get other varieties of banana in grocery stores?"

I laughed. "Sometimes. I have tried them when I could."

"Why only sometimes?"

"If a product doesn't sell well, stores won't continue to keep it in stock. Not even if people's lives depend on it."

She looked both disbelieving and disgusted.

"Don't tell me you're surprised by that," I said to her.

"I shouldn't be," she replied.

The Hartford Courant lay on the coffee table.

What the Small Gray Visitor Said

As usual, Kavi and I had read it all, except for the sports section. That one we had made a game of with the cat, laughing as Bagheera ran under it a few times. Ileandra had read it, too.

"Your news sources all show a stubborn refusal by many national governments to accept the need for change. If anything, it is going in the opposite direction. Nationalist politicians are isolating themselves from any other point of view, pursuing selfish policies, and ignoring the advice of intellectuals. This will lead to ruin. They seem to think that hoarding resources and advantages for a select few, and behaving with a complete disregard for ethics, honesty, and accountability will work for that few. Meanwhile, little is being done to stop this. Worst of all, abortion laws are being attacked, pushing the likelihood of unwanted births and an increase in population in the wrong direction. Beneficial laws are being undone. Too few are fighting this."

"So…you've noticed."

I was beyond frustrated at what had been happening.

Then I continued, "We had a great government for eight years, and so did many other nations during that same time period. Environmental protections were broadened, more national parks were established and existing ones expanded, reproductive rights were protected, and big business was somewhat reined in. However, toward the end of that time, the opposing political factions got fed up with the democratic process. They could not get their way, so they dug in their proverbial heels and refused to follow the law. They refused to follow the U.S. Constitution by refusing to seat any judges or justices until their party held a majority. Now they have it and are working to undo the benefits wrought by the previous party. They want to pretend that it's the 1950s…or earlier."

Ileandra thought that over for a moment. "That is insane."

"Yes, but they just don't care. And it's exhausting to see. It's exhausting to see the damage being done, and to know that not enough conservation will be done – or enacted – to stop it. Instead of conservation, we have conservatives, who seek to conserve a past that should remain in the past. The damage done to the ecosystem is what brought on coronavirus. We humans got too close too often to the deepest, wildest areas in nature, invading habitats that are not ours to mess with, cutting and burning them down, and consuming wild animals that ought to remain not just exotic but left alone, and what did we get?! A zoonotic disease – and not the first one that we've encountered. And to top it all off, this idiot administration – if it can even be called one with any accuracy – dismantled the pandemic response plan left in place by the previous one out of sheer spite against it."

I paused for breath, then went on with my diatribe.

Ileandra just listened, but with rapt attention.

"Right now, a nationalist government is in power in our country, and we are seeing that in others – quite a few others. This tends to happen in times of scarcity, or at least perceived scarcity, and due to human overpopulation and ecosystems collapse – all thanks to use and abuse of our planet by too many humans using too much space and too many resources, plus making junk and just throwing it away rather than reusing it – we actually are living in a time of scarcity. Soon we will all feel it, including those of us living in so-called 'developed' nations."

"Why are nationalists preferred? I mean, how is it that they come into political power? And what are they like?"

"I guess you really are wrapped up in your scientific endeavors to the point of not noticing the intricacies of human societies. Okay. I'll keep going." I was enjoying this anyway, so why not just unload my frustrations in this conversation?!

I went for it. "Nationalists are selfish, elitist, insular sorts with short attention spans and a gross disrespect for facts, education, and self-discipline. They are haters of groups other than their own, but very clever at concealing that fact from enough of their voters to get elected. They capitalize on the short attention spans and prejudices of their voters, including a propensity for superstition, which is shown in religion."

The alien had noticed that. She said, "Yes, I've seen what are called 'televangelists' on your communications networks, and huge cults called Catholicism and Islam. Those cults infest legal systems in many nations. But I thought that yours kept religion separate from law and government."

I replied, "We are supposed to do that. It's part of our Constitution. But the nationalists, pandering to their religious base, are working hard to change that. They are packing federal and state courts with judges who know the law but don't care. Meanwhile, the educated liberals are vilified by the nationalists as elitists. That includes people like me. We get labeled the 'educated liberal elite' – and that's not meant as a compliment."

"It should be," Ileandra remarked.

"Well, yes and no. The 'elite' part suggests exclusion of 'most' people. That's not good. Our policies, however, are inclusive and protective of everyone, not just a few. But instead, thanks to lies and short attention spans, we now have a criminal government that legalizes crimes. You can tell that it's a criminal enterprise by looking at the way that the hate group members talk. The ones currently occupying our highest political offices talk the exact same way that the hate group members do. That's not a coincidence."

"How else can you discern that criminals are in office?"

"They simply refuse to enforce laws that they are sworn to enforce, thus refusing to do their jobs. We study the backgrounds of these people to learn all about them, their motivations, etc. Then we can understand their not-so-hidden agendas."

"What agendas?" Ileandra was looking more and more unsettled by all this. Good. I wondered what her planet's history was like – if it had any parallels.

"One example is in the education system. Our schools, from pre-school through high school, should be focused on providing the best basic education possible in the STEM disciplines, which are science, technology, engineering, and mathematics, along with history, literature, art, and music so that students will understand how those STEM subjects fit into the world and why they matter…and be able to speak and write comprehensibly about them all. Science can't be shared if you don't know how to write and speak coherently."

"Agreed. What is actually happening?"

"Superstition, also known as religion, is creeping in, and the branch of our government in charge of education is actively working to make that happen by diverting funds to schools that teach religion and run a culture of it. This affects science education, because if the science conflicts with the religious teachings, the science goes and the religion stays. Religion is all well and good if treated as part of one's culture, but to believe in it to the point of having it rule your life is toxic. It addles one's thinking and destroys one's capacity for logic and reasoning."

"Your people, and those in other nations, are becoming terribly divided, just as they did before major wars."

"Yes. It happened before, and it's ramping up to happen again. We have become so divided that, when the religious nationalists found their unreasonable behavior criticized by the secular, educated, liberals, they decided that they didn't care anymore, and wouldn't listen to logic. Logic got in their way. They reacted with emotion, heaping yet more of that on after responding to policies that shared resources with anxiety."

"Why the anxiety? That is a specific emotion."

"They fear change, they fear that they won't be a majority anymore, they fear that that won't be okay, and they don't want to try it. They don't want to share the world with others, even though other cultures and other ethnicities and other sexual orientations are part of the world that we all live in. Nature doesn't care how they feel. It just is, and makes the world with everyone in it. But they resist it. There will be trouble."

"Why is this allowed to continue?!"

"The followers of the populist nationalists don't realize – because they don't study history – that it is not the liberals who are a threat to them. Yes, the liberals change old ways in favor of new ways. But it is the populists who will kill them. And they can't rely on escaping that by being physically, culturally, ethnically, or otherwise similar to the populist politicians.

What the Small Gray Visitor Said

There is a saying: 'Those who don't study history are condemned to repeat it.' We're seeing that repeat now. It's beyond depressing."

Ileandra's eyes widened. "This is appalling. It is what happens on any planet that goes through a collapse. It happened on mine, so long ago that the historians only have a vague sense of how it felt. They teach us the facts, of course. We had a terrible famine." She seemed lost in unsettled thoughts. Then she added, "But humans have made so many advances in science, medicine, technology, and other disciplines. These populists show disdain for all that. Why?!"

She was getting a bit emotional.

I felt burned out. "They are the resentful ones who are not educated, and they conflate education with elitism. They feel excluded from the respect that comes with being someone who knows how viruses work, so they refuse to cooperate with it due to their own most unreasonable and dangerous sense of inferiority – even though the educated members of society only seek to keep others safe with the knowledge that they have studied and worked to acquire."

"No wonder the Earth is having so many problems!"

"Herr Pumpkingropenfuhrer, our sociopath of a pseudo-POTUS, talks like a member of the hate group known as the Ku Klux Klan, and calls Confederate generals, who committed treason against this country by fomenting and fighting a Civil War to split it apart, heroes. But this pandemic is making people finally see him for what he is: an incompetent, self-aggrandizing, monster who cares only about promoting himself, the good of the nation be damned." At least I could have some creative fun with the name of the Idiot-in-Chief.

She knew. "Herr Pumpkingropenfuhrer?"

"Yes. It's a name I created for him. He's very orange, like a pumpkin – a gourd that you have no doubt encountered in your line of work – he gropes women in a lascivious, sexual way without permission from them – women he does not even know, which makes it unmistakable – and he is a hate-mongering authoritarian bully, just like Adolph Hitler of Nazi

131

Germany was. Hence the name I created. It seems to cover all the angles. I could see what he was from the start – a fraud and a monster. I'm extremely impatient with everyone else. I expect them to be as capable of seeing that, as fast as I did, even if they're not. My uncle calls him the Orange Moron, by the way."

"I realize that most humans are not well-educated, but why would they fail to see what's wrong about him?"

"Selfish insecurities add up to a deliberate failure. There are people who actually think that if other groups get rights that they ought to have had right along – that they lose an unfair advantage over those other groups by being put on an equal level with them."

"I see. You must vote him out, or he will cause a famine."

"I know. I will vote against him, but that isn't enough. Thanks to the Electoral College, which negated the people's majority vote last time, it won't be enough to prevent a collapse of ecosystems, economies, and societies. And I think I will live to not only see but also experience all of that. Huma selfishness and the determination to get things – money, space, resources – and pressure to each take as much as the previous generation while we have greater numbers than the previous generation – will crash our ecosystem. When I am not feeling apathetic, I feel angry and depressed about it all.

"Yes, that is a terrible obstruction in your electoral system. Yet you keep writing."

"Yes, I keep at it. Maybe I'm not so apathetic after all. I can't help it. The Ogallala Aquifer, which runs from north to south through North America, is being sucked dry by overuse. This is caused by a combination of human overpopulation and agriculture – both big agribusinesses and small farmers, who are the first to lose out. Ecosystems collapse doesn't just affect people south of our border, where it's hotter and drier, namely in Central American nations. It happens in the complacent United States, too. And what will happen when our ecosystem crashes due to drought inland and sea level rise shrinking our coastlines but massive human relocations within the contiguous United States. This will compress our numbers into a miserable existence of overcrowding. It won't be pretty."

I paused for breath. Would writing about it really help?!

"Iran has reversed its policy on birth control, withdrawing access to it from government-run medicine. It's still available in private ones, but few can afford them. The leaders of Hungary and Turkey are actually pushing women to have four and five children each, and Hungary is giving out government benefits if they do so. These politicians actually think that their people are underpopulated! And our idiot politicians are doing their best to take away birth control access and abortion. Brazil and Mexico now have populist leaders, too."

Ileandra seemed to know my thoughts, which I was getting used to.

"It has to make you feel better to write about it. You write for yourself, for your readers, and you hope it improves your species and the conditions it lives with or you wouldn't do it."

"It does make me feel a bit better. I have some readers, and it's better than just sitting back and watching the world go to hell – literally, not in the religious and superstitious sense."

"What else do you do? Besides your café chat group?"

I thought about that. Then it came back to me. "Well, you know that I watch irreverent liberal political comedians on television. They keep my mind focused on what matters while keeping me calm. I watch one of them on weeknights. The other one has a very different show, because it's not on commercial television. It's on cable television. He invites professors, journalists, scientists, lawyers, judges, and entertainers on for a discussion panel in each episode. Both do stand-up comedy-commentary on what's going on in the world, and they are excellent."

Ileandra was staring at me, a bit amazed, which was an expression that was bizarre to behold on an alien's face. Her eyes were already huge compared to a human's, and this only made them more so. She looked like a caricature of herself.

"You are the best possible human I could have met when I couldn't get back..." she trailed off, staring into space.

"Yeah…it's pretty bad, isn't it?" I said, laughing ironically. She looked up at me. "Yes, but you offer some hope."

I laughed a very rueful laugh. "Seriously?"

"Yes. Your writings and other efforts are not a waste. Our people have similar things in our historical records. Please keep going with what you do."

I stared at her, considering this. And I felt a bit better.

"Oh, I will," I told her. "Do you know if your planet went through this as your people transitioned from what they once were, physically, mentally, and socially, to what you are now? You couldn't always have been physically weak, this technologically advanced, and with your emotions and impulses so toned down as to not rule your society."

She looked at me for a moment, surprised.

"You are very observant."

I grinned. "It's a good thing that most humans can't get a good, close-up look at you." I paused, then added, "Or not…"

She laughed ruefully. "Perhaps not."

Then she responded to my previous comments.

"I know on a theoretical level, from reading our history, that we went through a terrible time of collapse such as your planet and your people are now going through. But I have not studied it in depth. Few of us do, because we do not need that many to run a government. We need more scientists."

"I remember when we had scientists occupying government posts. It was just a few years ago, with our previous, liberal, educated, attorney of a president in charge."

"And now it is run by the ultra-nationalists, business-and-profits-first capitalists, who, from what I have seen on your internet and televisions, are not experts, are quick to make changes that aren't legal, and care more for resource extraction than anything else, with no regard for future generations' difficulties from that. They don't take this virus seriously."

"Yes. They are living for today, and damn tomorrow."

She smiled, finished her smoothie, and asked, "Might I ask you to take me grocery shopping with you? I would like to see what varieties of bananas we can find besides Cavendish."

I grinned.

"Okay. Maybe tomorrow. I still have a lot to do here today. But prepare yourself for a shock at the excess of it all. Brands, quantities, and so on. Also, most of it isn't the produce section. That's just one sixth of the store space."

"That's fine. I'll see it all. You have to shop in those other sections anyway."

"Good. It takes lots of ingredients to make smoothies."

Ileandra nodded.

I got my grocery list ready.

Ileandra laid out her hoodie and cap, tucked her sunglasses into her shirt front, and put one of the face masks I had made for her in her pocket.

At least no one would mistake a petite little female such as herself for a gangster. She would, I hoped, seem only to be avoiding getting too much sun and taking in too much bright light. She wouldn't be wearing those glasses in the store.

As long as she didn't make prolonged eye contact with anyone else, she should be able to pass for human without a second thought, we hoped.

"So...you're all set for tomorrow's excursion," I said.

"Yes."

"Good."

I turned back to the computer and checked my e-mail.

The client had replied – all paid up. I prepared a receipt, e-mailed it, and turned my attention to the pile of fabric.

"Okay," I said, "let the fun begin! I love sewing masks."

Ileandra got up, brought the coffee mugs over to the kitchen sink, and commented, "Only two hours have gone by since you started working. You have already gotten a lot done."

I glanced up. We had had coffee and were looking at a huge pitcher of smoothie. I didn't care about lunch. I could just keep going and going, I realized.

"I'm going to get more done before the day is out," I said, and started sewing. Right now, I was so hyped up and ready to keep working that I really didn't care. I just wanted to sew masks and expand my patterns list for customers.

It felt better to make the masks than to worry about getting sick with coronavirus, and made me a little less stressed out about the world in general.

Hours went by. I felt a burst of energy that I had no intention of letting go to waste. The fabric patterns were beautiful, and I was looking forward to sewing them all. Could I really get that much done? Only one way to find out.

I picked up the one with a blue background that had honeybees and butterflies working on pink roses and lilacs. I pinned a piece of white cotton gauze to the back of it, top and bottom, cut some elastic cord for ear-loops, and started to sew. Forty minutes went by.

Done!

I got out the camera and its cord to connect it to the computer, and positioned the small wooden end table, which I kept under the corner table where the cat's bed was, in the middle of the room. I kept nothing on it because its sole purpose was for photographing completed masks.

I shot the image, shut off the camera, replaced the lens cap, and sat back down, tossing the finished mask into a cloth bag from Barnes & Noble that had the original cover of Harper Lee's *To Kill a Mockingbird* on both sides.

Ileandra watched this procedure in silence.

Then her eyes went to the actual book in my bookcase.

I noticed and said, "Go ahead – read all about racism in the United States. There's also a book on Jim Crow laws, which have been removed from all state and federal statutes, but that's a good background history book to go with the novel."

She took both books out and started to read.

I took a piece of fabric that depicted cotton bolls.

Thirty-five minutes later, I was photographing that mask.

Some fabrics were quicker to sew than others for some reason...usually because the thread snagged less in them.

Ileandra was done with the Jim Crow history by then and was starting in on the novel.

What the Small Gray Visitor Said

I took a piece of fabric that depicted cats smiling. Only the cats' faces were white; the background was black. It only took a half-hour. This fabric was smooth to work with.

Ileandra was not finished reading that novel.

I grinned. "Fiction takes you longer, huh?"

She looked up. "Yes, it does. It's not just straight facts. I have to consider culture and emotions and linguistic context."

"Let me know if you need any help."

"I will, but it's going well."

"Okay. I loved that book."

I photographed the mask and picked up the next piece of fabric: raspberry-pink rosebuds on black. The thread snagged a bit, so this mask took forty minutes.

We each paused for more of the blackberry smoothie mixture, then went back at it, with me sewing and her reading.

Bees on a cream background with flowers strewn here and there next...half an hour and done.

Feathers on light blue took another half-hour.

Outer space fabric with tiny stars and space dust.

A garden thick with pink and white roses, with only the green leaves of the flowers to offset them.

Golden bars of music swirling on black.

Foxes, sitting up and smiling at the viewer.

A rainbow of butterflies. Great for Gay Pride Week.

Even so, this would be beautiful all year long.

Ten masks later, I paused.

Time to upload all of the images I had taken.

I sat down at the computer and did the deed, saving them, labeling the images, and uploading them to my website. After that, I fussed a bit, posting them to the Face Mask Boutique page in just the right spots. It looked good.

I saved it and shared it and tweeted it and pinned it and posted it to Instagram. Then I put the camera away and went into the dining room.

"What are you doing now?" Ileandra asked.

She had finished reading the novel.

"Laying out a jigsaw puzzle," I said, and picked up one by the Pomegranate company with a colored-ink drawing by Edward Gorey on it. It was an untitled one from 1965. The artist himself sat front and center with a tiger-striped cat in his lap, while a man in a nightshirt, fast asleep, levitated in the sky above over everyone else. Death was among the characters, on the left edge. I quickly turned each piece right-side up.

Bagheera appeared with a "MrrrrOW!" on the edge of the table, leaping abruptly up to see what I was doing. When he saw, he got off immediately. He was a smart cat; he never messed with my puzzles. He even found missing pieces for me!

Ileandra stood by, watching all this.

"Your cat is very intelligent," she remarked.

I smiled. "Yes, he is. And he cuddles nicely, too. He just purrs, smiles, and relaxes into the cuddle. He's a great cat."

Bagheera sat down next to me and smiled.

I could hear him purring loudly.

I slitted my eyes back and smiled with my mouth.

The garage door opened, and Kavi rolled in.

I looked up, startled. I had gathered all of the border pieces and started to assemble them. "What time is it?" Then I pulled out my pocket watch. It was six o'clock!

Ileandra was sitting across from me.

Kavi came into the kitchen and saw us, and the masks showing out of the top of my bag in the TV area, and walked over to me…and hugged me.

I hugged back. My arms felt heavy.

"Yves said he got his edit from you at what was 10:30 a.m. here," Kavi said. "How many masks did you make today?"

"Ten," I said.

Suddenly, I felt a bit dizzy, and didn't want to work on the puzzle. I was abruptly out of energy. What had happened?

Ileandra was still sitting across from me, but she was asleep! Her head was down on the table.

Suddenly, I realized what it was.

We had both had coffee, and I had been riding on her caffeine-driven high all day. No wonder I felt drained.

What the Small Gray Visitor Said

A little alien body wasn't able to tolerate a jolt from coffee. Kavi seemed to take this in without me saying it.

"I saw the coffee cups in the sink. Are you okay?"

"Yeah...but we should move her to a sofa to rest."

We did that, carefully.

She slept right through the sounds of Kavi and me cooking. Well...Kavi did most of it. I was a bit shaky from the day's burst of activity.

She slept until we were halfway through dinner.

Then she smelled the food and came over to the kitchen table to try some of the sauce from the curried spinach and chick peas, the dal, and a bit of basmati rice.

I cut up some mangoes and we all had some.

Soon, we were both feeling like ourselves again.

"No more coffee for you, Ileandra," I said.

She grinned. "Agreed. Once is enough for me."

Hours later, we turned on the news to check up on things.

The travesty of a U.S. president had been on Twitter again, running his thumbs with nothing intelligent to say.

His tweet was repeated with much amusement by the late-night comedians. What he said was that he didn't want mail-in ballots available to all, due to his worry about fraud.

We all knew that he was really just afraid that, if more voters had access to a mail-in ballot, they would vote for someone else – anyone else. "Any Responsible Adult" was a well-known political slogan by now.

But what made this tweet so hilarious was what he had typed: "MILLIONS OF MAIL-IN BALLOTS WILL BE PRINTED BY FOREIGN COUNTRIES AND OTHERS."

Kavi and I both turned and looked at Ileandra when the image of that tweet flashed across the television screen.

"Others?!" I said. "The only 'others' would be aliens!"

If ever an alien had been in danger of losing emotional control over her facial expressions, it was now. She managed it, however, and said, "We have no such plans."

"Prime directive still in force, huh?" we said.

"Absolutely."

When James Corden came on and actually said the words, "He must be talking about aliens," we all laughed.

Genetically Edited

Ileandra sat in Arielle's car, strapped to the front seat. What was she doing here, she asked herself? This was crazy, going out anywhere! She should hide...

She was wearing a pair of periwinkle blue cotton pants with pockets, a long-sleeved, crew-necked lavender tee shirt, sneakers that had been hastily purchased at a thrift shop (the laces had been a source of confusion, but she had eventually gotten the hang of tying them properly), and a pastel blue hoodie.

Her bees-and-floral face mask was in her lap.

The sneakers had a floral pattern that fascinated her. The soles and laces were white, contrasting sharply with the multi-hued shapes on them.

The sunglasses and cap, which was also in a floral pattern (not a match – it was also from a thrift shop), were in her lap.

Arielle was dressed in linen pants that were equally fascinating to look at: they had many different threads to their weave, in hues of pastel blue, lavender, and pink. You had to look closely to see all that. The pants also had pockets, in which the human had put her house keys, pocket watch, flip-phone, and tissues. Her tee shirt depicted Ruth Bader Ginsburg, her favorite U.S. Supreme Court justice, who was saying, "Never underestimate the power of a girl with a book."

The ear-loops of a face mask poked out of Arielle's right pants pocket. It was made from the rose garden fabric. She kept the mask folded in half, and would pull it out and put it on when she arrived somewhere and got out of the car.

"I won't wear any pants, shorts, skirts, or dresses without pockets," the human woman had informed her.

Ileandra had been intrigued to hear that. "Why wouldn't clothing come with pockets?" she had asked.

Arielle had found that hilarious. "The fashion industry is why. It exists in order to sell more, more, more stuff, so it keeps changing styles. It mass-produces clothing, usually in poorly ventilated workshops in non-industrialized nations, complete with a lack of fire-safe exits and stable building structures."

Ileandra had actually gaped at her when she said that.

But she had come to expect to hear appalling things about how humans set up their habitats, so she had said nothing.

All this had taken place a half-hour before, when Arielle had emerged from her closet with that fun tee shirt on. Apparently, the human woman reveled in wearing tee shirts that had beautiful images and memorable words on them.

"Lots of humans revel in that," she had said with a laugh.

Now they were in her car, a blue Mercedes sedan, and Arielle pushed a button on the visor above her seat as she turned the vehicle around in the driveway.

So that's what that odd curve-shape in the driveway is for, Ileandra noted, as the vehicle turned to face forward and move toward the street. The garage door closed behind them.

The car moved down Tiger Lily Lane, around a couple of curves in it and out to a stop-sign at Nod Road. Arielle pushed a rod that jutted out from the right-hand side of her steering wheel, and a low clicking sound could be heard. A light also flashed on the car's dashboard. She planned to turn left, Ileandra realized.

Ileandra also realized that she had no familiarity with what was on the ground. Everything that she knew about was what she had seen at night and from above, while her ship had been cloaked.

The brightness of the late-spring day suddenly hit her eyes as the car pulled out onto Nod Road, which was a minor thruway. She put the sunglasses on.

Arielle glanced at her. "Are you okay?"

"Yes."

Arielle nodded and drove up the road. She was wearing a loose, long-sleeved, thin, dark pink cotton sweater that had an embroidered floral pattern, and her reddish-brown hair was down long, held out of her face by her sunglasses.

Apparently, the car's visor was enough for her.

They came to a big intersection at the foot of the small mountain and waited at the red light.

All of the vehicles were waiting, because someone on foot had pushed a button on one of the poles across the street and to the left. He wore a white jacket with white buttons up both sides of the front, and carried a notebook.

Arielle glanced at her guest and said, "That's a chef. He went over to the hotel to plan a meal, and is now coming back to the restaurant to our left. It's part of the same business."

White lights shaped like the outline of a human flashed, and the chef started across the road. Ileandra thought that that outline looked just like the ones of the forensic crime shows that Kavi liked to watch on television.

A few cars waited at each point in the intersection.

Ileandra looked at the drivers through her sunglasses, grateful that they hid her eyes. Hopefully, it was not obvious that she was studying each one.

A tractor-trailer waited to their right, its driver planning to go up the mountain. This was called Route 44, she recalled, and also Albany Avenue, though Albany, New York was several hours away from here by this slow mode of transport.

The driver of that huge truck was a large man with tattoos on his arm, which rested on the edge of the truck's window. He wore a black tee shirt, black sunglasses, and his hair was starting to turn white. It was cropped short.

He glanced down at their car, and Ileandra briefly panicked. Then she realized that he was looking at Arielle.

She glanced at her new friend and considered her appearance. Arielle was definitely what this species considered attractive as a female, with long, thin wrists, a long neck, and hair that wisped around her face.

She tried out her telepathy on the driver, and almost laughed out loud. The man had noticed the rings on Arielle's left hand – rings that Ileandra had been told represented her friend's engagement and wedding to Kavi – and had lost interest. He was looking at the traffic light again, waiting impatiently for it to turn green.

Arielle was waiting in the right-most lane, with her signal on again, this time for a right turn.

Another car pulled up next to theirs.

In it was a woman who looked to be Arielle's age. She glanced into their car, focusing on Ileandra.

Ileandra stiffened, and Arielle noticed.

Arielle had advised against wearing the mask inside the car.

That would just cause amusement and second glances, and second glances meant more scrutiny. That would be bad.

"Don't worry," she told her. "Passing glances don't give anyone in the next car much information. You could seem like an elderly woman, or a child, and this other driver won't have enough time to scrutinize you further before the light changes."

And she didn't! It changed, and Arielle stepped on the accelerator. The car swung to the right, heading west on Route 44. The other woman's car went straight, and she thought of them no more.

But what would happen when they got out of the car?!

Ileandra could either wait in the car, or go inside and sit in the waiting area. If she went inside, it was the law that she take off those sunglasses. But she would have the mask on, so that would solve the problem, she reminded herself. He would trade one covering for another.

They would be getting out of the car soon.

Their first errand would be to the bank.

Arielle had some questions to ask in the bank, and she intended to go inside and talk with someone about them.

The human woman had already informed her that face masks went against every security precaution banks had. "We look like we're ready to rob a bank with these on," Arielle had said. "In fact, that's exactly what a cousin wrote to me when he e-mailed a photograph of himself and his wife wearing masks that I sent them a few weeks ago. I'll have to briefly show my face from a distance of at least six feet just once for the people working inside the bank just for security purposes."

Ileandra thought about that as she rode along.

What the Small Gray Visitor Said

Soon, the car pulled into the bank's parking lot, and Arielle found a spot. "Well? What do you think? Will you come in?"

It was impulsive and foolish, and something that she would never be able to do once she got back to her own people. She still planned to do that…somehow. She was a scientist, she told herself. She should see what she could.

"Yes!" Ileandra replied, putting on her mask and trying to get out of the seat belt. She couldn't.

Arielle laughed one brief laugh and pressed the red release button. "Easier said than done. There. You just have to get used to it and press the right spot, and hard enough. Here, try it again." And she actually put the hook back in there!

Ileandra realized that her friend was trying to teach her a bit of independence in her habitat, and she relaxed a bit. Sure enough, one hard push down the center next to the hook made it let go. The seat belt's strap receded into the molding in the side of the car.

Now for the door-handle. That opened without a problem.

Arielle was already out of the car, walking around to meet her. "I'm going to close the car door for you," she informed her guest. "It just might be too heavy for you, and the car has to be closed and locked when we're away from it."

Ileandra nodded, and fastened her face mask into place.

Arielle secured the vehicle, and they went inside.

The human woman put on her mask as they reached the door, which she pulled open and held for the little alien.

Arielle glanced down at Ileandra.

With a start, Ileandra remembered that it was time to take off the sunglasses and let people see that part of her face.

She had been warned that not doing so would actually bring more attention, and negative attention at that, than nonchalantly removing the sunglasses.

She took them off, folded them, and tucked one of the earpieces into her shirt, just as she saw Arielle doing.

People were walking around in the bank, glancing at them, then glancing away, clearly with their own financial business on their minds. When she snooped a little into their thoughts, that was exactly when she found!

She wondered why, and snooped a little more.

Money was inextricably linked to humans' survival and sense of safety, it turned out. No wonder they didn't spare a thought for her short stature or wispy blonde hair or huge blue eyes. They had more important things to focus on than a slightly odd-looking woman.

She began to relax as she followed Arielle over to a place with cushy chairs and a low table.

After a minute or two, a plump woman with dishwater-blonde hair appeared and invited Arielle into her glassed-in office.

Ileandra was left to sit there alone, with nothing to do.

Fortunately, no one had asked to see her face.

So far, so good.

A woman walked by, done with her business at the tellers' counter, tucking things into her handbag. She was dressed in what was obviously fashionable clothing. It was tight on her figure, with no room for pockets. Her face and hair were heavily coated in cosmetics. It was a sharp contrast to Arielle's more natural, designed-for-comfort style.

The woman noticed Ileandra's gaze, and gave her a brief, polite, unconcerned smile (it showed in her eyes above her own mask), zipped her handbag shut, and moved on before Ileandra could make herself return the expression.

She would have to remember to do that in the future.

Meanwhile, she was astonished that that had been the extent of the interaction. The banker had given her that same smile, and then focused on Arielle.

Apparently, she could blend in enough to see this habitat!

With nothing to do – no reading material on the table and nothing else nearby – Ileandra's mind wandered a bit. She realized that she could hear the conversation between Arielle and the banker, whose name was Marin.

Arielle wanted to open an account to store her earnings from making and selling face masks.

The banker, however, wanted to sign her up for a credit card, which Arielle didn't want.

The banking details were technical and meant little to her, but then the conversation had turned to pleasantries and questions about Arielle's books.

"So much detail! How do you keep track of it all?!" Marin asked, awed by Arielle's rapid rattling off of bank history. She had just explained how the Glass-Steagall Act of 1933 had created a separation, or divorce, between commercial and investment banking, and then lamented its reversal in the 1990s, which had laid the grounds for the economic meltdown that came a decade later.

Apparently, bankers at this level didn't do anything more than mechanical transactions – basic functions that, though necessary to the everyday lives of a bank's users, did not require the intellectual intricacies that high-level bankers had to operate with. This banker's job was to sell more services.

Arielle had no intention of signing up for any.

If she wanted them, Ileandra discerned via her telepathic eavesdropping, she would go to a financial advisor, not a low-level salesperson. This woman was a tool of a larger system, one that could use and abuse unwitting customers.

Ileandra smiled to herself as she heard the conversation. It was polite, but Arielle was wise enough to stick to her book topics and not say all that about sales pitches.

Instead, she heard her friend answering the question that had been asked.

"It's what an Aspie is designed to do: gather, store, keep track of, and access masses of data. My brain is like a racecar. Society used to be set up to benefit people like me in terms of career success, but now it goes the other way, helping neurotypicals more at making a living."

Marin was all agog. "What's an Aspie?"

"Oh! That's a person on the autism spectrum, with Asperger's. We talk. We were, most of us, very annoyed that it was removed from the DSM manual, so that it was taken out when version IV was updated to be version V. It got lumped in with autism as a general thing. It's just a normal, minority model of a human brainstem. The majority model is called 'neurotypical'. There are other models, also, but those are the main ones."

Marin stared. "So, this is how you remember all that?" she asked, referring to Arielle's earlier barrage of data.

"Yes. Lots of famous Aspies have done important things with banking and law. Alexander Hamilton, one of this nation's Founders, was an Aspie. He set up the Department of the Treasury and our first banks. James Madison was another; he wrote the U.S. Constitution. Thomas Jefferson wrote the Declaration of Independence."

Ileandra could see that Arielle was thinking about continuing to say that a Scottish economist had written *The Wealth of Nations* and that he was another Aspie, and that James Madison had read through 300 law books that Thomas Jefferson had shipped to him from Paris in order to decide what to put in the Constitution, but changed her mind when it was clearly too much for Marin.

She was letting Marin talk instead.

Marin said, "I just remember facts that are near and dear to me, and forget the rest, such as what I need in order to do my work, things about my friends and family, and that sort of thing. You seem to remember all that and much more. How do you do it? Not that I'll remember your entire answer later."

Arielle explained that it was a matter of access to more areas of the brain, enabled by having more connectors on one's brainstem going in more directions. "Aspie brainstems look a lot different. *60 Minutes* did an episode on it in 2011 that illustrated that with some MRI scans. It was incredible."

Marin was very cheerful and amazed all at once.

Ileandra felt almost sorry for her, being unable to do with her brain what she and, apparently, her human friend Arielle could do with theirs.

This was valuable insight into the human condition.

It was not the same for her people.

Her people were, it was now clear, all Aspies.

148

But, she realized, they couldn't have always been that way. Her attention returned to the conversation in the glassed-in office room, and Ileandra realized that Arielle had finished her business. The account was set up, and Marin had given up on inducing her to open a credit card account.

The conversation wrapped up in the glassed-in office, and Arielle came out of there, saying her good-byes and thanking Marin for all of her help.

She came over to Ileandra, smiling from the fun of that social interaction, and said, "Okay, that's done. Let's go."

Ileandra stood up, nodded politely to Marin, who nodded back at her with barely a second glance, and they walked out of the bank into the bright sunshine.

Ileandra hastily put the sunglasses back on her face.

She was still getting used to the thought that this rule was about preventing bank robberies, and not to spot aliens. Once she had understood that, she had calmed down and acquiesced.

She was getting used to the idea that she would be less easily spotted for what she was if she did nothing that caught other humans' attention.

The next stop was up the street and across, at a store called The Fresh Market.

They needed groceries, including a lot more ingredients for smoothies. Arielle and Kavi did make those before Ileandra had arrived, but not on the scale that they needed to in order to keep Ileandra fed.

They got out of the car, with Arielle reaching into the back seat first to grab two bags with pretty photographs on the outsides, with flowers on one and berries on the other. The logo for the store was on them, too.

"Connecticut finally caught up with France and other smart countries and banned those stupid plastic bags that grocery stores used to give out. Actually, this one and another one, called Whole Foods, never used them, but now all of them have stopped. We bring our own bags in now."

Ileandra replied, "I have seen the damage done by those bags. It's chocking your ecosystems. But...you know that. I've read your books, and seen what you post on the internet about it."

The human woman grinned. "Yeah...you've moved in with the wrong human if you were hoping to convert one who isn't awake to the problem. Then again, I am the safe option."

"Indeed, you are."

They went in, and Arielle took a small shopping cart that consisted of a metal frame on wheels that held two of the store's green plastic shopping baskets. More plastic. Well, this wasn't one-use plastic that would be thrown away to pollute.

The inner doors slid open and a profusion of beautiful colors confronted them. The produce section of the store was full of the most wonderful raw foods that would make excellent smoothies.

Arielle headed straight for the little plastic boxes of berries, checking them for freshness and choosing red raspberries – "My favorite," she said with a smile – blackberries, blueberries, and strawberries. She would recycle those containers in a blue bin in the garage, which she had pointed out as they had gotten into her car to leave.

That wasn't the best solution, but that was the only way that the store presented the berries.

"Soon, if you're still here with us, the local farms will have harvested their berries and we can go get some of those. The quality and flavor are even better, and the containers are made of rough green cardboard instead of plastic," Arielle told her guest.

Ileandra considered this, disapproving of the need for any plastic at all. "Why do grocery stores not use those also?" she complained.

"I wish they would, but human laziness gets in the way."

Arielle paused, thinking.

Ileandra watched her thoughts, fascinated as the human worked the problem out.

Apparently, if shippers bothered to use wooden crates – or even reusable plastic ones – shaped in such a way as to accommodate open cardboard boxes of berries without crushing them, there would be no need for these clear boxes that were made out of processed fossil fuels, which wouldn't decay for millennia…or longer.

A thought flashed through Arielle's mind, along with a memory of a news article, about a teenage girl who had just won a science prize for inventing a container made of processed fish scales. It looked just like the plastic ones, but broke down as biodegradable material within a week or so or being discarded.

Then, just as rapidly as the thought had run through the human woman's mind, a sad feeling followed. The problem was getting most humans to make laws requiring its manufacture and use. There were just too many people involved, and too many of them were either too lazy or too connected to financial gain from the old system, unwilling to let go of that personal benefit and make the change.

"You can sense and feel what I'm remembering and considering, can't you?" Arielle asked, looking at Ileandra.

The alien woman smiled a sad smile. "Yes, I can."

"Well, that saves us a lot of time, at least."

With that, Arielle forced herself to cheer up.

Fascinating how humans keep themselves functioning.

This one chose to take breaks from such negative realities by seeking sensory enjoyment, Ileandra observed. She watched as Arielle went over to the complimentary coffee stand, took a standard-sized paper cup, and poured herself a small amount of coffee from an urn labeled "Georgia Pecan", added some milk, and drank it.

The human woman tried all of the flavors – there were four of them – the same way, then threw the cup into a garbage bin.

Ileandra inhaled the aroma, but declined to drink any.

She wasn't about to cause a repeat of the marathon work-session that that had caused Arielle to churn out previously.

Arielle got the cart and resumed filling it with all sorts of fruits. Soon they had oranges, bananas – only Cavendish bananas were available, they noted with disapproval – and avocadoes.

151

What the Small Gray Visitor Said

"Hopefully our idiot president won't offend the Mexicans so that they cut us off from avocadoes," Arielle said. "We import most of them from there."

Ileandra stared. All these different nations meant barriers to access to things that were technically possible to share.

They continued to shop.

A woman glanced at Ileandra, who had hung her sunglasses in the front of her shirt again, copying Arielle.

The woman was older, with chin-length, gray-and-black hair that framed her head in a slight pouf, glasses, and a light covering of cosmetics. She pushed her cart past the cheese display as Arielle measured out some cashew nuts.

'That poor woman,' Ileandra heard her think to herself. 'She must have some genetic disorder, not to have grown right. No one is that short anymore – not since the 19th century.'

And with that, the woman's thoughts went to her grocery list, and she wheeled her cart around to the deli counter!

It was really that easy to pass for human?!

Incredible.

Sure enough, that same woman caught up with her husband and muttered the same thing to him. He glanced in Ileandra's direction, then looked away quickly as she met his gaze. Ileandra actually found herself annoyed by this, and realized that it showed in her returned gaze. All the better for her cover story!

She waited until Arielle was getting milk and orange juice to whisper to her about that.

Arielle looked at her. "We humans aren't as hard of hearing as you think," she replied, glancing around. Fortunately, no one else was within immediate earshot. "If you were trying out for spy school, you'd be rejected." And she grinned.

With a start, Ileandra realized that she had been careless.

She would have to wait until they were in the car to talk.

She did just that, saying nothing else until Arielle had collected everything on her list, paid for it, wheeled the cart out to the car, put the bags into her trunk before speaking again.

"What's the matter? I hope you're not mad at me."

"No! Of course not. You just reminded me to be more careful, that's all." Ileandra was thinking of other things by then, anyway.

"What are you thinking about?"

"Ice cream. I'm willing to try it., even if it makes me sick."

Arielle stared at her, trying not to laugh.

"You knew I was wishing for some, didn't you?"

"Yes." Ileandra was enjoying doing things like this.

"You're having fun with your telepathy – way too much fun!" Arielle said, glancing around to make sure that no other humans were within earshot, which they weren't.

Ileandra nodded.

"Okay, fine, Live dangerously. Let's go next door to J. Foster Ice Cream and get some. We can eat it in the yard around the side, facing the trees. They have tables outside."

And they did. Arielle got toasted almond coconut chocolate chip ice cream, and Ileandra got a berry flavor that promised tastes of blackberry and strawberry and blueberry. There were some whole berries, which she had to chew.

Her small teeth weren't used to doing much work.

Fortunately, berries weren't much work.

She had often wondered why her people lived on liquid nutrition.

Then she noticed that Arielle was running her tongue over her teeth very carefully after enjoying her ice cream.

"Are your teeth okay after eating that?"

"Yes. I just want to keep them that way. It's not good to just leave anything, particularly sweets, on one's teeth for half an hour, or close to it. It's better to completely eat it off, or, if that's impossible, to floss between teeth and brush the stuff away with a toothbrush. I'm okay, though. I got it off." With that, she picked up their now-empty dishes and little wooden spoons and napkins, and threw them into a rubbish bin.

They walked back across the ice cream shop's pine-needle-covered yard and back to the grocery store's parking lot, where Arielle had left the car.

"No sense burning fossil fuels to move the car to the ice cream shop's lot," she had said as they walked to it.

They got in, with Ileandra managing to pull her door shut hard enough to satisfy Arielle that it was securely closed.

When they got back to the house, however, Ileandra was sorry to realize that she could not lift a grocery bag and carry it inside. Arielle did that, carrying both heavy bags at once.

"I didn't actually expect a little alien woman to be physically powerful," she said, thumping the bags onto the kitchen counter. "You have so much technology to deal with every task, after all, that you can get by with that."

Ileandra looked at her. "You mean we have become completely dependent upon it."

"Well, yeah, okay, but you can't have everything. You can either not use it and stay overpopulated and unable to remediate the damage wrought by too many people using too much of everything, including what the ecosystem can produce, or you can use it to fix all that. And in the process, you have to trade something off. Physical strength is what you traded. I'm sure I'll find out what else you traded off as your stay here continues."

Arielle was putting the food away as she said all this.

Ileandra watched her, memorizing where it all went.

Maybe she could help with some housework…

…wait, what? "Traded?" she asked.

Arielle shut the last kitchen cabinet door and the fridge, folded the grocery bags up, and put them by the door to the garage. "Yeah…just like Nature makes Aspies trade off abilities that neurotypicals have as their dominant ones. We each have the same, but it's like a scale. We Aspies have much more data storage, access, and manipulation ability than neurotypicals do, but the trade-off is that we don't intuit our way through social interactions. We are the inverse of them."

Ileandra was startled. "Are you sure you have no telepathy? I was thinking about Aspies vs. neurotypicals. It was your conversation with that banker that was the most interesting thing of our trip outside."

"I knew you would appreciate that." Arielle grinned. She started lining up ingredients for the evening meal, including a mango lassi. She was going to cook curried salmon, basmati rice, and spiced spinach.

And she didn't have to say that to Ileandra.

But Ileandra had to say a few things to her.

"While you were having that conversation, I was realizing something about my people that I had not thought about before."

"Travel will do that to you," Arielle said without looking up. She was busy getting her cooking equipment out.

"What?"

She grinned. "Remember, I used to do tours at the Mark Twain House. He's a famous American author and humorist. He was also an Aspie, and he was great at observing the human condition. Or, more accurately, it seems, it is the condition of sentient beings of whatever species. He said that 'travel is fatal to prejudice'."

Ileandra considered that.

"Yes, it is. But I was also thinking that my people have no neurotypicals. We are all Aspies."

Arielle looked up from her ingredients at her.

"What did you do, genetically edit them all out?"

"Yes."

"Wow. Human corporations talk of editing us Aspies out. I don't like that. I have written about the folly of it in my books, and will keep on doing so."

She paused, because Ileandra was staring at her, horrified.

The alien said, "Your species won't survive without the Aspies. It is your Aspies who have enabled technology to develop. You are so deeply entrenched with technology at this point that it is the only way forward to the health of your planet and your future existence."

"Yes, I know," Arielle said, with a hint of sarcasm. "We Aspies are so cool that we likely invented wheels, figured out that fire could help us to cook food, developed food storage and so on, and I can name Aspie after Aspie who did or invented or wrote or discovered this and that. However, we also need the neurotypicals. As frustratingly incapable of intense focus as they are, they have their strengths. They get things done, and implement things that we create and think of. We need people with both kinds of brainstems."

"But too much of an appetite for sex and food leads to more consumption of resources through more reproduction. It is not managed or controlled, however much access your laws and science give you to birth control."

"True, but maybe you need to watch a bit more of *Star Trek*. Spock, the Aspie character, is half human, with the strength to match a genetically engineered Khan Noonian Singh. Add the emotion he felt when he thought that Kirk, his best friend, was dead thanks to Khan, and he was able to defeat him, thus enabling Dr. McCoy to use Khan's DNA to heal Kirk."

Ileandra considered that.

"I think you're right. We have lost some important things."

"Such as what? A lust for life? That can lead to overconsumption of resources, brought on by too much sex, which causes too many people to be produced."

"Yes, that is how and why we lost that. But...I think we may have taken it too far. I don't know from personal experience how bad things had gotten when there were too many of us, using too much, and causing so much damage. I just know about it from our history."

Arielle responded, "There is always a lot of emotion and suffering in history, and that can get left out of the short summary version of it. You have to really think about that to take it into account. Someone experienced that – painful hunger caused by insufficient food, cold and/or radiation sickness from one's predecessors having used up all heating materials and energy sources before new and safe methods could be invented and implemented, and so on."

Ileandra thought about that.

What had the transition period in her planet's history felt like to experience, physically, mentally, and emotionally? How had it been socially? How had it felt as each genetic iteration was created?

People had to live with gradually waning resources, dying.

People had to adapt to having amped-up telepathy due to genetic manipulation, and the social problems that that had created.

People had to live with the next genetic iterations that came as a result of living with that increased telepathic ability, iterations which scaled back emotional responses and physical strength, and amplified mental acuity.

Ileandra knew that her society prized mental acuity above emotion, but they hadn't forgotten emotion.

They remembered what damage it had caused.

They remembered what joy it had offered, and traded it away to dispense with any further damage.

That was what they had lost.

It was okay to remember the joy now.

It was safe now.

Maybe when she got home, she could share that.

She looked at Arielle, watched her cooking an evening meal for Kavi, and knew that these humans shared that and were doing what they could not to contribute to the damage that her people had focused on so intently as to lose the joy.

Life was supposed to be enjoyed, not simply lived.

Her people had the option of balance in that now.

They just didn't know it anymore.

Arielle and Kavi knew it still.

Their problem was that too many around them sought to have all that, yet it wasn't feasible.

And they understood what was threatening them.

She felt sorry for them, and worried for her friends.

She hoped that they would not be impacted directly by that when she went home.

Study in Rhapsody

Arielle had a lot of work to do.

Her parents and uncle had come over for dinner again last night, which had seriously cut into her work time, so she was anxious to spend hours working on an edit of a novel. She said it was about a vampire.

After a lengthy explanation of what a vampire is – one in which Ileandra was required to suspend disbelief and just accept the implausible as plausible in the interest of what humans consider to be fun – she understood the concept.

More importantly, the alien understood that her hostess had to work. Yet the human woman paused to see if Ileandra would have something enjoyable and engaging to do! She has already done plenty for me, Ileandra thought.

"You could watch movies in here and keep me company," Arielle said, turning on the television. "Look – all you have to do is go to the Movies-On-Demand channels and pick something that doesn't cost extra. If it says 'Watch for Free' it doesn't cost extra."

The alien looked at the screen.

There were so many choices that Ileandra didn't know where to begin. Also…

"Won't the sound distract you from your work?"

Arielle laughed. "No. I keep familiar movies on all the time when I'm working. It doesn't surprise me because I know the shows, and it calms me."

That settled it. She would watch movies all day.

But which ones? "What movies do you recommend?"

Arielle looked like she was in her element.

"Outer space ones, of course – preferably ones that teach you some human history – and something that shows you human culture, too."

She scrolled through the options.

Then she paused. "Here they are: *Hidden Figures*, *Apollo 13*, *First Man*, and *Bohemian Rhapsody*."

What the Small Gray Visitor Said

Aside from the title that invoked the Apollo Space Program, Ileandra had no matrix, no point of reference with which to understand those titles.

But not to worry; at her guest's clueless gaze, Arielle proceed to expound on the selections she had cited.

And she got out the book version of *Hidden Figures*.

"You can see the differences between a book and movie. The book is always the accurate version of the story; the movie is the entertainment version, sometimes with the order of events rearranged in order to make the story more exciting and thus sell the movie to more viewers. I don't approve of that, and I want the facts, so I usually read the book to correct my understanding of it all. It's fun, too."

Ileandra didn't ask why not just read the book.

Clearly, fun was the starting point.

Ileandra decided to follow Arielle's method and see what she could learn. Part of the point of this exercise was, after all, to settle into an activity that would encourage Arielle to focus on her work and edit all day.

The other part of it was to understand humans.

What actually happened was that the human took lots of breaks, using the bathroom, getting coffee, making smoothies, walking around, petting her cat, looking up, stretching, and watching the alien watch the movies, then explaining things that the alien didn't seem to understand, but in the end, she got half of the book edited. So, Ileandra supposed that it was, in fact, a productive workday for her.

Ileandra would have just worked straight through and edited more, but that was different. A human clearly needed more time to do her job, and could not sit perfectly still for hours on end.

Arielle was obviously making substantial changes to the book manuscript; there was no doubt that she was working. But the point of a vampire novel still eluded her.

As she read through *Hidden Figures* and watched the movie, Ileandra didn't have many questions…other than the one about the reason why Arielle had an editing job.

Why would another author need this done?

The movie ended, and Arielle got up to pet Bagheera, who had settled into his basket and was staring at them both. Then she took her coffee and juice cups to the kitchen.

Ileandra watched, looking curiously at her computer.

"What are you thinking about?" Arielle wanted to know.

"Sorry…I can't let you surf the internet for a while. I've got to edit a lot more of this today. I can't keep this client waiting much longer. She'll need to go over what I've done and tell me if it's okay or not. I'm trying to keep her meaning and intentions intact while helping her tell her story."

At last – an opening for asking her about the edit!

Ileandra considered how to pose her question.

"I was wondering why this edit is necessary. I'm trying to understand your work."

Arielle put the clean and dry cups away and looked up. "Oh! I see. Well, this client is not good at writing, but she loves to do that. The story is her idea and no one else's, so if she is serious about making a marketable book out of it, she must pay someone who is good at writing to fix her manuscript. And she is. This is really important to her. She will get credit for writing it, and I will get paid for helping her do something that matters to her."

"And she doesn't want to just do something else?"

Arielle looked at her. "Spoken like someone who is not an artist. We who are authors love what we do, and we want to be remembered and admired by other humans for our creativity. Take that away, and all the joy of work goes away. Joy is indispensable."

Ileandra thought about that.

Her work in botany had an element of joy to it, but it was different. It was tied to finding a plant that was viable in her home ecosystem, and as a food source that would actually nourish her people. Those moments when she succeeded in finding the right plant were joyful.

But it was not something that was created out of nothing. It was something that was discovered after trial and error.

Arielle was watching her think. "You're considering joy very carefully, aren't you?" she asked with a knowing grin.

Ileandra looked up at her. "Yes, I am," and smiled back. "I have felt it when I have found the right plant, after much searching and analysis."

Arielle nodded. "I spend months on each book that I write, and then another week or so polishing it and formatting it. It's not an instant gratification activity."

So, she understood.

Ileandra smiled, and the human woman started making a strawberry orange smoothie.

That came out really good. Thin, but delicious.

Ileandra would have to remember this combination.

Arielle laughed. "I discovered this combination decades ago. That's funny; I am broadening your gastronomic horizons with this visit."

"Is that what this is? A visit?" Ileandra asked.

"Well, we shouldn't just keep calling it a 'stranding' and dwell on the negative aspects of it. That's not good for anyone. I mean, why induce or amplify anxiety? We might as well enjoy knowing each other until you can go home."

"Yes. You are right." Ileandra stared into her glass, inhaled the enticing scents of the juice, and drank some more. Food this enjoyable was still new to her. "Thank you."

"If you are interested in watching a human who focuses on the grind of hard work while striving toward a glamorous goal, watch *First Man* next. It's about Neil Armstrong being the first human to land on Earth's moon. He didn't let emotion take him over until he knew it was safe to do so – when the goal was achieved. Even then, you will see that he waited, and waited, and waited until every step was completed and the entire goal was achieved, because to do otherwise was just too dangerous. The other astronauts could afford to feel the thrill of space travel more than he could, so he put that off, but he definitely felt emotion. He was just careful and cautious, and it paid off."

"You are an excellent movie critic," Ileandra observed. "That is exactly the sort of thing I want to observe. That woman in *Hidden Figures* – the mathematician behind the success of the Mercury Space program – was fascinating. It was also fascinating to see it pointed out and demonstrated that..." Ileandra was not sure how to phrase this.

Arielle stepped in, and suddenly the alien understood the value of a wordsmith. "...that Nature has absolutely no interest in how human culture views which individual it places talent and ability in?" she grinned. "I love that. It's one of my favorite things to observe in movies and in history...and in herstory."

Ileandra was impressed. "Yes! That is it; now I see the value of having an editor. I could not say that, but that is what I meant. Human society favored white males, and yet Nature ignored that and put the ability to manipulate and understand mathematics in a black woman. That was what made the movie so engaging. Well, that and watching humans learn to safely go into and return from space. All of it..."

"So...are you ready for more of that?"

She picked up the remote control, scrolled through the movie options, found *First Man*, and paused with her fingers over the controls.

'I have to edit more. I'm aiming to get halfway through this vampire manuscript before Kavi comes home. Some days I just steam my way through a job, so that other days I can relax a bit. Then I get back to it when I hear from the client. Oh, and after she pays the next invoice." Arielle grinned at that last bit. "Got to get paid, and not be stupid about this...working for oneself is tricky that way, but I'm doing okay at it, and I love it."

Ileandra nodded. "I'm ready."

"Great!" Arielle hit the 'Play' button. "Enjoy the music, too. That's part of the show. They give out awards for the best original film score at the Oscars each year. The Academy Awards is the official name of those prizes, but the statuette looks like a little, golden, naked, standing man, who is named Oscar."

She put a dish of canned cat food on the floor as she said this. "GOOD boy, Bagheera," she said, and petted him. Bagheera had been walking around on the kitchen counter, meowing and purring and trying to rub on her until she had caught on and fed him.

Now, the cat rushed over and started eating.

Ileandra caught a glimmer of a thought in the human's mind and suddenly realized that Arielle had known all along that her cat was hungry. She had simply been determined to methodically take care of one task at a time – smoothies, then cat food…and to enjoy interacting with her pet.

Her thoughts jumped back to something that Arielle had just said.

"Why is it called an 'Oscar'?" Ileandra asked, feeling a bit guilty for the delay she was causing Arielle in getting back to work.

Arielle, however, didn't mind. "There are several theories, all outlined on the award's Wikipedia page. You can look later, in the evening, but for now, I shall wickedly make you wait with your question left unanswered, because I have to use the computer."

Ileandra nodded, smiled, and returned to her spot on the sofa to watch the movie.

It was all true, what Arielle had said.

Neil Armstrong was portrayed as a man who had emotions, but who also refused to let them dictate his responses to any stressor in his life, no matter what. It saved his life and that of David Scott, the astronaut who was with him aboard Gemini 8. And he refused to let the thrill of setting down in the Moon's Sea of Tranquility overtake him and distract from a safe landing there.

He was an unusual human.

Arielle got up and stretched and pet her cat when the credits rolled, and said, "Neil Armstrong may have sacrificed demonstrations of emotion too much; he and Jan ended up divorced. But he probably couldn't help it," she added.

Ileandra considered that.

And she thought about the other scientists that she spent her life with aboard her ship. They really didn't communicate much. They certainly didn't talk about issues in such depth as Arielle did with her.

She had another thought, and Arielle was up and walking around, so she voiced it.

"Do you talk about life in such depth of detail with Kavi?" she asked.

Arielle looked at her, then smiled. "Not so much. But that's probably because we're been married for a couple of decades and already hashed most of that out long ago. It's like we're in agreement about all that now, and it's old stuff to us. If a movie reminds us of it, I bring it up, and go over some of it again, and he just nods and smiles. He laughs a bit, too. He loves these movies as much as I do. His mother has commented that if she mentions a movie, he's usually seen it…and so have I."

Ileandra listened, and thought about discussing such things with a certain male scientist – one of the ones who had been with her when she was stranded. She had definitely seen him looking back in alarm, toward her hiding place, as he was reluctantly beamed back up to their ship.

But he never communicated with her other than to pass samples and laboratory equipment back and forth, and to share views of them through a lens.

It left her wondering whether or not there was any reason to try to communicate with him more.

She would have to get back to her ship first, though.

They paused for lunch, which meant solid food for Arielle – leftovers the evening before, when the humans had taken a ride to the grocery store together – and a carrot-almond-butter smoothie with turmeric and pinch of cayenne for Ileandra.

What the Small Gray Visitor Said

The alien had insisted upon staying home alone and trying to contact her ship. Nothing. But she hadn't really expected to contact it. Her real motive had been to induce the humans to go out and spend some time alone together.

Yesterday had been June 18th – their wedding anniversary. Kavi had said that he had wanted to buy Arielle flowers, but that he couldn't in the pandemic. Florists were closed.

There really wasn't much that they usually did that they could do this year…or until a vaccine was available.

And now they were stuck, as the alien saw it, with her.

Who knew how long they would have her with them?! She felt like an intruder into their lives, accidental though her presence here was. Yet the humans continued to be genuinely happy to have her with them. She knew it, because of her telepathy. It puzzled her a bit, even though she realized that they were enjoying a rare secret, one that most never had.

Who knew how long they would have her with them?! She felt like an intruder into their lives, accidental though her presence here was.

She picked up the remote control, scrolled to *Apollo 13*, and started that movie as Arielle returned from the bathroom and settled into her chair.

The human woman was making good progress; she had edited a quarter of the novel. Another two movies, and she would have met her work goal for the day.

Arielle glanced up and said, "This one is more for pure enjoyment than anything else. It's a show of America being determined to manage a crisis on the strength of its own resources on its own. And the music is awesome. You'll hear some famous, old favorites of rock songs."

Another new experience: having classic songs pointed out. Ileandra let it run. It started out with instrumental music, but soon a rock song was included.

When that movie was finished, she was duly impressed.

Arielle showed her another book, *Lost Moon: The Perilous Voyage of Apollo 13* by James Lovell and Jeffrey Kluger.

Ileandra's first question was, "Why did this Jeffrey Kluger also write the book? Why not just the astronaut?"

Arielle smiled. "Remember why I'm editing this novel? Astronauts are engineers, not writers, but the story is Jim Lovell's. He needed help, and the helper was given credit. Kluger must have contributed so significantly to the writing of that memoir that his name belongs on the cover. Scientists must make whatever they write accessible – intelligible – to others, or it's useless. That means, at the very least, having an editor work on whatever they publish. In fact, the day that you appeared in my garden, I had just edited a journal article that Kavi wrote. 8 pages, and yet it was not polished enough to publish. It will be published, though, and we are looking forward to seeing it in a few months."

"Kavi needs help with his writing?" Ileandra was incredulous. "But he speaks perfectly."

"Well, yeah, he's born and raised in America, and he has a high I.Q., which one would expect of a research scientist, but he isn't a wordsmith, and even someone who writes can go so fast that they skip a word that they are absolutely sure that they included, because they thought it. No one can edit their own work."

Ileandra understood at last. "I see," she said, nodding.

A half-hour went by in silence, while Ileandra read the book and looked at all of the photographs. She suddenly realized that she had just taken in the story the same way that Arielle liked to do it. She could see why it was worthwhile.

Now, what was that last movie? *Bohemian Rhapsody*?

"What is *Bohemian Rhapsody* about? It doesn't seem to be about outer space," Ileandra said, putting the book down.

Arielle looked up from her computer and gave her a big grin. "It's not." She stretched, stood up, and moved to the sofa. "Don't worry, I'll get back to work," she said, looking at Ileandra's face.

Ileandra realized that she had been looking askance at her hostess for not working, and hastily stopped that. "I'm sorry. I didn't mean to look at you like that."

What the Small Gray Visitor Said

The human woman laughed. "That's okay. "I'm going to get halfway through this book before the day is out. I can tell now. I'm pausing to tell you something really cool about this movie. It's about the formation of a rock group from Britain called Queen, and it is named for the most famous song, written by their lead singer, Freddie Mercury."

"He was named for a planet?!" Ileandra was surprised.

"No, that was the stage name he legally changed to. His original name was Farrokh Bulsara. He was a Zoroastrian Persian-Indian guy. You'll get his biography from this movie. I wanted to tell you that the fight between the group in the early 1980s is entirely made up, just a device used to point out the other talents of the other members. It was the STEM disciplines rock group that needed a pure artist. When they took on Freddie, they got that, and the group was complete. It was also like a family to them."

"STEM?"

"Science, Technology, Engineering, Mathematics."

"Oh…an acronym."

"Yeah…I don't know a lot of those. Like, texting – I don't do that. Don't ask me to take a quiz in emojis – emoticons." Arielle grinned.

"Can most humans in your culture do that?"

"Yes – it's a very neurotypical pastime. But back to this movie…I will tell you a fact from this movie that brings outer space into it, about one member of the group besides Freddie. The other guys are all English. The lead guitarist, whose name is Brian May, holds a Ph.D. in astrophysics. His thesis, which I looked up online, is about the movement of cosmic dust in the astral cloud. He went back to school 36 years after starting it and finished."

"Fascinating," Ileandra said, sounding hilariously like Mr. Spock. She had been binge-watching *Star Trek* episodes off and on since her arrival, so she knew what she was doing, but she still couldn't help herself.

Nevertheless, Arielle giggled.

Ileandra wondered, "Why didn't he just finish that degree earlier?"

"He was busy making a living as a rock star. Rock stars get rich. You'll see. But after a while, he wanted to finish, and he had the luxury of time and plenty of money to just go back to school and finish it, so he did. He's a vegetarian now, and an environmental activist."

"What about the one whose name is for the first planet in your solar system?"

"He's dead. He contracted HIV, an auto-immune disease, and came down with AIDS, which is what you get when the condition gets out of control. Treatments from thirty-five years ago were still experimental, so they couldn't save him. But he was so well-loved that it helped spur scientific efforts to improve them. If he got AIDS today, he would have a much better chance at a longer life."

"He is dead, yet this movie was made, and did very well?"

"Well, yeah! People loved him, and the music, and the rest of Queen lost a member of their chosen family. They miss him. They have found another front-man singer, named Adam Lambert, but there will never be another Freddie. Every person is unique. That must be true for your people, too."

Ileandra thought about that. She hadn't thought about that much before. The goals of her people as a whole were such a powerful force in her own world that it had not occurred to her before.

But now she realized that it was true.

"Yes. It is," she said, staring at nothing in particular.

"Well," Arielle said, getting up and sitting back down at her computer, "enjoy the movie and the songs. This is a study in creativity and enjoyment, and the reasons why it matters. I love it, and I hope you do, too."

Ileandra watched it, and she did.

She had never expected to love anything quite like that, but seeing thousands of humans feel like they personally knew a man just because he had composed a song and could sing it beautifully, all while inviting them to sing along and feel the sensation of togetherness with him did that.

It was a new sensation to her.

She liked it – a lot.

Arielle saw her watching, open-mouthed in amazement, as Queen's attorney-agent, Jim 'Miami' Beach, sang *Radio Gaga* with his arms up, and looked like he had happily lost himself in that song when it ended.

"What does that expression on his face mean?" the alien asked her.

"It means that he got emotionally high off of that song." Ileandra looked back at the screen quickly.

Yes, that was it.

She had never felt that.

"Did you feel that, watching this movie?" she asked.

"Definitely. I don't need to go to a crowded venue to get high, either. In fact, I don't think I would like that. Movies, when well made, get me high like you just saw Miami get."

Arielle looked at her at the end of this little speech.

"I know you're not like Mr. Spock. You can feel it, too, and don't mind acknowledging that. It's just so new to you."

Ileandra smiled back. "Yes. Yes, I do, and yes, it is."

The human was halfway through the edit of her manuscript, as she had planned, and they heard Kavi's car pulling into the driveway.

Arielle saved her work, backed it up, prepared an invoice, and e-mailed that and the half-edited file to her client.

Ileandra went right over to the computer to look up the Oscar statuette on the internet.

Arielle laughed as she went to greet her husband.

She knew that the alien was not easily distracted.

She also knew that the information would disappoint Ileandra with its indefiniteness, but one couldn't have everything.

A Summer of Protests

The summer was shaping up to be one of outrageous, historically significant human and civil right violations, accompanied by rising infection rates as large numbers of people came out to protest them.

The protests had been against the requirements to wear face masks and to maintain social distancing, and going on for the past few months, as governments across the United States had imposed shut-down orders.

That had seemed idiotic enough, but these idiots also refused to wear face masks because it impinged upon their "freedom". There was no freedom to infect others!

They carried Nazi and Confederate flags and assault rifles.

Ileandra had reviewed the political events leading up to this point, just so that she could make sense of the news, and asked me about that.

"Oh," I said. "That's been on as much as the protests. There are always a few assholes. I looked that up a while ago. There are some reports that radical, right-wing, alt-right recluses with huge fortunes are providing the financial resources for this nonsense. But then, a month ago, something else had happened – something that had taken the focus off of the pandemic."

"You mean when a cop in Minnesota murdered a black man by putting his knee on the guy's neck, cutting off his air supply, as he pinned him down on the pavement of a city street in plain sight, on camera, while his colleagues just stood there."

"Yes." Protesters were now congregating in large numbers all across the nation. I wasn't someone who went to protests, not even before the pandemic.

"Why is that – why don't you go?" Ileandra asked, as we sat in front of the TV, watching it live on CNN.

She had stopped surveying every channel when she realized that I found it exhausting. Now she just picked a channel and stuck with it – but not Fox News, which I had disparaged as Fixed News and Fox Noise. Then I had shown her the miniseries starring Russell Crowe about Roger Ailes, the monster who had made that network the alt-right, fact-averse, travesty that it was today, called *The Loudest Voice*.

Properly appalled, she was done with that channel.

"I don't like crowds," I told her. "I'm a loner. I don't like being out among large numbers of people making a lot of noise. That's part of being on the autism spectrum. So, instead of doing that, I vote for the issues that these protests are about. I keep educating myself about them, signing petitions, and making posts, tweets, pins, and other shares about them. My books and blog pieces are all supportive of these liberal policies, too."

I paused, then added, "The trouble with all of these protests is that, correct though the protesters are about their demands for social, political, and legal changes, they are also risking the spread of more coronavirus cases. It was all very amusing to watch MAGA morons attend rallies for fascist, alt-right nonsense with no face masks, but the liberal protesters, who acknowledge the risk, aren't being careful enough. They wear masks – most of them – but they are not six feet apart from each other."

"So, you fight from your computer, and with your vote."

"Yes."

"You've got it covered, then." The alien smiled and turned back to the news coverage.

"I guess. Those cops should be fired and prosecuted – all of them, not just the one who actually committed the murder. Too often, police have delayed on charging perpetrator cops with murder and arresting them for it. So have prosecutors."

Someone was being interviewed about slogans. She was standing on the edge of one of the crowds, at Union Square in New York City. She said, "Black Lives Matter…don't say that All Lives Matter, because all houses are not on fire."

Ileandra looked at me again.

I grinned. "She's right. I'm fine. I can go out in the world and interact pretty much fearlessly with a cop, but if I were black, I would not trust a cop. Kavi is Indian, and he has been profiled. He once drove with a stomach cramp to the pharmacy to buy something for that, and a cop noticed him behind the wheel of his car, looking miserable and dressed in loose, old clothing. He followed Kavi all the way there and back home again, then realized that it was nothing and left."

Ileandra was gaping at me. She realized that and closed her mouth, then opened it to say, "Couldn't the police officer see that he wasn't feeling well?!"

"No. It was from a distance, and Kavi was in his car – not the Mercedes he drives now, either. It was when he was in graduate school. The car was okay, but it didn't project a message of wealth and professional success. He looks very different now, driving his dark blue Mercedes, dressed like he stepped out of an L.L. Bean catalogue. I went online and taught myself how to give him a nice haircut at home so that he won't have any trouble driving around while barber shops are closed for the pandemic. I don't want anything to happen to him."

She thought about that.

"This is not anything that happens with your people, is it?" I asked her.

"No."

"As I remember my research about aliens – a thing I did just for fun when I was in my twenties, but in as much depth as I could manage it – you don't have such problems. I found that there were many different aliens, I guess from different planets and solar systems, perhaps even galaxies for all I or any other human could know, each with different agendas, and most not here to kill us, though some were here to experiment on us, hence the abductions. But I didn't sense anything like racism among any of you. Was I right, or wrong?"

"You were right."

"But what about your people's past? Did it ever exist?"

The alien didn't even need to think about it. "Yes. It did."

"What is your planet like now?"

"That's over with, long ago."

What the Small Gray Visitor Said

"What are the lingering effects of that, though?" I couldn't help myself. I was horrified by what I might find out, but I couldn't stop.

She looked at me uncomfortably, and I sensed that she wasn't sure whether or not she should answer my question. But, after considering it, she made her decision.

"Our planet went through many resource wars because of something like racism, plus nationalism, plus whatever other form of insular thinking and emotional insecurity causes wars."

I stared at her, taking that in.

"And what effect did that have on its ecosystems?"

She looked at me silently.

I looked back at her.

"It must have had some effect," I prodded. I wasn't the sort of person who accepted silence as confirmation of anything.

She answered me at last, "It killed most of our plant life."

I felt a bit sick. But I wasn't the least bit surprised.

She knew that, of course.

"You said 'most' plant life. That suggests that not all of it is ruined. I mean, your people are still alive, and you obviously need to eat plants. I've got to buy more ingredients for smoothies again." I think I said that more to make myself feel better than for any other reason, to calm myself after what she had just told me.

It worked, sort of. She smiled bleakly back, and said, "Yes, some plants are left, but not enough varieties to sustain us."

There it was: confirmation of the reason why she was a botanist who collected plants from Earth.

She 'heard' that and nodded.

I got up to pour out more smoothies for us.

We were drinking blueberry-mango ones, with cinnamon and cardamom.

While I was at it, I looked through the fridge and wrote up a grocery list. I wanted to call it in to Rosedale Farms, just up the road, and perhaps see a friend who worked there.

"Are you going out?" Ileandra asked.

"If I am, I'm bringing you with me, but it's not necessary to go just yet. We can stay in today."

It had been a month since her arrival here.

We had gone grocery shopping each week.

Kavi had insisted, after that first incident with the caffeine and the pile of work I had churned out so abnormally fast, that Ileandra never drink anything that we hadn't approved.

He had abandoned all pretense of diplomacy and hospitality when he demanded this.

"Ileandra, you could forget not to drink coffee – or worse, something alcoholic – while Arielle is out driving. With that telepathic link you two have, you could get her arrested for drunk driving, or cause her to crash the car and injure herself or someone else…or even get someone killed. If you got my wife killed, I would never forgive you."

I hadn't told him about what had happened the second evening, when my family had brought pizza and beer, and she had drunk half a bottle of it.

It was just as well.

But she remembered, and was quite horrified and upset even before Kavi had gotten to the end of his warning.

I felt it.

Her assurances and promise to not drink any stimulant or depressant, and to comply with that rule about staying with me when I went out, had satisfied him.

For better or for worse, I had a constant companion all summer. No chance that I would get lonely!

I came back to the sofa and sat down to drink my smoothie.

Bagheera was on the end of the sofa closest to my computer desk, sleeping, but he woke up when I sat down. The cat moved over to be closer to me.

He never sat down in my lap, because I was too ticklish, but he loved to curl up tight against me and purr and then fall asleep there. I loved that right back.

I sat back against the back of the sofa and stared into space. "I'm procrastinating. I should be doing more of the edit of that vampire novel. I'm three-quarters of the way through it. And after that, there's a couple of short stories from another client to edit. I think he's on pot – marijuana – for inspiration as he writes them. They're really weird science fiction."

Ileandra turned away from the protests on CNN and gaped at me.

"Someone writes fiction while under the influence of a hallucinogen?"

"Yup."

"Why?"

"Maybe he's worried about not being able to come up with anything unusual without it. It's the only explanation that makes sense."

She raised her eyebrows, seemed to wonder about that, and then decided to just watch TV again.

I laughed.

I was feeling a bit burned out.

It was good that I had gotten so much work done lately, but I just wanted to sit today and relax. The problem was that I tended to feel guilty unless I was working all of the time.

Kavi called it the Protestant Work Ethic.

He liked that term. It was something that he had heard a bit too much about in school in Philadelphia. For some reason, his parents had sent him and his sister to a private Episcopalian school. That phrase was tossed about there a lot.

I stared into space some more.

Ileandra broke my reverie with the comment, "The problems of racism, sexism, phobias of other cultures, and the drive to out-reproduce anyone who is different from one's own group are systemic. Your planet's ecosystem may end up like that of my planet if this isn't fixed. My people failed, until their numbers were decreased."

'Were decreased' …by what means? War? Policy? Both?

Maybe I could find out more about that.

For now, I said, "Agitating peacefully for social change has done a lot to transform human societies in the past century. But we do need an unpopular population policy, one that causes crushing disappointment. To get that, we would need something to happen that would convince a majority of humans of the necessity for it, or nothing will happen."

"What has been done in the past century?" the alien asked.

"Oh…now you're getting me into my element," I said.

I began to talk about women getting the right to vote, the end of segregation, gay rights, the Stonewall Riot, the fact that I had a trans cousin in New York City, and lots of details about all of that.

"Gay Pride is likely called off due to the pandemic, though," I said wistfully.

The rainbow butterflies fabric that I was offering as a face mask option was beautiful – white with all different butterflies in flight. I had meant it as a choice for the Gay Pride celebrations in late June, even though the idea of actually holding a parade with large numbers of attendees seemed foolish. Even masked, people would still be too close together!

"It's sad. I know how much fun a Gay Pride Parade could be. I attended one myself, years ago, when Kavi was doing some work in Manhattan at the Cornell Medical School's hospital. Music from the 1980s blared as colorfully costumed drag queens danced on floats. The mayor, wearing a white polo shirt, beige cargo shorts, sneakers, and knee socks, walked in the parade while drinking a large coffee. He seemed to enjoy being there. It was fun to watch, and pretty!"

I was getting a bit tired, and my mind wandered.

A lady in Hawaii had already ordered a rainbow butterflies mask. She had told me that their governor was smart and careful, and had required everyone to wear a mask in public from the outset of the pandemic. As a result, Hawaii's rate of infection was flat.

Rainbows meant something different in Hawaii, though, which predated Gay Pride: the sight of a rainbow meant that an alii was traveling. The alii are members of the native Hawaiian aristocracy.

Rainbows are for everyone. We can all enjoy them!

What the Small Gray Visitor Said

Come to think of it, I had rainbow dogs for another pattern, but I just liked the colors. I wasn't a dog person per se; I liked to have cats and visit other people's dogs, leaving the care of the dogs to them. The point of that fabric option was to please face mask customers who loved dogs.

I had given Uncle Louis a mask in that pattern, and he had actually smiled happily when he got it.

Uncle Louis didn't show much of a reaction about much, even though I loved to talk with him about many topics. He just wasn't very demonstrative. That was why it was such fun to give him that mask.

I glanced up and realized that Ileandra had 'listened' to all of that. More like eavesdropped to it, I thought, deliberately projecting that to her.

She smiled and looked at her smoothie, and took a sip.

But our connection didn't stop. She couldn't help it.

As statues of Confederate racists were being torn down, I had read an article in National Geographic that asked the question, "How much history [of the racist past] should be taught?"

I was surprised by that question.

My response was, "All of it!" We should never forget any of the details or contexts or white trash inferiority complexes that drove hate crimes, nor the sufferings of slaves, runaway slaves, slaves who sued for their freedom such as Dred Scott (and lost!), slaves who escaped and went back 19 times to rescue 300 more people from that misery, including her parents (Harriet Tubman), and so on.

Remember it all!

I looked at the alien.

She had 'heard' all that, too.

Enough of this. I started speaking out loud again.

"As I gather my thoughts about this, another blog post is forming in my mind. I could also write a book chapter about this, I suppose, but that's a project for a later time."

"You aren't writing one now?"

"No, but I may have a topic after you go home. I don't want to write anything until you are safely back. Then it won't matter, because you won't be affected."

Ileandra's eyes widened. "You think ahead a lot, about consequences."

I grinned. "I try. I wish most humans did that. My father remarked recently that the Confederate flag ought to have been banned as a term of the surrender of the Confederate Army and government. I agree with him – it would have saved a lot of trouble later on."

Reports about angry Southerners who wanted that flag displayed openly in any venue they chose had been aired for the past week or so as it began to be banned in quite a few.

Ban it along with the Nazi flag, I thought. It was in the same category of hate and shamefulness.

Ileandra was watching my thoughts and the news like a tennis game, I observed.

She laughed. She had seen a tennis report on the national news a couple of nights ago.

"So," she said, as the news reports got repetitive and nothing new seemed to be forthcoming, "tell me more about the history of human societies and the changes of the past century."

"Oh, okay…" I thought about how to continue. Then I decided.

"Social, political, and legal change has only come, it seemed, with a wrenching of rights out of the clenched hands of a selfish, insecure minority that sought to control things by not sharing with others."

"Women did not get the vote by asking nice and sweetly. Our foremothers insisted upon it – demanded it. They broke laws that disadvantaged them until the men gave in. They shamed Woodrow Wilson by publicizing the forced-feeding in prison of Alice Paul, their leader."

"And they had not been perfect."

Ileandra asked, "What do you mean by that?"

"Many had been racists. Alice Paul was one. It was disappointing to know that Alice Paul, with all of her graduate degrees, was such a jerk."

"What did she do that made her a jerk?"

"The usual selfish, insular nonsense. The white women suffragists had had to share the victory with black women, including one of their own, Ida B. Wells-Barnett, a journalist who reported on lynchings. Someone had to tell the world about those crimes. Before the vote for women was won, she was told that she was not welcome to participate in suffragette marches. She made herself a picket sign and simply walked out into the street and joined them. At that point, the suffragettes just all kept marching together."

Ileandra went over the computer again and looked both women up.

"We can watch a movie about them later. It's called *Iron-Jawed Angels*. It's named for the force-feeding device used on Alice Paul."

Black Americans – apparently, calling them "African-Americans" didn't work for everyone with dark skin, because their ancestors were also from other places besides Africa, it had recently been pointed out – had also not gotten rid of segregation by asking nicely. They had broken the Jim Crow laws repeatedly until those were ended.

But there were plenty more racist problems to solve.

Oops...I had lapsed into thought again.

No problem. Ileandra had 'heard' all that.

I talked about gay rights. It was late June, after all.

"Gays and lesbians rioted on the night of June 27th, 1969 – well, early in the morning of the 28th, actually – at the Stonewall Bar in Greenwich Village, Manhattan because a plainclothes cop had punched a drag king (a cross-dressing lesbian) named Stormé DeLarverié in the stomach as she stood outside. She immediately knocked him flat, setting off the mêlée. The LGBTQ community had had it with police harassment. They had just attended Judy Garland's funeral – she was a famous singer and actress – so they were out in large numbers, and the police had decided to follow them around. Last year, the New York City Police Commissioner actually made a statement about it, saying that the police had been wrong to bother them."

"So how did that improve life for the LGBTQ people?"

"It's now illegal to harass people for not being heterosexual," I replied. "No one gets equal rights just because the ruling group feels like being nice. We each – each group that is not white males – have to insist upon it."

"It seems to take a long time – and it may take you too long to save your ecosystem. This is what is keeping the focus off of that problem, this inability to share the world with each other. Each group wants to take too much for itself."

I looked at the alien.

"You would know; your people went through this."

"Yes, we did, though the details are not studied as much as you have studied them. They are ingrained into our collective memory and thinking, though."

"That's the problem here – not enough collective memory and thinking. It fades over time, and there are always those who just don't want to change. And they reproduce, perpetuating their drive to continue selfish, destructive practices. I want a population policy, and only the educated, secular thinkers seem to see the need for it and act accordingly. We need more of that – much, much more."

I paused.

"I would like to see it enacted into law," I said.

That felt the safest, the most effective, and the most permanent. It had worked well with voting rights, desegregation of schools, restaurants, transportation, and whatever else, and resource allocation, and it needed to be applied in many more facets of society.

We sat and drank another cup of smoothie, I petted the cat, and then we did watch that suffragette movie.

I had given up on the idea that I was going to get much work done today. It was a Wednesday.

What the Small Gray Visitor Said

Kavi was probably working hard in his lab, and here I was, enjoying a visit with a friend, hanging out in the living room, goofing off.

"You've been doing lots of work!" Ileandra said, refuting my self-imposed guilt trip. "You've also sewn enough masks that if someone contacts you and asks to buy any, you could just pack up some of what you already have."

I laughed. "Yeah…as Uncle Louis says, I have stock."

The movie was over, and it was mid-afternoon.

I checked the computer, clicking through the e-mail, the Facebook notifications, and a post on my overpopulation group's feed. Someone had posted a story about the Uighurs in northern China.

"Oh, you are going to love this, Ileandra," I said, my voice dripping with sarcasm.

She picked up on it.

"What is it?"

"China has a population policy. It also has the largest population on Earth, at 1.4 billion people, with India a close second, at 1.38 billion. But back to China. Its majority ethnic group is the Han people. A minority is the Uighurs, and they are Muslims. China has been putting the Uighurs into concentration camps if they insist upon having more children than the population policy allows, and doing forced sterilizations to stop them, while allowing Han people to reproduce just a bit more than the policy allows, unchecked."

Ileandra looked both puzzled and disgusted. "Why?"

"They do it to practice a subtle form of cultural genocide. It's more of the human propensity to not share. The idea is to enable the Han, from whence the ruling class comes, to out-reproduce other groups. That way, policies that suit the Han will be made, and to the exclusion of other groups' interests."

I turned to the comment thread and added some input of my own:

Each population policy effort must be looked at in detail to see its real intent: in this case, it is about suppressing another culture in favor of the ruling one. That is not right. The numbers of both should be dropped. China has the largest population on the planet, and is plundering the fisheries of the seas around it, and attacking the fishers of other nations, pushing them out of the way militarily at sea where no witnesses can prevent them - only watch. Any population policy will cause anger and crushing disappointment to those who want more kids. I really don't care about that, and in fact that reaction angers me. But to use the policy to try to stamp out another culture also disgusts me, and I built the policy in my series of novels about overpopulation to work against that idea.

Leaving people to choose whether and how much to reproduce always leads to them choosing to reproduce and many to reproduce several times. This is killing our planet. If a population policy causes crushing disappointment, so be it...but not one like this, aimed at stamping out another culture. It must be applied equally, so that there will be some of everyone.

The alien leaned in to read what I had added.

"You are not likely to prevail, even though you are right."

"I know, but it's fun to annoy people with my ideas. At least it will induce them to think outside of their comfort zones. It's all very easy for me, a child-free woman, to say the things that I do, but then, that is why I am child-free. It's deliberate. I must practice what I preach, anyway."

Ileandra grinned. "You annoy people?"

"I'm the sort of liberal who annoys – with or without planning it that way – conservatives. I get accused of having drunk the Kool Aid, which means sucked up the policy platform like it's the sweetest, most perfect thing without questioning it, even those I do question it."

"How do you annoy people? Just by having a different point of view? And what do you question?"

"I don't agree with ripping down every last monument, because it smacks of rewriting history and forgetting it."

"Keep the U.S. presidents' monuments, but add details to their plaques, even if that costs some more money. Include that they owned slaves, and whatever shameful details go with that."

"When I saw a historic marker for a former slave market on a trip to the South, I thought – and said – that there was something missing. What was it? Crime scene tape. Families were ripped apart there, and other crimes against humanity committed there."

The alien nodded. "That makes sense. Remember it all."

We went into the kitchen and I laid out pasta, hot peppers, mushrooms, plum tomatoes, capers, garlic, onions, and a few other ingredients for a sauce called puttanesca that Kavi and I liked to eat sometimes. Time to have it again.

Ileandra watched me.

"What else has changed for the better for women?"

I smiled. "You love to get me going, don't you?"

I thought back to my college days, when I had majored in women's history and minored in women's studies.

"I want things that used to be a problem for women, and still aren't done by most: I want to be married with my own last name and the courtesy title of "Ms." rather than to be known as my husband's wife with my own surname hidden as a mere initial. I really abhor the courtesy title of "Mrs." It is a holdover from Puritan times, when property owners were addressed as "Master" and "Mistress" – always with the man's last name – hence the "r" in "Mrs." The title is spelled "Misses" when written out today."

"Fortunately, I can have what I want now without being harassed about it. It's commonly accepted now. I am Ms. Desrosiers, not Mrs. Ravendra. I would find that galling, and Kavi respects me for it rather than feeling insecure or slighted. Only men with weak egos would feel slighted."

"Yet there was a woman in the 1950s who wanted to use "Ms." rather than "Miss" (she was single), and her parents' response was to cut off funds for her college tuition. They cared that much about controlling her. It was crazy."

"There are actually people who want to return society to the way it was in the 1950s. I got an e-mail from some older,

183

distant, Republican cousins to that effect once, complete with artwork from that decade. It depicted cozy, wealthy, middle-class towns that were occupied by white people."

"I wrote back to point out that the only people who were happy back then were heterosexual, Christian white people with a patriarchal lifestyle. Everyone else was unhappy, and the attitudes of conformity intensified that."

"A close family friend of ours had her life ruined by that. She was raised in a religious family, and coerced into attending a conservative, Christian college. At least it offered instruction in music, which is what she wanted. She learned the technical skills necessary to be a lovely soprano singing teacher, plus a teacher of the flute, the clarinet, and the piano."

"So far, so good," Ileandra said. "Then what?"

"She met an engineer there. He proposed to her."

"How did her family and his respond to that?"

"Her family was very pleased. So was his mother."

Ileandra said, "I sense something bad coming."

"You sense correctly. His mother knew that he was homosexual back when society expected gays to pretend that they were heterosexual and just lie to themselves and everyone else, their happiness and that of others be damned."

The alien stared at me, appalled.

"His mother didn't care that marrying a woman would ruin that woman's life. So, our friend did not find out what she was signing up for, and she married that gay engineer."

"What happened to them?"

"It didn't last. You can't hide from yourself, nor hide it from the world. They had two kids before they ended up divorced."

I started to cook the pasta sauce, thinking as I worked.

It's not fair to anyone for society to be the way that it was.

And there are people who want to go back to that!

They want to control others.

It's flat out wrong.

A little while later, I was done. I filled the pasta pot with water, added a little salt, inserted the drainer section, and replaced the lid. I would wait until Kavi was home to boil the water and cook the pasta.

Ileandra asked, "You said that radical, right-wing, wealthy donors control politicians. That's not everyone. What about the others?"

"There are liberal politicians. And other corporations than just the ones controlled by right-wing conservatives. But they can be slow to act, because they are reluctant to give up any profits. Money is poison in large quantities, even to those without poisonous, controlling attitudes."

"So what can be done?"

"The trick is to hit corporations – the big donors to conservative politicians – in their wallets. The more that consumers refuse to do business with a corporation unless and until it adopts liberal policies and practices, the more likely that corporation is to change."

"One example is the decision not to post any more ads on Facebook until all hate speech is expunged from the site. Ads are how that leviathan company makes its money."

Ileandra glanced at the computer. She had been looking around on that site, and it was still up on the screen.

I continued my diatribe. "It's working, too. Facebook's founder and owner just lost $7 billion of its net worth. Of course, he has $72 billion more, but hitting him in the wallet may finally induce him to make a regular policy of removing hate speech. Other social media platforms have done it, so why not Facebook?!"

After all of that had been hashed out, Ileandra had one more question.

We had gone out into the back yard to pick some nasturtiums and to snip some fresh chives.

She broached in a less direct manner than I used.

I had been called blunt once – by the engineer dad of my best friend from college – and he had meant it as a compliment.

185

But I could see why she laid out a preface to her question.

"Arielle…I found an organization on the internet of people who believe in aliens. But I haven't heard you talk about them."

I looked at her.

"If you mean MUFON, the Mutual Unidentified Flying Object Network, there's a reason why not."

She said, "I do mean MUFON."

"Did you read the Wikipedia entry on them, or did you just visit their website?"

"I just visited their website. Why do you ask?"

"It's better, when researching a topic, to visit not only a primary source, which, in this case, is their website, but also secondary and other sources, such as ones that discuss them from an outside point of view. If you had done that, you would have seen that they are unscientific and have blatantly bigoted views of other religions, races, and cultures. If I joined them, I would be interacting with the same sort of idiots that want to keep the social, political, and legal aspects of society as they were sixty or more years ago – with all of the negative effects that go with it."

Her mouth dropped open. Then she shut it. "I see."

I scooped up the nasturtiums and chives and stood up.

We went in, and the alien immediately went back to my computer to look up MUFON on Wikipedia.

I laughed and started making salads.

Our visitor had found that she could eat them, as long as I put nothing other than olive oil on them.

Nature Is Indifferent to Our Desires

I often laughed when I found people railing against whatever it is that Nature does that does not suit them.

"It's not fair!" wailed the real estate brokers of Florida land, land at sea level, land that will cease to exist for sale in a few decades. Literally: a few decades more is all that it has.

Nature doesn't care. Nature is an indifferent force, after all. There is nothing we can do to deter it.

We can attempt to shape it to our desires, building dams and levees and dikes to hold back the rising seas after we have heated up the atmosphere and thus caused the ice shelves to melt away. But it was our very attempt to make our planet accommodate us that led to the melting…and the pandemic.

Cases were spiking in midsummer as the effects of reckless refusals to maintain social distancing were being felt, and many people were dying of it. People were learning the hard way that gambling that they wouldn't get sick didn't pay off.

Whenever I thought of the concept of global warming and climate change – two names for the same concept – and remembered that it is manifested with both intensified hot and cold seasons, not just the hot ones – it was as a year of them.

And I thought of a year of the four seasons as a suspension bridge with one high beam supporting it. Winter is that high beam, like a hump of difficulty to be crossed, while the other cables that arc down from the supporting ones represent the rest of the months. The lower the arc gets, the closer the year is to the warmer, easier, comfortable weather of the year – summer. But summer has its own difficulties, such as hurricanes and tornadoes.

But this year, as the year went to the lowest, shortest cables, I looked up at the sky and felt anything but easy. How would we get Ileandra back there?

And was this only an accident, or was it actually a reconnaissance mission? I didn't want to be naïve.

But I still hoped it was only an accident.

I liked her.

A Surprise Visit from the In-Laws

It was a Friday morning, late in June.

Our current plan was to hang out over the weekend and enjoy the garden, the kitchen, and some movies at home.

However, the garden had a bit of growing to do before it could offer much more than a few meager clippings of fresh herbs or a crop of strawberries. Raspberries – my favorite – wouldn't be available until late July, but then we would have red, golden, and black raspberries galore.

I talked about that over breakfast happily.

"What will you do until then, though?" Ileandra asked, trying to eat oatmeal.

We were all having that for breakfast. I had cooked up a pot of it, with shredded coconut, cinnamon, and cardamom, and drizzled some fresh local honey over it before pouring milk on the lot of it.

Ileandra let hers cool off even more than I did, and that was saying something. I couldn't abide anything that burned my tongue, and had warned her to wait. That was unnecessary, I quickly realized. She probably had less tolerance for hot food than humans did.

Kavi, however, was shoveling his oatmeal into his mouth at a brisk pace, all the while scrolling through updates from his phone. He was going to leave for work soon.

I looked back at Ileandra.

"I'll do what you've seen me doing: shop in the organic produce section of the grocery store, plus as some special ones on occasion, such as Whole Foods or The Fresh Market, but now that it's summer, I can go to farm stores. That's the best," I said, imagining the wonderful things I could find at Rosedale Farm.

"Rosedale Farm?" Ileandra asked, hoping I would talk about that.

I realized that she had read the name from my mind telepathically.

So did Kavi. He glanced up at her.

She suddenly realized what she had done. Again.

"Oh! I'm sorry."

She looked flustered.

Kavi looked annoyed.

I found myself thinking of every *Star Trek* novel I had ever read in which Spock had thought about the ethics of living with his telepathy…and laughed

"You really can't help it, can you?" I said. "Well, try, and don't worry. There are worse things you could have read from someone else's mind and blurted out loud. I'll show you which of my *Star Trek* novels talk about this. And I know you know what character's musings to look for," I added with a grin.

Now Kavi looked like he was about to crack up.

"Are you sure you're not Earth's first space diplomat, Arielle?" He grinned at me as he asked that.

"Sign me up," I said.

Then I thought about Rosedale Farm again.

My friend Sylvia worked there when she wasn't out on some gardening job. She hired herself out to various homeowners, usually elderly women with once-gorgeous yards who couldn't physically handle the demands of keeping them up on their own anymore.

Ileandra was doing it again – reading my thoughts.

I could tell because she looked a bit panicked by them.

"I'm going to call Rosedale Farms and ask the shop to gather a list of items for me, and then pick them up. Come with me and see it," I said to her. "It's not the same as other years…thanks to the pandemic, I can't just use the tongs and take a few cider donuts and look around the shop, gathering items at the register, but I can call ahead and pay, and go get the freshest, best, locally grown foods. At least it keeps them in business and local people fed with organic ingredients."

She looked hesitant. "I should wait in the car."

"You're a botanist who collects this stuff. You have a chance to see it as we humans use it. You have that cute hat and some face masks. Sylvia is not going to get too close of a look at you."

She looked at me again, took a deep breath, and said, "Okay. I'll come with you and see it." She smiled.

The alien had been trying all of the sauces and soups that I made, and was no longer losing weight, and had particularly enjoyed the chilled curried carrot soup that I had served yesterday. She looked about as healthy as she had when she had arrived, and perhaps more so.

My list was just about ready to call in when the phone rang.

It was my mother-in-law. She was interesting – a retired historic preservationist. My father-in-law was a retired endocrinologist. I liked him. They had emigrated from India with their parents as children, and lived near Philadelphia.

She was calling to say that my sister-in-law, her husband, and their kids, who lived near them, were about to drive up for an impromptu visit. Jasmine was 10, and Karan was 6.

I should have expected this.

After being on lock-down for the coronavirus, people all over the country, and all over the planet for that matter, wanted to see each other in person again.

"Great!" I said. "When will they get here?" And how would we explain Ileandra, I thought?!

"Early this evening, I think," Jodhaa replied.

It would take them roughly six hours of driving, but add rest stops and checking into the hotel in Avon, which was about 10 minutes away from us, tops, and that meant around dinnertime.

Aiesha made the most delectable Indian meals – wonderful, full-course meals – though she would have to eat my French-American cuisine for the evening. It was unrealistic to think that I would have time for anything else, and I had already made mushroom velouté soup. I had a ratatouille, too.

Aiesha called next. "Don't worry about us," she said. "We will maintain social distancing. We have been wearing the beautiful masks that you made for us."

"You're planning to just drive all the way up here and then possibly just drive right back?! I want to feed you and visit!"

"That's very sweet of you. I want to visit too...but let's take that risk. If it doesn't work, we can stay at the Marriott Homewood Suites for a night. If it pays off, we can visit for the weekend, and I love your food!"

She did. I believed her. No one asked for recipes if they didn't like your food, and she had done that, several times.

I had a quick discussion with Kavi, and then spoke again.

"Why don't we plan on the tests being positive. I'll go shopping for more food, and we can eat outside, and have open windows a lot – it's summer, after all. That way, assuming this works, we can have a nice visit."

There was a brief pause, and I heard her confer with Sunil, her husband. Then she spoke again. "That sounds great! I would rather not have to cook in that hotel suite, but I would have done it if you and Kavi had asked. After all, we're impulsively driving up, pretty much unannounced."

I laughed. "It's okay. You said you haven't gone out into any large crowds, and have been careful."

"We have been very careful. We're just burned out from being careful and isolated."

I'll bet they were, I thought, but they were smart to do it.

We had two guest rooms available, but they had only used them a couple of times, and that was before the pandemic.

Usually, they stayed at the hotel – but not with the intent to cook in it. They ate with us when they visited.

There wasn't much point in visiting without doing that!

But I was glad they chose the hotel.

I found that less stressful because it was less work for me.

It freed me up to both cook and bake for the family and to watch my mother-in-law work when she took over the kitchen, and enjoy her food.

Aiesha's culinary talents were on a par with her mother's and mine. Her work at the office was temporarily stopped, and she had been homeschooling the kids.

"How is that going?" I asked, curious about the logistics.

"It's going pretty well," Aiesha told me. "I can design at home, on my computer, with software just for the task, but sometimes I have to visit a site. I can bring the kids and have them sit in the car while I look at it, then go home and work on the design. They're good about coming along with me."

"That's good!" I said. "Are they interested in what you're doing?"

She laughed. "Jasmine is, but Karan isn't."

Well, he was only 6.

Sunil, Aiesha's husband, was very nice, but he didn't cook. He was also an aerospace engineer, which made him fun to talk with. He was also homeschooling their kids.

"We miss you," Aiesha said. "See you in a few hours!"

"We miss you too. See you for dinner," I told her. "I'll make you some more masks, so you have a change of them. Have a safe trip!"

I began plotting to buy enough ingredients to work with, taking out cookbooks and writing down what I needed on a list. Soon I knew exactly what to ask Sylvia to gather for my order at Rosedale Farms.

Kavi watched me, smiling.

This time, the parents-in-law were not coming.

They were the same age as my own parents, and they were sticking with the lock-down habits until a vaccine was found.

All this gave Kavi extra motivation to find one.

He was looking forward to this to visit; I could see that. But the reason behind it – why they were driving all the way up from the Philadelphia area – was so that Kavi could give them coronavirus tests.

The plan was for him to conduct the tests from their car in the driveway. They would wait while he ran the tests back at the lab, then either leave immediately if any of the tests were positive or come in and stay…and go nowhere else.

At least mine were only ten minutes away, and the only people they ever saw were Uncle Louis and us, so we could visit with them.

Family visits with my in-laws were fun, even though I felt a bit of tension with my mother-in-law. She never spoke to me about it, but I suspected that she was peeved at me for not having kids…as if that were up to her.

Kavi had told me firmly that he didn't want kids either, and that it was not up to his mother. "And I'm not that dutiful of a son," he would add with a devilish grin.

I loved that.

I completed my list, called the farm to read it off to Sylvia, and stuffed it into my handbag.

Kavi had watched all this while he drank his coffee. Now he gave me a hug and a kiss goodbye and went out to the garage. We heard the engine of his car start, and watched it pull out of the driveway and disappear down the street.

Ileandra was standing in the middle of the room, ready to go, but looking concerned.

I looked at her. It was obvious what was worrying her.

"Don't worry. You'll be fine. I've told them that you are a friend who lives alone and had a bad fall, so we took you in. They know you're here. Just limp around a bit."

Ileandra looked a bit startled.

"Yes," I added. "You will get plenty of sympathy and not too much scrutiny. Enjoy it!"

It was about a five-minute ride to get to Rosedale Farm. We got into my car, and drove off into the sunshine. We opened the windows partway, to circulate the air. That was supposed to help protect us from the virus, so we did it.

It made sense to do everything possible to not catch it, even though the virus was still being researched. It was maddening to know just enough about viruses to have some ideas as to how to protect ourselves, but not enough specific information about this particular virus. That meant that all of our precautions might still fail to pay off.

We passed the crop field. Corn was starting to grow on it.

The strawberry patch was now covered up with straw.

"There's your beam-up site," I said to her, unnecessarily. "They grow strawberries in June, and then corn after that."

She gave me a little smile, and I realized that she had known that anyway.

I realized that, when we were finally able to drop her off to be picked up – beamed up – the corn would be tasseled, and so high as that she would disappear into it.

Meanwhile, on the opposite side of the road, construction equipment occupied the small, concave, tamped-down-dirt area by the river. A narrow area of tall, leafy trees was all that was between it and the river. The construction crew was walking all around the place.

As I paused at the stop sign, I thought, little did they know that they were holding up an alien departure, and that I had her in the car with me.

I continued driving as soon as it was safe to cross.

In no time, we were there, smelling fresh produce as we approached the stands, and I was picking up what I would need to work with, all packed in brown paper bags.

Sylvia was there, and Ileandra met her without fuss.

The alien wore her bee mask.

So did Sylvia! I had given her one just like it.

They enjoyed that, and Sylvia didn't notice anything non-human above the mask. Of course, the hat helped.

I had told Sylvia that I was helping someone who had injured herself and had no relatives to take care of her. Kavi had checked our guest for the virus, of course, so Sylvia had accepted this explanation without any more questions.

And since I had brought cooked food for six weeks to Sylvia when she had surgery on her shoulder, she had believed me. It was entirely plausible that I was helping someone else this way. I felt a bit guilty lying to her, but what could I do?!

I would just have to wait until the visit was over, and then I could tell her the truth. If she even believed me...

Once we had the food, we came right back, and I started cooking.

I had some frozen shrimp, and everyone liked my shrimp and grits recipe. It was more of a Louisiana one than pure French, so it was a bit spicy. I toned down the spiciness for my mother, but I wouldn't do that this evening. That was why my husband's family enjoyed it.

What the Small Gray Visitor Said

Once I had that in order, I picked out some masks for Aiesha and Sunil – raspberry pink roses on black, and outer space fabric. While I was at it, I bagged up more masks for Jodhaa and Harendra; pastel blue with tiny blue rosebuds for her, and musical notes in gold on black for him. He liked sitar and orchestra music. For the kids, I would have to sew new ones, so that they would be small enough. I trimmed some fabric to their measurements, and began sewing rose garden and Star Wars ones.

I tried not to think about having to turn them away because of the pandemic as I sewed.

If we had to do that, I was going to give them the masks anyway – in ziplock bag that I would have to toss through the car window.

I delivered them to customers that way anyway.

But I tried to be optimistic.

I imagined the tests being negative and kept sewing.

We would find out in a few hours anyway.

Costume Damage

The coronavirus tests had been negative, and we were enjoying our visit.

Aiesha and I were cooking.

It was a good thing that my parents liked Indian food.

They had lived in London, England, while my father completed his M.Phil. in city and regional planning at the University of London, and while he did so, they had fallen in love with that cuisine by eating at many vegetarian Indian restaurants. It was inexpensive, which was what had gotten them to try it. Well, that and the Indian architects who were his roommates before their wedding.

It was the second evening of Aiesha, Sunil, Jasmine, and Karan's visit.

We had not hugged them, and they had not touched us. They had worn gloves and masks to use rest rooms on the way to Connecticut. Aiesha washed the gloves in hot water and soap every time they were worn. I did that, too – it was better than choking birds with our personal protective equipment!

They had gone straight to the hotel, wiped down every surface, and used the bathroom there before coming here.

We had seen them after that, for a dinner on the patio.

There was a slate-and-concrete patio off to the left of the back door, just outside of the breakfast nook. Luckily, we hadn't had any major storms that necessitated putting the outdoor furniture away. It consisted of an oval metal table with eight chairs. We need two more, though, and Kavi added them from the kitchen table.

We were having a party. It was Kavi's birthday.

Aiesha and I had collaborated on a beautiful meal together…while wearing our face masks.

It was difficult, and I kept lifting the mask away from my face from time to time to get a whiff of fresh, cooler air.

So did she.

I looked forward to a lovely evening of feasting on dal, basmati rice, curried treats that both of us had made, complete with mango lassi, and a mango kulfi with chai. Aiesha would make the chai. I had made the kulfi.

Ileandra wandered over to see what we were preparing.

She had her bees mask on, and she remembered to limp.

She had also been wearing a hat whenever the in-laws were here. It was odd inside, but she just said that she had smacked her head and didn't want the part where the EMTs had cut her hair to show, and Aiesha had bought the story.

Kavi was very impressed when the alien had come up with that. When we were getting ready for bed last night, after his sister and her family had left, he told me, "She must have been reading a lot of the fiction in your collection!"

She had, indeed.

At least she didn't overact. It was a decent performance.

I was wearing a beautiful, long-skirted dress with pockets, all cotton, which had a detailed, true-to-nature pattern of raspberries in all three colors: red, black, and golden. Each leaf was drawn in two hues of green on a sky-blue background, and honeybees worked over the fruit.

I loved it.

But Ileandra was wearing a tee shirt from the Mark Twain House and dark blue pants.

No way was she going to wear that tonight, I decided.

I insisted that she come upstairs with me.

"Let's see what I have that fits you," I said, opening my closet. Some of my dresses were shorter than others, and even if they looked a bit long on her, they would look okay.

She looked startled.

"Can't I just wear this?" she asked, "Or can't I wear one of those other outfits you found for me?"

Thus far, in her brief forays into local thrift shops, my mother had found some sweatpants and linen capri pants, and a couple of shirts that had daisies and butterflies, but they were far from suitable for a dinner party.

"No, definitely not," I said, pulling out a dress that depicted strawberries on pastel blue. "Try this on."

It no longer fit me, and it had long straps hanging from the waist, made of the same fabric as the rest of the dress. They were meant to be tied around the wearer's waist, ending in a bow. Thus, the smaller size, still large on the little alien, would not be a problem.

"Your clothes are so beautiful," she said, suddenly sounding almost wistful. "They show the plants that our people are trying to grow on our world by collecting them from yours and cultivating them in laboratories. But they look so different under our artificial lights. Here, they look at their best – as they are meant to look."

"Well, they are at home, in their natural habitat here," I replied, helping her into the dress. "There. Have a look at yourself in the mirror. You look beautiful!"

The alien turned and stared at herself.

With her face mask on, she looked almost human, except for the egg-shape of her head, and the large size of her eyes, but I had an idea for disguising that. I swept up the top front of her hair and attached a bronze bee clip to it, making a slight pouf that framed her face prettily.

She turned her head from side to side, considering it.

"Yes, that will conceal the differences in the shape of my head sufficiently. Thank you," she said, smiling up at me.

I smiled back. "You're welcome. Keep the dress; it's not too long on you."

It hung just above her ankles, and the tips of her shoes poked out. They blended in decently with the rest of the ensemble.

I handed her a light blue sweater that hung open in the front, with no buttons, and the effect was complete.

Hopefully, when my mother saw her, she would approve of this look.

She was far better than I at putting outfits together.

But I was not bad...

...and maybe I could learn to sew dresses at some point.

For now, though, it was still just face masks.

We went back downstairs, masks in place.

My parents and uncle arrived soon after, and my mother exclaimed over Ileandra's appearance, and stopped herself just in time from saying that she looked almost human.

Instead, she managed to say that Ileandra's hair looked almost grown in, worn in the style I had arranged it into.

Kavi, my father, my uncle, and I all gave her a look that said, "Nice save!"

We went outside and sat down at the patio table to eat.

The moment of truth came when it was actually time to eat. What would Ileandra do?

She was eating more and more solid food, but still nothing like the quantities that a human would consume.

And what about the mask issue?

She lifted it, inhaled the aroma of the beautiful array of delectable dishes of food, and said, "It's smells wonderful. I haven't been able to eat much for weeks. Do you mind if I take a small plate of it and sit on my own with it? Food still makes me feel a bit uncertain, but I'm eating more and more as time goes on."

Aiesha didn't find this odd at all.

It was a performance worthy of an Academy Award, I thought.

Ileandra 'heard' that and smiled a slight smile behind her mask.

I grinned, letting Aiesha and the others mistake it for solicitous hospitality, and dished out some of everything onto the alien's plate, handed it to her, and added her spoon.

She thanked me and took her plate and her seat cushion over to the edge of the flower bed, sat down facing slightly away from us, and settled into place.

I explained this away as just more social distancing.

Sunil looked unconvinced but, fortunately, said nothing.

Ileandra waited until we were eating to lift her mask and try the food.

Somehow, I could sense that she was really enjoying it.

Well...I knew how!

I had positioned everyone so that Aiesha, Sunil, Jasmine, and Karan had their backs to the flower bed as they sat at the table. But Karan kept twisting his head around to look at Ileandra.

"Karan, don't stare at her. That's not polite," his father said. But he snuck a few more looks at her.

I was a bit worried.

We enjoyed the meal, however, and Kavi thanked me and Aiesha for it more than once.

The dessert had been a work of art that Aiesha had let me create, even though she was the expert at Indian cuisine. It looked almost like something she could have made.

I wasn't bad with kulfi, though. Aiesha complimented me on it profusely. It was a mango, cardamom, saffron, and pistachio ice cream, sculpted into individual servings, each the shape of a pyramid. There were crumbled pistachios on top.

My mother was pleased to see how impressed Aiesha was.

My father was pleased to eat his kulfi.

Uncle Louis just ate it, and said, 'It was all right."

My mother almost kicked him – classic Uncle Louis!

Nevertheless, everyone from Philadelphia looked at him.

I almost laughed. Almost. But...I grinned and told them, "If it's not cheesecake, he says 'it was all right'. If it is cheesecake, Uncle Louis says 'it was really good'."

That did it. Everyone laughed, including Ileandra.

Kavi was very happy with his birthday dinner.

When he helped me clear the plates away, I whispered to him that there was more kulfi in the freezer, though not sculpted into any shape. His eyes lit up in anticipation.

Ileandra had eaten her entire serving over by the flower bed, and had definitely enjoyed every bit.

It was a very pleasant evening.

That is...it was pleasant until we finished cleaning up, with Jasmine's help, and realized that Karan had disappeared for a while.

The men were all sitting in the living room with the cat.

What the Small Gray Visitor Said

They hadn't been watching Karan.

I was annoyed.

Where had that kid gone?!

With everything cleaned up and put away, my mother, Aiesha, Jasmine, and I headed into the living room.

The men were full enough, except for the free-flowing chai that Aiesha had made yet more of.

We each had another cup, except for Ileandra, who was no doubt feeling rather full.

"Where is Karan?" his mother said, pouring some more into his cup. "He left his Star Wars mask on the counter."

We had opened all of the windows after it got dark, so that we could continue to visit.

"Maybe he's in the bathroom," Sunil suggested.

"No, he isn't," his sister said. "I'll bet he's sneaking around upstairs."

I looked at Kavi, horrified. What if he found Ileandra's bag?! She couldn't keep it high up.

That was exactly what he had done.

Ileandra had dashed upstairs, abandoning all pretense of a limp, to check on her things.

The bag had apparently not retained his Karan's interest, but he had found her small gray environmental suit, and attempted to try it on.

She met him on the landing halfway down the stairs.

I was right behind her, followed by Kavi.

Karan had torn it open in order to step into it.

A huge gash went down the front of it.

The head covering was awkwardly pushed over his head, and we could see his tee-shirt through the opening.

I wasn't surprised that his head fit into the head-piece of the suit, but he was still little, and it did.

I was horrified. The suit looked ruined.

And I was furious. This was why I hadn't had kids.

"Karan!" I roared. "You had no right to look through anyone else's things, much less touch them. You have ruined that suit! Ileandra needs it to work on rare plants!"

Kavi looked slightly less stressed when I added that last complaint. At least it made an excuse for the suit's existence.

Aiesha appeared right behind us, saw her son and the suit – and the head-piece with the obvious alien head to it – and completely overlooked that…we hoped.

Jasmine appeared right behind her mother, and looked like she approved of the scolding her brother was getting.

"Get out of that suit this instant!" she shouted at her son.

Sunil appeared in the hallway, along with my parents and uncle, who were fascinated to see the suit.

Fortunately, they made no comment, even though they knew what that suit was.

Sunil looked critically at it, and I was really worried now.

He was an aerospace engineer.

How much did he know about space suits?

But he focused on the damage to someone else's property instead. It looked extensive, and he was embarrassed.

Good – on both counts!

People who had kids should never relax and assume that they won't do anything long enough for them to actually do it!

Karan looked terrified.

I didn't care.

He stepped out of the suit.

Ileandra rushed up to the landing, grabbed the suit, and ran up the rest of the stairs and into her room.

Karan said, "I just wanted to try on her costume."

"Please tell Ileandra that we're very sorry," Aiesha said. "We'll go back to the hotel now." To her son, she said, "You will apologize to her tomorrow."

The party was over.

Ileandra sat in her room, stunned and horrified.

It wasn't the condition of the suit that upset her.

She could easily fix that with her tools.

It was the fact that the suit had been seen by several people.

Her human friend had been quick-thinking as she scolded the boy.

She was suddenly exhausted.

Just as she was thinking of taking off the dress and looking for her pajamas, Arielle knocked on her door.

"Come in," she thought, and started to say it out loud.

But the human woman had heard it anyway, and came in.

The moment after she turned the doorknob and entered, Arielle did a double-take. "You didn't say 'come in' out loud..."

Then she saw the suit again.

"Can you fix that?"

Ileandra tossed it aside, onto a chair by the window.

"Yes. It will be as if nothing had happened to it."

"Then you're upset that they all saw it. So am I."

"Yes." The alien paused, then added, "But you were very quick and clever with that lie you concocted."

"Was it really a lie? Or just a partial truth?"

Ileandra did a double-take.

"You're right. Protecting me from rare plants that could cause a negative reaction is part of its function."

"What happened that day that I found you – no poison ivy where you were?"

Ileandra finally smiled.

"No poison ivy. Well, some, but I know what that is and avoided contact with it."

"It looks like something that abductees claim that was worn when they were taken, though."

Ileandra looked at the human woman.

She had been wanting to ask this question for weeks, but afraid to do so.

She sighed. "We had to know whether or not we would have immune responses to microbes that humans carry. We didn't hurt any of you."

Arielle stared at her. "Scoop marks explained at last..."

I was stunned.

How could it be that easy to find out?!

Was it even true?

"Do you need any help getting out of that dress, or with the barrette I put in your hair?"

The little alien looked up at me, surprised that I had changed the subject while feeling so terrified.

She knew my reaction. She felt it through our link.

"That would be nice. Thank you."

She stood up, and I unclasped the barrette and unzipped the back of the dress. It was a little big on her, even though it just fit. I guessed she just wasn't used to it.

I needed a mundane distraction from the shock of the end of the evening.

"Well, good night," I said.

"Good night," Ileandra said. "Thank you for everything."

I nodded, and backed out of the room.

I went into my bedroom.

Kavi was in there, getting ready for bed.

I took off my dress, got my nightgown, put it on, and went into the bathroom.

Then I just stood there, staring into the mirror, not seeing anything.

Kavi came up behind me and hugged me.

"Thank you for a great party. You're very clever; I think even Sunil bought your explanation for that suit."

I met his eyes in the mirror. "He'll reconsider that later. There's no pretending that that suit doesn't look like a small gray alien from outer space."

Kavi hadn't let go of me yet.

He rested his chin on my right shoulder and leaned his head into mine.

I leaned back.

"We can't undo anything. Let's just hope it's okay."

I told him what I had just talked about with Ileandra.

"Wow." His eyes widened. I saw that in the mirror.

Yeah... "I know," I said.

"No, I mean, you figured it out so quickly," he said.

I dismissed that. "So she says."

But I could sense that it was correct.

What the Small Gray Visitor Said

Ileandra changed into her pajamas, and picked up her small gray environmental suit. Next, she opened her kit bag, and took out some tools.

It was nice of her human hosts to be so concerned over the condition of her suit – she did need it, just in case of some catastrophic ecological event or encounter with careless humans that spewed air pollution – but she could fix it in short order.

Her mind wandered as she worked.

The natural world on this planet was currently getting a break from human activity and the pollution it caused. Air was cleaner due to less motor vehicle use. But...journalists were not able to catch the wealthy corporations in the act of illegally burning and clearing more forests during this shut-down because of travel restrictions.

She hoped that this wouldn't mean she would miss gathering more species of plants before it was too late...that is, once she got back to her people, and back to work.

After a few molecular manipulations, it was as if nothing had ever happened to it. The suit was worthy of a spacewalk, if necessary, a deep-dive into the Mariana Trench of Earth's Pacific Ocean, or a walk through an area undergoing a volcanic eruption.

She rolled it up, put everything back into her bag, and put the suit and the bag back into the drawer where she had been keeping them.

A moment later, she took them out, dragged a chair over to the closet, slip its pocket door open, dragged the chair inside, climbed on top of it, and pushed the items onto a high shelf. Then she backed out of there, shut the door, and put the chair back across the room.

Such lengths would be necessary until the visit from the human children was over.

There were very few children where the alien was from.

They weren't needed very often, and when they were brought into existence, they were quiet, causing no such problems.

That wasn't to say that they weren't curious.

Everyone she had ever known, with the exception of many of the neurotypical humans she had been meeting lately, was curious.

But they were careful, too.

That carefulness was largely missing on Earth.

Of course, that was why her people kept coming here: to study the results of carelessness, immediate gratification, and a crippling lack of curiosity.

The small proportion of humans who were curious, careful, and who delayed action until they had made certain that the results of careful planning would be beneficial and not damaging wasn't enough.

That was what made this planet such a useful one to study. They needed to understand how their planet had gotten so depleted of fertile growing soil, flora, and fauna that could live healthy lives, and clean air and water that Ileandra's people now spent most of their time working to repair it.

It had been several millennia since the damage had been done, and still, they were working to repair it.

She wondered if it were possible to save her own planet.

And she was horrified to find that she had a close-up view of the same thing happening on another.

Well...she must not shrink from what was unpleasant.

That never solved anything.

She would just have to observe some more of it.

She would do that while she was among the humans.

She had done that before, and she would do it after.

She was determined to hang on until there was an after.

She would get home.

That bridge would be repaired eventually, she knew.

She hoped it would be done soon, though.

What else might happen?!

Who else might see something, and what might they say?!

Overheard

Ileandra was not a noisy person.

Being an alien who often worked in secret, at night, on another planet – and who was now stranded on it – meant that she had had lots of practice at moving soundlessly.

She was naturally stealthy.

Right now, that meant that she did not cause the slightest distraction as she moved down the staircase – not a sound that would catch anyone's attention.

Kavi was arguing with someone, and she didn't want to interrupt or disturb him.

Thus, their conversation continued as Ileandra moved, unnoticed, across the landing, down the second half of the staircase, to a spot on the last few steps. She sat down.

It was late the next morning, and Aiesha, Sunil, and their kids were back.

Ileandra had gone back upstairs when they arrived, rushing to get her forgotten face mask after Arielle had given her a chocolate almond smoothie for breakfast.

She had waited upstairs until the sounds of breakfast had stopped, wondering how to face them after rushing up to Karan the night before, giving him a shocked, angry look, snatching back her small gray suit, and running up the rest of the stairs without a word to any of them.

Kavi was sitting in the back den, drinking Indian chai (she could smell it), and arguing politely but in a tone of resentful beleaguerment. The alien realized that he was video chatting with his parents, who were back in Philadelphia.

Arielle was out in the garden, picking berries.

The strawberries were ripe, and spectacularly red.

The alien could see her friend, smiling as she plucked berry after berry, dropping each one (well, she paused to pop one into her mouth from time to time) into her green cardboard container.

The human woman couldn't hear her husband and in-laws.

That was just as well.

Ileandra could.

"Why can't you at least consider applying to a hospital in Philadelphia?!" his mother asked him. She sounded angry and sad, and frustrated.

"You could easily get a position there, and in a big city, the pay would be about a hundred thousand dollars higher," his father put in.

Ileandra could see Kavi from the bottom of the staircase. He was sitting on the far sofa, with his back to the windows.

She moved out of view, and sat back down on the staircase so that he wouldn't notice her. He seemed to be more interested in where his wife was just now, though; he kept glancing nervously out into the garden, watching to see if she were about to come back inside.

Ileandra didn't think she should show herself just now.

Better to wait until the subject changed...

...better to let him think that the repair to her small gray suit was taking a lot longer than it actually had...

...and she had finished it in just a few minutes last night.

She sat there, listening to Kavi speak out loud.

She couldn't help but hear him. It wasn't telepathy.

"Because I'm happy here, because I already make half a million dollars a year, and because I won't move Arielle away from everything and everyone that she knows," Kavi replied.

He looked annoyed, cornered, and like someone who was being patient in a situation that would end soon enough.

"Ah, there it is!" his mother said, a bit too loudly.

Arielle, out in the garden, glanced up, looking confused.

Ileandra, worried, eavesdropped on her friend's thoughts and mood. But it was okay; the human woman could barely understand the conversation from outside. It was only the tone of the conversation that Arielle could hear from outside.

A small plane was moving around overhead, birds were chirping, and children in the yard to Arielle's left were bouncing loudly up and down on a trampoline.

So that was where they were – they had found friends to play with. She briefly trained her telepathy on them, and found that the neighbors – the parents – were keeping the kids apart, maintaining a proper social distance. They were requiring masks to be worn and turns to be taken, always with the visitors six feet apart from themselves and their children.

Ileandra turned her attention back to Kavi.

Kavi's mother was talking again. "You cater to your wife's autism too much! This is why you aren't more famous in your profession! This is why we have no grandchildren from you!"

Kavi's father made a slight sound of objection, directed at his wife. "Don't harangue him about that! I like Arielle."

Ileandra realized that he didn't want to…alienate…his son. What a word, "alienate"! It could mean to offend, to put someone at an emotional distance. And their son already lived at a physical distance.

She thought about that.

Alienating Kavi did seem like a foolish move.

Why not have what they could of their son?

Why push for more when he would not yield it?

Humans would do that, she realized. If they wanted something, that was it – they would pursue it ceaselessly, no matter the cost, no matter the detriment to what they already had, be it a relationship, an ecosystem, or whatever else.

This was what her people had given up.

What, she wondered, had they lost that was good?

There was always something.

Kavi was having none of it.

"I don't have to justify myself to you. I'm not a child. I'm happy, Arielle is happy, and we know what we want. I love living here, and I don't want to move back to a city. The air is cleaner here, and it's not all about me. Arielle is settled here, comfortably, near her parents, not too far from her aunt to visit from time to time, and she can write. Her books and her business are doing well."

"Why can't she write somewhere else?!" his mother continued. "Why can't she do that while raising children?! Or working in a law firm with that degree of hers?!" His mother paused to think. "Of course, now she is too old to give you a child. Why do you stay with her?"

Kavi looked furious now, but was containing himself. He didn't want to alienate his parents completely, even if he wasn't going to live as they wanted him to.

"You know perfectly well why I do that. I love her. She is a fascinating person, an excellent cook and baker who likes to experiment and give me food adventures, and we don't want kids. We want to travel, pursue our careers, and not add to the human population. Arielle can give you the statistics more readily than I can, but you know that our species is in overshoot – well past the Earth's carrying capacity for us!"

Ileandra could almost feel a sense of disinterested exasperation from his mother, even though she was far away.

From his father, however, she sensed something else: an appreciation of the logic of this statement.

Apparently, this was not a new subject.

Kavi's mother would not give up, however.

"I don't care about all that. I wanted more grandchildren. You are educated people, and educated people are the ones who should be adding to and continuing our species. Never mind what the others do!"

Kavi laughed.

"Amah, you are educated, too. You know that if we all do that, there will still be far too many of us humans. And why don't you just enjoy what you have, instead of berating me for not giving you what I don't want? It would not be you who would have to actually live with the choices that you would make for me. It would be me, and Arielle."

Kavi's father spoke up. "Jodhaa, you do this on every call. Our son is right. Now promise you won't bring this up to our daughter-in-law. No good can come from it."

Ileandra could sense that sanity was at last reaching this obstinate woman. She said to her husband, "All right, Harendra. You know I'm just disappointed. Who will inherit their things? Who will carry on their stories?"

"Our extended families can do that," Kavi replied. "Or Arielle's books can help with that. Lots of authors end up sought after by historic preservationists like yourself. They can leave their documents, artifacts, memorabilia, and whatever else to a museum…or have one started later."

Ileandra heard a deep sigh.

It was definitely from his mother – his 'Amah" – that was what Indian people called their mothers.

She was glad to have been taken in by humans who weren't from just one culture. This was interesting.

And she was able to learn about the push to reproduce, no matter the cost to the ecosystem.

She needed to study outside of her chosen field more.

Botany could only teach one so much…

"Tell Arielle we said 'thank you' for the beautiful face masks she made for us," Kavi's mother said.

"Yes, please tell her," his father said. "The feathers pattern is beautiful, and very comfortable. I get lots of compliments."

"I will. She's sending you more. Bye, Amah. Bye, Baba."

A moment later, Ileandra realized that she had been sitting on the bottom stair for several minutes, lost in thought.

Arielle had finished picking strawberries. She had not heard what her in-laws had been saying, thanks to her husband watching for her and monitoring his own conversation.

Kavi had strictly enforced an unspoken rule with his parents, hearing them out without allowing them to upset his wife. And now the video call was finished.

Ileandra stood up and walked toward the kitchen just as Arielle came inside with her berries.

"I'm going to make a fresh strawberry tart for tonight's dessert," Arielle announced. She sounded happy.

She looked at Ileandra first, wondering about the suit. "Is your Small Gray suit going to be okay?" she asked.

Ileandra noticed the capital letters in Arielle's thoughts and smiled. "Yes, I fixed it. It's as good as new."

Arielle breathed a big sigh of relief. "Oh, good!" she said.

Aiesha came inside just in time to hear this exchange. The alien realized that she had not heard the tone of the words "Small Gray".

Jasmine was right behind her mother. The 10-year-old girl had caught what the topic of their remarks was, and said, "Karan had some nerve trying on your suit! That was so rude!"

Her parents glanced at her as she flounced into the living room to look at her aunt's books, but said nothing to her.

After a few minutes, Jasmine went back outside.

Instead, Aiesha said, "I'm so sorry, Ileandra. We will punish him when we get home tomorrow, and he will apologize to you himself when he comes in."

Sunil added, "He certainly will. I had a lot to say to him about the ethics of touching other people's property without their permission, plus damaging their work materials. I'm very glad that you were able to fix it. It looked damaged beyond repair. We felt terrible about it."

Etiquette was a fascinating concept to observe.

It preserved her secret nicely, and the suit, too.

Ileandra nodded, smiled politely, and said, "Thank you."

The human woman opened the cupboard and took out a package of sliced almonds, almond extract, a bottle of rosewater, and some seedless strawberry jam.

Kavi got up from the sofa, came over to her, put his arms around her from behind, and kissed her on the cheek. "That sounds great. My sister and her family haven't had that before. Have you?" he asked them.

Sunil got up and carried his empty tea mug over to the kitchen sink and said, smiling, "No, we haven't. It sounds delicious, and I'm sure it will be. Nice tee shirt, Arielle!"

It said, 'Don't annoy the author. She may put you in a book and kill you.' Arielle grinned. "Thank you!" she said.

Aiesha joined her sister-in-law at the counter, nodded and smiled at Ileandra, and agreed that she would like to have a slice of the tart. She had come back toward the house just in time to hear her mother badgering her brother, and looked through the window at him sympathetically as she came around to the back door. The alien had seen her from the stairs.

Ileandra wondered whether her own disapproval of Jodhaa's words showed on her face, then decided that she didn't care. Scientists couldn't always keep their views out of everything. After all, we were people too, she reasoned.

Aiesha could read all that without telepathy, she realized with a start. Neurotypicals functioned by intuition, she had read, and now she was watching that in action.

Fascinating.

She looked away, at the beautiful, ripe, juicy, red, perfect strawberries, and smiled to herself.

Hopefully, it looked as though she were just admiring them, not thinking about other things.

Not Arielle, though.

She was putting the ingredients for a sweet, buttery tart crust into the food processor, tossing in a little cinnamon and cardamom that weren't listed in the recipe, and she was happy.

Her sister-in-law was reading the recipe.

"You added cardamom?" she smiled a happy smile.

Arielle looked up. "Yes. I love that spice."

Aiesha shook her head, but it was an apropos gesture. She approved. It was obvious that the two sisters-in-law liked each other. That was something for her human friend at least, Ileandra thought to herself.

"Are you going to watch me bake?" Arielle asked. "One at-home chef watching another?" she added with a grin.

"Yes, I am." Aiesha grinned back.

Kavi was standing across from where his wife was working, leaning against the counter with his tea mug.

Kavi started making another batch of chai tea in a large pot on the stove. It didn't take him very long to mix water, milk, whole pods of cardamom, a few slices of ginger, some raw, granulated sugar, and to steep bags of Darjeeling tea in it. It smelled wonderful.

Tea was a stimulant, but Ileandra didn't care.

What was wrong with having a cup of it on occasion?

They weren't going out anywhere, and she would have other things with it. She wouldn't cause Arielle any trouble if she enjoyed some…just a small cup, not a big one.

If she experienced withdrawal symptoms when she went back to her people, she would get through them. It wasn't as though she were having caffeine every day among the humans.

Kavi seemed to sense that she wanted some, and shared the finished chai tea among five mugs.

It was delicious and warm without being too hot.

The alien was surprised that he didn't object to her having anything with caffeine, but he informed her, "This doesn't have that much caffeine, and it's early in the day."

He had only given her half a cup of chai.

That explained it. But it was just enough.

Arielle was busy shaping the buttery crust dough into a tart pan and putting tin foil over it. She poured clay pie-weights into this, put the tart shell onto a baking sheet with sides, and put it into the oven.

Next, she paused for a sip of chai, and then took over the stove to make a toasted almond custard.

"Most bakers don't work from scratch like Arielle does," Kavi told Ileandra, watching her watch his wife. "My mother works that way, too."

Aiesha smiled. "Yes, she does. I go back and forth between memory and recipes."

Kavi hung around watching as his wife took the tart pan out of the oven, removed the pie-weights and foil, poked the crust again with the fork a few times, and put it back in for a few more minutes.

Arielle was definitely better off here, in her own sphere, and happy near her own mother most of the time, with her own friends and chance to develop her career as she wanted it, not as others wanted it.

Kavi was a good husband. He had his own career, he was successful, and he thought of his wife's career at the same time.

Humans could live well, Ileandra thought. They didn't all make wrong choices.

The tart's almond filling was fully cooked. It smelled as good as the chai tea, but different: nutty, with milk and egg yolks in it, and, of course, refined white sugar.

"Would you like to taste it?" Arielle asked. "I could give you some on a spoon to lick," she offered.

Why not? "Okay," Ileandra said. "thank you."

It tasted good!

She couldn't dare enjoy much of it, she thought, realizing that she shouldn't get too used to human food. It was a luxury that she would miss once she got home.

The oven timer dinged.

Out came the tart shell. Perfect!

Aiesha said as much, leaning over to inhale the aroma.

Arielle hulled the strawberries, except for a few.

"These can decorate the top," she explained.

Kavi laughed appreciatively. "My wife likes to photograph her dessert art. She uses it in her blog," he explained to his sister and brother-in-law.

Arielle took out a small saucepan, and a whisk, and filled it with strawberry jam and rosewater. She turned on the burner, blended and melted the contents, and assembled it all on a beautiful plate of stained glass that depicted pink roses.

Sure enough, she got out her camera next.

"My father, the expert amateur photographer, has fully equipped me with a great camera, so I might as well use it," she said with a grin, shooting several images.

She checked them on her computer, saved them, and put the apparatus away.

The back door banged open and shut.

Jasmine was back from the neighbors' trampoline.

She went over to look at the fresh strawberry tart.

"Oh wow, Aunt Arielle! This looks and smells terrific!"

She and her aunt smiled at each other.

"Thanks!" Arielle said. "Did you want to look at a book? I saw you looking before, but not touching anything."

Jasmine looked rather pleased with herself. "Unlike some people," she said, glancing in the direction of the trampoline sounds. She was indicating her brother. "Yes...you have some interesting fairy tale books."

There were French fairy tales, Russian ones, Danish ones, German ones, Celtic ones, a Persian one...Ileandra wanted to read a few of those herself later.

"Go ahead and read some. I trust you to be careful."

Jasmine grinned, said "Thank you," and went back to the bookshelf. She took out a beautiful, illustrated book called *The White Cat*, another called *Scheherazade's Cat*, and a collection of tales entitled *Don't Bet on the Prince*. Once laden with reading material, the girl flopped onto a sofa and opened a book.

Aunt and niece got along well, Ileandra thought.

Aiesha admired the tart at some length also.

She looked at her daughter and said, "I wish I could get you to learn to make desserts this nice!"

Jasmine glanced up and said, "I will eventually."

Karan raced in, banging the door shut.

He had stayed a couple of extra minutes with his new friend next door, and his father had let him.

But now Aiesha and Sunil looked at each other.

Then they looked at their son.

"Karan, I think you have something to say to Ms. Ileandra," his mother told him.

The little boy looked up at her. She was less than a foot taller than he was, but it was enough.

The boy felt awkward and ashamed.

"I'm really sorry, Ms. Ileandra. I won't touch your things again," he said.

Everyone looked at her to see whether or not the apology had been accepted.

It had.

"Thank you, Karan," Ileandra replied. "I appreciate that."

"But you were able to fix your suit?" Jasmine asked. It was a rhetorical question, aimed at her brother. "Don't trust him!"

"I have," she said, "and he won't find it again."

Everyone laughed.

"Good!" Sunil said with a grin, looking at his son.

I Don't Eat Reese's Pieces

It was evening.

Dinner had been a joint effort between myself and Aiesha. We had had an Indian-French fusion meal with garlic cilantro naan, biryani rice, curried chick peas, coconut shrimp curry, and bindi masala, also known as curried okra, followed by my strawberry tart.

It didn't go together, but no one had cared.

It had been eaten once again out on the patio, with Ileandra over by the flower beds. She had eaten the sauce from everything, plus a dollop of tart filling topped with strawberry sauce. She had even eaten some strawberries.

After dinner, we had decided to watch a movie with our masks on and the windows open, even though it was a bit less comfortable without the air conditioning. I loved the fresh air, though. I kept lifting my mask every now and then for a gulp of it. Masks were a bit hot to wear for long periods of time.

We were sitting in the front of the big television in the living room, enjoying a movie.

Karan had been allowed to choose it.

At least that meant no issues with anything not rated PG.

He had chosen...

...*E.T. The Extra-Terrestrial.*

Kavi, Ileandra, and I had all nearly lost it when he did.

Kavi had clicked the "Guide" function on the TV remote control, shown us all the grid of channels and movies playing for the evening, and scrolled through while asking Karan what he would like to see, all while surreptitiously watching his sister's reactions to the choices. One wrong look from her, and he would skip an item.

The rest of us had just watched this proceeding in silence...until Karan had made his choice.

And why wouldn't he want this one? Elliott, the main human character in the story, was a very relatable one, and the orchestra score by John Williams was well-loved by all.

What the Small Gray Visitor Said

It seemed strange to be watching it after only a few weeks, with an alien in the room, and with four humans who, at least officially, didn't know that one of us was an extra-terrestrial visitor.

Sunil glanced at each of us.

I suspected that he had understood what that small gray suit actually was, but had had no chance to do anything more about it, and he wasn't saying anything.

Kavi managed to click the selection without calling undue attention to himself, but he couldn't resist making eye contact with me – wide-eyed with amazement at our situation – and then with Ileandra. I did the same simultaneously.

We all seemed to suppress gales of laughter at once.

I'm sure she felt ours brimming to the surface, and squelched just as fast as they had risen.

I don't think the other three in-laws caught on.

I hoped not!

For some inexplicable reason, as the movie started, and Elliott lured E.T. into his home with Reese's Pieces candy, Karan turned to look up at me.

"Aunt Arielle, would you ever help a stranded alien like that? I mean, would you get one to come inside like that?"

I gaped at him for a moment, then smiled, and said, "Well...I don't eat Reese's Pieces, but I would help, if I met one who needed it."

Jasmine listened to this exchange, looked pleased, and turned back to the movie.

No one else so much as glanced up.

They just kept watching the movie.

I went into the kitchen for a moment to laugh myself silly...silently. I couldn't help it.

Kavi joined me a moment later to do the same thing.

We held onto each other and collapsed onto the kitchen floor, sliding down into sitting positions next to each other, leaning again the cupboards.

We laughed until we couldn't breathe, then took deep gulps of air, and laughed some more – without our voices, of course.

If we had laughed with our voices, I'm sure the others would have noticed.

When we finally calmed down enough to look around, Ileandra was sitting against the cabinets across from us.

She, too, was laughing – and being careful not to be heard doing it.

We got up and went back to watch the movie with the rest of the family.

The next morning, Aiesha and her family were to drive back to Philadelphia.

They came over for breakfast first, though.

It was a full breakfast, which was very American, though I made a few French treats. In France, people just had café au lait and a croissant, but what the hell – I was part Irish, and we were all hungry in the morning.

I made crepes with all sorts of sweet fillings: fresh strawberries, raspberry jam, and chestnut paste. I also made omelets with scallions, heirloom tomatoes, hunks of brie cheese, and mushrooms. Karan's didn't have mushrooms.

Instead of chai, Kavi made a huge pot of hazelnut coffee, and lots of fresh-squeezed orange juice. We put out the half-and-half cream for the coffee, and granulated sugar-in-the-raw in the sugar bowl.

Thus sated, we all sat out on the patio with our coffee for a while. Ileandra wandered around the garden, and noticed with a wistful note in her voice that the honeysuckle bush wasn't in bloom.

"It was when you arrived," I said, "and it will bloom again before the end of the summer."

She listened to me, nodded, and continued to pace around the back yard. The herb garden was flourishing now.

Sunil watched her.

The alien was wearing her floral bee face mask with the black head-ties, but no hat. With a start, I realized that the oval shape of her head must be obvious.

Sunil glanced from her to me.

Aiesha had gotten up to use the bathroom, and Kavi was in the kitchen, cleaning a few things up. He didn't have to go to his lab today.

Sunil was still looking at me, I realized.

"What are you thinking about?" I asked him.

"Aliens."

I froze.

"You have a small collection of books on aliens in your living room," he said, and I breathed a little easier. "When did you get those?"

I laughed. "In my twenties. I have read them all, cover-to-cover, and I save all of my books, grouped by topic. It's probably been twenty-five years since I actually opened one. Why do you ask?"

I thought I knew perfectly well why, but I wanted to make him say it.

"I just wondered. I mean, I know that you did your law thesis on outer space issues, but aliens...that's not a scientifically proven topic, so that's different."

"I read all that stuff before law school, for fun. When I find a topic that fascinates me, I study it intensely, and remember what I read. But I moved on from aliens because it couldn't be proven, and I had no interest in delving too deeply into an area that seems to be populated by conspiracy theorists and crackpots who aren't taken seriously. That's not the kind of life I wanted, however much logic I saw in some of what I read."

"Some?"

"Well, there was an astronomer who thought she had figured out, after talking to an abductee, where in the universe those particular aliens were from – namely, the Owl Nebula – but I just didn't see any point in expending any more energy on it after reading everything. I mean, what was going to happen? I'm not interested in chasing lights to see if they are actually U.F.O.s and possibly getting abducted. Carl Sagan didn't believe that we are alone, but he didn't do that, either."

"So, you believe that we are not alone?"

I looked at him. Was he mocking me, or did he just know?

"I have believed that we are not alone since at least the year that the *E.T.* movie came out. I was twelve then. No…probably earlier. I was eight years old when *Star Wars* came out, and my mother took me to see it. She just knew somehow that I would like it. I wondered how she knew… Anyway, even though our space program could only take humans as far as the moon at that point – it still can't! – the whole idea just made sense to me."

Sunil nodded.

I looked at him now.

"How about you? You're an aerospace engineer: what do you really think? I can guess that you must love it all, working with the tools for going to outer space and back, but what do you think about aliens?"

"We are not alone," he said.

I had another thought.

"You know I study human overpopulation and ecosystems collapse."

"Yes. What about it? How does that relate to aliens?"

"Sometimes, people in the online chat group that I administrate bring up the idea of humans developing space travel capability, finding another Earth-like planet, and exploiting it for its space and resources. They suggest this rather than scaling back our species' consumption of our own planet and making do with what we have here. I always point out that we could very well get to another Earth-like planet only to find that it is already inhabited by another sentient species like us – one that is using the space and resources."

Sunil smiled.

"No wonder outer space law appeals to you, and that you wrote your thesis on it."

I laughed. "That thesis dealt with our own orbital ecosystem, which is riddled with human-caused junk. We've made quite a mess, plus laws to regulate that mess, but what we really need is for someone like you to develop a vacuum cleaner for outer space."

Sunil grinned. "We're working it."

He paused.

I knew he was about to say something else.

"So...what would you do if you found a stranded extra-terrestrial?"

Damn. He knew.

I looked at him.

He waited.

"I would help that alien to get home, even if it meant some waiting was required, and write nothing about it until the deed was done. That way, the alien would be safely home, preferably with no provable evidence left behind that the Men in Black – if they really do exist – could bother me with. After that, I could write the story as fiction and sell it. I'm really not interested in being treated as some ridiculous crackpot. It's not worth it. It's far better to be an author of science fiction."

Sunil looked at me.

"Fair enough. I looked forward to reading your book."

We walked out to the driveway to wave good-bye to Aiesha, Sunil, Jasmine, and Karan, and it felt odd not to give them any hugs or kisses...but we didn't.

I was actually relieved to see them go just so that I could turn the air conditioning back on, and felt a little guilty about that. Oh well...

...I could cancel that feeling out by the fact that I had given them another pair of face masks and a note for Kavi's parents.

When I had started this face mask business, it was just to mask the family, and I had done that – once each. But each face ought to have a change of mask, so that while a washed one was drying there would be another, so...I sent two more.

They were beautiful, and I had shown them on a video chat with a smile just before Aiesha and her family left.

"Very nice," my mother-in-law had tersely said.

"That's beautiful! And medical-grade," my father-in-law, a retired doctor, had said with a sweet smile.

I was very glad that Kavi was happy living in Connecticut.

Night Frights

Kavi and I were in our room.

We had just come upstairs after watching *The Late Show with Stephen Colbert.*

The in-laws had left in mid-morning, and the three of us had been alone for the rest of the day.

The visit had been fun, and we had enjoyed creating and eating several great meals and trading stories.

But...we were glad they had gone home.

None of us wanted to let them know that, of course, but the fact was that we had an alien houseguest, and the stress of pretending that she was just a human visitor recovering from a fall at home alone, unusual of an excuse for her open-ended stay with us as that was, made for constant tension.

We had managed not to slip up, but were not confident that it could be kept up indefinitely.

Hence (at least on my own part) the relief that they were gone.

We went into our room, and Kavi tossed the larger, decorative pillows that finished the look of the bed in daytime mode into a corner.

Bagheera leaped onto the bed, walked into the center, and flopped there to watch us get ready for bed.

I came out of the bathroom in my pink cotton nightgown, smiled at Kavi, and stretched a hand out to pet the cat.

Then I froze.

There was a Small Gray in the hallway.

We hadn't closed our bedroom door, so there was nowhere to hide.

Kavi glanced at me, looked out into the hall to see what I was staring at, and froze too, his mouth open in shock.

I looked around in the hall at the rest of the area, half-expecting to see at least three more Grays there.

Had they beamed directly into our house?!

Had they levitated themselves in?!

A moment later, I remembered that Ileandra had gone upstairs – using the stairs to walk up here – before we had.

"Ileandra?" I said. "Please tell me that that's you."

My voice sounded strange – like it had lost volume.

For someone who had paid attention in acting classes in junior high and high school and who normally had a booming, confident voice that came up from my lower body and projected strongly outward, it sounded alarmingly, abnormally faint.

I realized that I was terrified, and forcing myself to calm down and speak rather than give in to the fear.

Kavi moved closer to me, keeping his eyes on the Gray.

A moment later, the Gray seemed to distort itself, and then the head tipped backwards as the front of the suit opened very neatly across the neck and down the chest.

Ileandra's head poked out, and she pushed the head covering with its huge, black, almond-shaped eyes away and stepped carefully out of the environmental suit.

I breathed a deep breath of air, and felt sincerely calm.

Kavi did the same – audibly.

Then we both felt quite foolish.

Ileandra looked like an odd mixture of apologetic and on the verge of uncontrollable laughter.

Then I glanced at my cat, who had not been alarmed at all, and sat down on the edge of the bed, laughing so hard that I couldn't stop.

Kavi started to laugh a bit, too.

Ileandra gave up trying to look apologetic and gave in to the urge to laugh, though she didn't laugh as hard as I did.

"I should have checked the cat's reaction to you!" I said, my eyes tearing up. "He didn't react, but what did we humans do?! We thought of every alien abduction movie and freaked out...even though we know you're already here."

"Sorry...I had to test my suit one more time."

"Did your repair work?" Kavi asked.

"Yes, the suit is fine."

"Awesome. Good night!" he said, and shut the door.

Fireworks

It was mid-July – Bastille Day in France.

It was another excuse for people to gather, inadvisable though that was.

It a couple of weeks after Aiesha and her family had gone home. Despite the risk, we had all succeeded at obeying the social distancing guidelines and avoided getting sick. If we weren't sick by now, Kavi said, that visit had been okay.

That was good news, though it was still frustrating not to fully understand how the virus worked – how it traveled, how it was caught, and so on.

It was hot out, and we were sitting inside, with the air conditioning on, watching movies. It was getting dark out.

Europe was closed to Americans, as many had abandoned social distancing for the holiday and given in the urge to engage in large gatherings on beaches and at public pools. The coronavirus pandemic had surged again, to over 3 million in the United States.

Feeling frustrated, I had commented about it to Ileandra. "You're going out of this world, and we can't even travel around our own planet. We wanted to go to Belgium next. Their food is even better than France's, and I want to try it."

She had nodded sympathetically, but said nothing.

What was there to say, anyway?!

I felt sorry for travel agents, who couldn't earn a living.

And I felt sorry for the tourism industry to some extent.

Well…I wasn't sorry that cruise ships were not able to run out to the open sea, past the 100-mile mark and into unregulated, international waters where they could spew raw sewage and dump plastic trash…nor go into Venice's lagoons.

It was the workers who had no visitors to historic sites and museums to show around, and the restaurants with fewer customers, whom I felt sorry for.

Travel to other countries had been shut down for months due to the coronavirus pandemic anyway, and now it was going to last even longer. Not testing for the virus would not make fewer cases of it exist, but that was the Orange Moron's asinine hope. Kavi ranted about it, disgusted, whenever the news carried that nonsense.

Planes still ran, but with fewer passengers. Planes had always been disease vectors, with air that was uncirculated and surfaces that were barely cleaned. It was no loss, giving up on trips with Kavi until a vaccine was found.

We had given up eating out, even though reopenings were starting, provided that people sat outdoors, on sidewalks and in sectioned-off bit of streets.

We had watched the July 4th celebrations of the past on public television this year – no new ones were aired.

Black Lives Matter protests continued.

So did the dismantling of symbols of white privilege.

I wasn't going to miss the statues and flags of the Confederacy, but there were some monsters who would.

Thank you for that, Herr Pumpkingropenfuhrer.

One of those monsters, when a Black Lives Matter march blocked the roads in Seattle, Washington on July 4th, drove at high speed at the edge of a crowd, and slammed into two black women, flinging them high into the air. Their shoes had gone flying in various directions, and they had fallen back down to the pavement with terrible injuries.

We all – myself, Kavi, Ileandra, my parents, and Uncle Louis – had seen it on the national news during our 4th of July dinner. We ate in the living room, where we could watch TV.

I was glad that we were in between dinner and dessert just then, because I don't see how I could have kept eating while watching those women's bodies get destroyed – if they even lived. They were in the hospital, in serious condition. Later, we found out that one of them had died.

"I hope that driver's life is legally ruined, and that he is never allowed to be happy again," I said.

I had read about the sort of people who would do such a thing. Our worthless POTUS talked just like them. They had been called "trash" for a long time, but it wasn't their lack of chances for a better life and a more advantageous position in

226

society that made them trash. It was the hateful things that they did that made them trash. It made me just not care about them.

After a while, the news had moved on to conclude with a reiteration of the fact that Americans could not go to Europe, and then added that they were going on road trips to national parks in recreational vehicles instead.

Ten days later, nothing much had changed.

But we did see news reports about masses of infected people in southern states such as Texas and Florida that had opened up too soon, anxious to "restart" the economy, only to have to close up again due to renewed outbreaks.

"You can't benefit from an economy unless you're alive and healthy," I kept saying to people online who fretted about lost livelihoods. Lost lives seemed to outweigh it all.

There were far fewer planes in the sky, especially at night. That didn't mean that there were none, however. Would the skies be clear enough for Ileandra to get picked up?

"Ileandra," I asked, "Isn't there another spot that we might take you to, one that your people could research, so that you could go home? I mean, we love having you here, but it is still risky, and I never know if we are feeding you properly. I don't want you to get sick from malnutrition."

Kavi was sitting in the living room, drinking his chai. He seemed lost in thought for a moment. Then he said, "Should we take a drive to see where else you could be picked up?"

Ileandra was staring at us both in amazement.

"No, thank you, but that will not help. And I am not becoming malnourished with you. You offer me a wider variety of nutrients than what I normally have access to, and it is more enjoyable. At last, I have learned what everything tastes like in its original form. Thank you for that."

We both looked at her. Every so often, she revealed a bit more about her life among her people. This detail was a tantalizing insight into alien cuisine...if it could be called that at all, I thought to myself.

She 'heard' that. "It's nothing like this," she told me. "It's concentrated."

I gaped at her. "You mean your food is like pills?!"

"Food cubes!" Kavi said. "Just like the science fiction of our childhoods…"

Now it was her turn to gape at us.

"We guessed it, didn't we?" I said, grinning.

Her shoulders sank. "Yes, you did. Then she smiled.

"So, what about the idea of a ride? Would they meet you in a different spot?" Kavi wanted to know.

BOOM.

Bagheera leaped off of the sofa, ran to the window, and landed in his cat bed. He stood upright in it, staring up at the sky. He was staring away from the mountain, toward the nearby golf course.

BOOM.

He wasn't scared; he just wanted to watch.

BOOM. BOOM. BOOM. BOOM.

We joined the cat to watch the fireworks.

"No. I will have to meet them in the same spot where I got lost. This is why I can't have you drive me somewhere else right now to meet my ship," Ileandra told us, watching the pretty colors. "Humans are staring up at the sky at night too much right now for that."

We looked at her.

Damn. She was right.

BOOM. BOOM.

"I have signaled to ask them," Ileandra said, realizing that we deserved a complete answer. "They agree that it is risky for me to be here, but we also agree that now is one of the riskiest times of the year to do anything. We don't usually visit this area during fireworks season. It's too heavily settled with humans."

"No open sky, no empty areas," I said, nodding.

BOOM. BOOM. BOOM.

Red, white, and blue bursts of fire cascaded out of nowhere, in pretty formations, falling from the sky.

We shut of the lights and watched in the darkness.

The cat settled down into his bed, crouching upright, watching it with us.

Space Junk

The side door screen slammed as my mother walked in.

"Arielle, quick – turn on the TV!" she said.

It was a quarter part nine in the morning, and Kavi had just left for work a half-hour earlier.

The three of us had had a nice, quiet breakfast.

I tended to catch up on news via the internet, reading it off of *The New York Times* and *The Hartford Courant*'s websites, and by checking my e-mail and Facebook and Twitter for personal stuff – all on my desktop computer.

Kavi listened to NPR on the way to work in his car.

Something really momentous must be going on for my mother to drive over and demand that I turn on the television.

I did. "What channel should I go to?"

"Local news. I've been trying to call you, but you never have your phone on!"

It was a standard complaint about me. I would turn it on, check my messages, reply to them, and then turn it off so that I could work without distractions. It usually worked.

But not today.

Ileandra was sitting on the sofa, looking at my books, because I had been editing a book on food insecurity by an econometrics professor. I needed to concentrate on that...

...and that was obviously not going to happen today.

Channel 3 WFSB News was galvanized with a story about an explosion in a huge condominium complex in downtown Hartford, Connecticut.

It had happened about an hour before rush hour could get underway.

Most of the residents had still been home, and now they were dead. Emergency crews had rushed to the scene, but the place was a charred wreckage, and a strange smell was emanating from the site.

It was obvious that no one was still alive in there.

"Wow," I said. "What could have caused that?"

"Listen!" my mother said, staring at the screen. "They've been explaining it over and over again."

The newscaster stood outside, in the graveyard of the historic church on Main Street that contained the graves of the founders of the city of Hartford. It was away from the cordoned-off area, so the emergency crews weren't ordering anyone away from that spot.

Emile Souza was talking excitedly but coherently into his microphone. "Eyewitnesses say that a bright streak shot out of the sky at 6:54 a.m. this morning. It was like a blast of light from space, one woman said as she walked toward the Wadsworth Atheneum, which, as you can see, is closed due to broken windows caused by a concussive blast from the object. Other buildings around the site of the former residential complex – now completely obliterated – also lost windows."

Ileandra and I exchanged glances.

As the reporter began to speak again, an emergency worker appeared at the edge of the screen and waved at him.

Souza paused to listen, then said, "I'm being told to leave the area now due to concerns about contamination." He began to walk toward Main Street, and the camera showed the Channel 3 News van. "What kind of contamination is not being disclosed, but we're going back to the studio just as a precaution."

The scene cut to the studio, where Darrin Maison and Carin Sutherland sat at the desk. Immediately, they began to speak, reading from the computer screens below.

They looked shocked and horrified, and it was at the latest, breaking piece of information.

"We are being told that Emile Souza is en route to Hartford Hospital, not our studio, for a checkup. The reason for this is fear of radioactive contamination, possibly from a satellite. That is what may have crashed onto a residential complex in downtown Hartford and burned it to the ground in minutes," Maison summed up.

His wife, Carin Sutherland, looked shocked. "Our own Pete Beckett lived in that complex. We are grateful that he was here in our studio, delivering a weather forecast, and not at home, when the object hit, and have invited him to stay with us." Pete Beckett was a popular, gay, blond, stubble-haired guy who lived with two or three cats. He was perky and lovable.

I looked up at my mother. "I met him once at Sur La Table."

"Oh yeah…" she said.

Sutherland was talking again. "He lost his three cats in the blaze."

We groaned, feeling no sense of surprise.

Sutherland went on, "At Channel 3 News, we would all like to send our deepest condolences to the friends and families who lost loves ones this morning in this disaster."

We flipped to other channels, including CNN and MSNBC, and found the same story being covered.

"NASA officials are now confirming that a satellite owned by Russia has failed and crashed to the Earth, obliterating a condominium complex in Hartford, Connecticut," a reporter from MSNBC was saying.

"Apparently, a satellite operated by NASA observed a satellite that its officials knew to be the property of the Russian government drop abruptly out of orbit and fall to Earth early this morning," Wolf Blitzer was saying. "There was no time for U.S. Navy ships to attempt to shoot it down, which would have required that they be outfitted with temporary equipment to do that anyway."

My mother looked at me, horrified.

"Mommy," I said, "don't you remember that being done during the George W. Bush presidency – successfully – to shoot down one of our own old satellites as it spiraled in over the course of two days?"

She shook her head, staring, mesmerized, at the TV screen. "No. What happened?"

"It was actually kind of funny, for two reasons. One was that Dick Cheney had just shot his friend, that lawyer named Harry Whittington Jr., over Thanksgiving, by mistake, so David Letterman joked that he was 'locked and loaded' to shoot the thing down. The equipment used to do that was described. It's something that a navy ship can be outfitted with when necessary, but it isn't standard. The other part of the story was that they missed on the first try as the thing crossed over Vancouver because an Aleutian tribe rowed out in a long canoe and catapulted a huge ball of flaming lard onto the deck of the Navy ship, causing such a distraction that they couldn't concentrate on shooting at the satellite."

"Why would they do that?" my mother asked.

"Oh…I remember that…" Ileandra said, letting me tell the story, but she was smiling a little.

"It was rather ridiculous. Whoever was tasked with preparing pamphlets in the language of this Aleutian tribe made a mistake and wrote that we were trying to shoot down their "sky god". Then the pamphlets were air-dropped over the island that this tribe lives on."

"They actually didn't know what a satellite is?!" my mother asked, turning away from the television to look at me.

"Yeah…they actually didn't know."

"So, what did the Navy do about that?"

"They calmly apologized to the tribespeople for communicating incorrectly, told them that they were trying to hit a broken machine, and that they had made a linguistic mistake when the pamphlets were written and had no interest in attacking the Aleutians' sky god. That worked. They got the satellite on the second try, and that was the end of that."

"So why couldn't they do that this time?!" she asked.

"I don't know," I said. "But we might find out as the story continues. Since it's Russia, though, we already know that they aren't that big on transparency. They didn't want anyone to know about it when Chernobyl blew up. They weren't going to tell the world; they were just going to put out the fire and act like they could handle anything and everything on their own."

My mother looked at me. "So, how did the rest of the world find out?"

"We had satellites. There weren't so many in 1986, but we had a few. We were like, 'Hey Russia – we have satellites, so we can see your nuclear plume from outer space! Your dirty little secret is out, whether you like it or not!'"

My mother hadn't wanted to watch that miniseries. It was very well done. "Maybe I'll watch *Chernobyl* after all," she said now.

Meanwhile, the news went on and on.

We watched shots of government scientists in radiation suits for hours, working to find, cool, and collect radioactive bits of debris. They had several trucks lined up all around the site, and a parade of lead boxes were being carried out and loaded onto those trucks.

Kavi called the land line phone after about an hour.

"We're watching it on the news here at the Health Center," he told me. "Radiation units are being prepared in case any of the workers get sick handling that debris."

"Do they need you to help take care of the patients?"

"No. At least, not at this time. If there are any genetic mutations due to the contamination, I'll probably be in on studies of those effects, but it's way too early for that."

"So…can you work on your coronavirus stuff, or what?"

"No one is getting much done, to tell you the truth."

"Are you going to stay and try, or not?"

"Probably not. I'll be home in a little while," he said.

My father showed up next. He had been out with his camera, photographing scenic vistas atop Avon Mountain.

Instead of going home with his images, however, he had decided to share them with me.

He got the input cord out of his camera bag and connected his camera to a USB port on my computer after I set up windows for the hard drives of both devices, and we copied the images over. We didn't move them; he would be saving them again later, on his own computer.

The results were fascinating.

He had managed to get distance shots of the plume of smoke from Hartford.

Kavi walked in, saw what we were doing, and said, "You could probably sell those photographs to *The Hartford Courant.*"

My father looked at him, then back at the computer screen.

I got to work labeling them all, but said, "I doubt it. Lots of people just send them in via social media. Asking for money would just seem crass. But credit is okay."

Kavi looked contrite.

My father didn't care one way or the other.

My mother wanted me to e-mail Channel 3 with the images anyway, so I started looking up ways to do that.

Ileandra came over and watched us click through the images – twelve of them in all – and then sat down again to watch the news reports.

Kavi started making a pot of chai tea – a big one.

We all sat there until lunchtime, transfixed by the news.

"Remediating the environmental damage is going to be a huge job," I commented. "You would think that having the DEEP (Department of Energy & Environmental Protection) a couple of blocks away would help, but the federal government is probably going to preempt any state inspection."

"It could be years before that site is usable again," my father chimed in.

"It will be a lot longer than that," Ileandra said. "Ideally, no one should live there for at least a millennium."

Kavi and my parents stared at her, horrified.

I just said, "Watch the *Chernobyl* miniseries and you won't stare at anyone who says that again. You'll understand."

Three pairs of eyes shifted onto me briefly, then went back to the television screen.

When lunchtime came, Kavi made us a huge pan of curried potato fries with black mustard seeds (forgetting that my parents weren't crazy about those!), tomato chunks, onion, and garlic. I cooked up a pot of curried chick peas and rice, and made a batch of strawberry-mango smoothie in the blender.

We watched the reports all day, forgetting that we were sitting on an unrelated and even bigger story – one that we couldn't share.

The 'story' sipped her strawberry-mango smoothie with us.

Café Chats Continued

The next day, the cleanup efforts in downtown Hartford continued to dominate the national news.

Ileandra and I were going to have another virtual café chat with Elise and Nainsi.

Whenever we held those chats, we opened the conversation by updating each other on our writing and editing projects.

This was going to be a bit frustrating, because I had not gotten much editing done on that food insecurity book. But it was okay; the client had been writing it for a couple of years, and didn't need it back for a few more weeks.

I was sure I could finish the job in two. The book was only twenty-four chapters, and a total of 310 pages, aside from front matter and end materials. And I was fascinated by the topic!

Today, however, news was still breaking on the fallen space junk, and that was too important to miss.

I wanted to get going on this virtual café visit just to see what people were saying about it. Elise and Nainsi might have had a chance to hear from other people, or I would just hear from them. Either way, I was excited, despite the horror of the crash, because I had studied this for my law thesis. I never thought it would be a reality, applicable to my home area!

But before we started, I was making a batch of smoothies.

Coconut milk, cardamom, yoghurt, almond butter, and a pinch of salt went into the blender with a spoonful of honey and a spoonful of rosewater.

Ileandra watched me make it with obvious pleasure.

"I haven't had that before," she said. "It smells good."

I smiled. "I'm creating a new recipe. I'm glad you trust me with your food."

She smiled back. "You are mixing only natural ingredients, and they are all safe to consume. What could go wrong?" she asked. It was a rhetorical question, of course.

I smiled without looking up at her, poured the smoothie mixture into two large containers that we could keep next to the computers during the chat, took the blender apart, and washed the pieces with hot water and soap.

I made sure not to use the set of two that had come with the machine, however. Ileandra and I were supposed to have come from separate places, properly socially distanced.

It was after lunch, and we planned to spend the afternoon chatting with Elise and Nainsi.

They had written to me on Facebook's chat box last night, wanting me to provide them with a legal hypothesis on what was likely to happen next with the mess in Hartford.

I had laughed when I read it.

"Now that the sky has literally fallen, they are taking outer space law and outer space issues seriously," I had said to my family and Ileandra.

"Have fun," they replied.

We had eaten lunch, dinner, and snacks with my parents yesterday before they had gone home, and Uncle Louis had joined us for dinner.

They could see why I was itching to hold another virtual chat café.

Anyone could.

It felt wrong, considering what was going on in Hartford, but that felt normal in an odd way.

Of course, any psychologist could have explained that one away. People who know about a disaster in close proximity but are unaffected by it personally tend to feel a vague, undefined guilt about going about their normal, everyday business.

I shook it off.

It was ridiculous.

This disaster had nothing to do with me.

It was just exciting and fascinating to see outer space law and space junk so close to home, and to be able to watch it and talk knowledgeably with people about it.

At half past two in the afternoon, Elise and Nainsi appeared on our screens, eager to visit.

"So," Elise started us off, "they are saying that the satellite is Russian, but they either don't know whether it was a spy satellite or some other sort of satellite. Does that matter?"

"Not for purposes of arbitration under the Convention on Liability for Damage Caused by Space Objects," I said, already enjoying this. "All that matters is that the nation that owned that satellite has been positively identified, and NASA has video proof. The treaty can now be applied to this case."

"How will it be applied? And has it ever been done before?" Nainsi asked.

"It has been invoked before – in 1979, when the Soviet spy satellite called Kosmos-954 crashed where the caribou range in northern Canada. But it wasn't really applied. The Soviets offered to come over and clean up the mess, and the Canadians and the U.S. said, 'No thank you, we'll clean it up and bill you for the work,' which they did to the tune of one million dollars. Scientists in radiation suits went out in the snow with lead boxes, collected everything, and analyzed it."

"Did the Soviets pay the bill?" Elise asked.

"I don't remember," I said, "but they were not happy that we got their fragments and were able to analyze the evidence, such as it was, of their orbital spy technology."

Nainsi and Elise laughed slightly. "I'll bet they weren't," Nainsi remarked.

"Tell us how the treaty works," she said.

"Okay. The United States will file a claim against Russia for civil damages, meaning monetary compensation for property and lives lost, and then the United Nations will assemble an arbitration panel of judges from nations that are not parties to this dispute. If the panel finds Russia guilty, it shall be held absolutely liable for the damages and be required to pay them to the United States. Then the families can apply to the U.S. government for the funds."

Nainsi stared at me. "Money. And the families can't just sue Russia themselves?"

"No. Our government sues on their behalf."

Elise said, "That is the standard procedure?"

"Yes – it's written into the treaty," I said. "Criminal law works the same way, though: the state always sues on behalf of victims. However, this will be a civil international case, so that means suing for money."

Nainsi was disgusted. "Lives lost, and it comes down to money."

"Money is all that can be given once lives are lost," I told her. "You're a ghost story author. You know that necromancy won't help. Once people are dead, there is nothing to do to reverse that. All that the law can offer is to stick it to the guilty parties by depriving them of as much money as it can get."

"And that won't be enough to hurt Russia."

I looked her. "A life-changing amount that helps the bereaved families will have to do. And it's still early yet for that. But we may just get there, and I must say that I am fascinated to watch this play out. It's never gotten this far before, and setting a legal precedent is going to make history. It's awful to need one, but we're going to get one…of some kind or other."

That produced sober looks from my listeners, but no further comments.

Elise and Nainsi checked their phones from time to time for updates.

It was mostly just more on the cleanup process.

After a few minutes, Nainsi asked, "What's it like up there, in space?"

I glanced at Ileandra, who actually knew from experience, but looked away quickly. Then I thought back to my law paper. "It's crowded at the height where most of the satellites are, with hundreds of them in orbit, plus debris moving around. At a much higher orbit, out of the way of all that, is the International Space Station. It's over 250 miles up."

They gaped at me for a moment, and then Nainsi asked, "How do they get up there without getting hit by all those satellites?"

"Well, NASA has something called the Deep Space Network, and the space agencies of India, China, Japan, Russia, and the European Space Agency all have one. They track every last one of them, including the debris. They just watch for a clear window of objects and time and launch through it."

"Fascinating," Elise said, doing an unconscious impression of *Star Trek*'s Mr. Spock.

I grinned and told her what I was thinking.

Everyone laughed.

We decided to invite some other people into the chat to see what they thought of the mess in Hartford.

And thanks to Elise, who had practically lived at the Barnes & Noble café before the pandemic shutdown, she knew just who to call. Soon our screens were filled with people who were sipping lattes and eating cupcakes or microwaved cookies. They wanted to simulate life at the real café.

One window on our video chat had a pair of blonde women at it (dyed brunettes, actually) who were politically right-wing and who wrote – but somehow never got around to publishing – young adult stories. For them, Elise had explained to me, it was more about the process of writing and the social interaction that came from discussing it with others for them than actually finishing and marketing anything.

We had found that out at some abortive – and aborted – writers' group meetings, and the group had then splintered. Hence our smaller chat group. Our genres and political leanings and ambitions just didn't mesh, but it was good to have met them and learned about them.

"So...do you think that the Russians made their satellite land on us on purpose?" one woman asked the other.

Her friend glanced up at her from her phone, which she had been texting on, startled, thought about that for perhaps a nanosecond, and then said, "I don't know. It's possible."

Her questioner nodded very seriously and went back to perusing the news on her own phone.

I wondered what sites she was focusing on...

Meanwhile, Nainsi looked at me. She had heard them.

"What do you think?"

Elise and Ileandra were looking at me, too.

I laughed. "No, I don't think that idea has any merit whatsoever. I mean, what strategic value would it find in hitting an old, modern-style, randomly-located residential complex full of educated, professional residents? Plus, NASA had a satellite watching at the moment the Russian one failed and it looked legitimately like it just broke down. Shit happens, as the saying goes. It doesn't always have to be deliberate."

Nainsi suddenly grinned, gave a brief laugh, and nodded.

Ileandra said, "Too bad most humans aren't as logical and measured in their thoughts as you are."

For a moment, I was horrified at her careless choice of words.

But then Elise spoke. "Now I know you're a fan of hers. She writes and talks like that about her own species all the time!"

I laughed, partly in relief and partly in agreement.

"Yeah, I definitely do that a lot, and in my blog."

Ileandra seemed to realize her close call, but she calmly said, "I know – I read it." And she gave a big smile at that. We could see her eyes smiling above her bee floral mask.

Maybe it was easier than I thought to hide an alien visitor in plain sight. Maybe hiding Ileandra would have been far more of a tip-off than anything else…

…in any case, no one seemed to want to think about that.

They were far more interested in the downed satellite.

Nainsi asked, "What other space treaties are there?"

I thought about that. My mind tended to be full of the orbital debris treaty, but fortunately, I remembered the others.

"There is one about the 'exploration and use of the moon and other celestial bodies'," I said. "It's a first-come, first-serve basis of use. The U.S. made sure to have the NASA astronauts plant its flag on the moon on July 20th, 1969."

Elise cracked up. "Of course it did. What other treaties are there?"

"There's a companion one on activities of states on the moon and other celestial bodies. I haven't read it, but I'm going to. Although…I can kind of guess what it might say."

The others nodded. No doubt, so could they. Logic is helpful that way...

"Come on, what else?" Nainsi prodded. "We expect you to know this." She was grinning.

I was having fun with this, so I didn't mind.

"There's a treaty about the registration of objects launched into space, so that we all know what's up there, but if spy satellites are actually listed as such, I'll be shocked. No doubt, they are listed as something other than what they are."

"Naturally." Elise nodded knowingly. "What's the point of a spy satellite if it has 'Spy Satellite' painted on it?!"

"Indeed." I laughed and sipped at my coconut smoothie.

Ileandra had finished hers.

I hoped she wasn't hungry.

She still looked thinner to me than she did when she first arrived, but I thought I had managed to put a bit more weight onto her as I had gotten more adept at making smoothies. I would never have honed my smoothie-making skills to this extent if she hadn't 'visited' us!

"Are there any more treaties about outer space activities?" she asked me now.

I looked at her.

"You mean to tell me that you haven't looked that question up? You usually have checked everything that I might possibly talk about!" I said to her with a surprised grin.

She grinned back. "No – not this time."

"Huh. Okay. So...there is one more. It's about rescuing astronauts. We have so many countries around the planet that are doing things in space: The United States, Canada, the European Union, Russia, India, China, Japan, and they aren't always friendly toward each other politically, even if we aren't at war with one another. But...in space, all such bets are off."

"What do you mean?" Ileandra asked.

"Well, the astronauts are scientists and engineers, up there to further scientific inquiry, and not at war with one another. They also aren't willing to put politics ahead of their efforts. Space is too dangerous for that. They count on each other for safety. If there is an accident, and they can possibly help one another, they will, and this last treaty is about immunity from legal consequences for doing so. The astronauts may rescue each other, and then they must bring the rescued astronauts and whatever equipment they are able to save back to Earth."

"Fascinating!" Nainsi said, "And to think that I usually don't pay any attention to outer space. I tend to think of it all as *Star Trek, Star Wars,* science fiction, alien conspiracy theories, and immature fantasy."

Ileandra stared at her. "Why is the topic 'immature' to you?"

Nainsi hesitated. "Well, um…" she trailed off.

I spoke up. "I can help you with that, because as I was defending my outer space paper during the law school seminar that I wrote it for, one guy muttered to the student next to him: '*Star Wars,* science fiction, *Star Trek*' in a rather derisive tone. At least that earned him a funny look from the professor, who had no use for jeering at people in his class. The intense enjoyment of a fascinating topic is a classic marker of being on the autism spectrum, yet jeering at it doesn't affect the validity of the data being presented. I knew I wasn't going to work in insurance – that I was too unconventional a person and personality for that – even though I didn't learn about autism and Asperger's until a year after completing law school."

"Wow." Nainsi was intrigued. "So that's why you became a writer and editor instead of an attorney."

"Yes. That's why. I love what I do, I'm good at it, and there was little chance of doing well doing the conventional, expected thing with the degree. Plus, I did have the satisfaction at graduation of introducing that professor to my family and hearing him tell them that I had convinced him, through my thesis paper, that outer space was connected to international environmental law. That was great."

"Congratulations!" Elise and Nainsi said.

"Thanks!" I grinned, happy about that memory.

Ileandra was smiling, too. "You did some real, useful good with that paper," she said. "But are those all of the outer space treaties? Are there none on interacting with people from other planets?"

No suspicion from the others. They just looked at me, waiting for an answer.

I answered, "Sadly, no, and I doubt we will make one now that the beginning excitement of the space race is over 50 years in the past. We would likely have to have confirmed contact with aliens for that to happen. And it would have to be a calm contact, between diplomats, not with ray guns pointed at us."

Ileandra didn't seem at all surprised by that. Maybe a little disappointed, but not at all surprised.

As we were thinking of ending the chat, a couple on the lower left of the screen decided to ask a question. They were in their late sixties, I guessed, and I remembered seeing them in the real café often, relaxing with books and magazines over a hot, chocolate chunk cookie and coffees.

The husband spoke up first.

"How long do you think it will take before there is any further news on legal proceedings about this satellite crash?"

I said that I figured it would be a few more days before any panel of jurists was seated.

They nodded, satisfied, but clearly eager for the next news report. I smiled and said I was eagerly anticipating the next one, too, voicing their rather obvious thoughts.

They smiled politely.

The wife said, "He's a retired attorney who worked in finance, some with the IMF, so he tells me the same thing."

I nodded. "Yeah...any legal process tends to be like a waltz so that the process of discovery and other preparations can be done carefully. No big show immediately, and all that, and then we might not even get to watch it."

But as we were getting ready to stop, which was around 4:45 p.m., a report by the Associated Press appeared saying that the process was underway.

Elise found it on her phone.

"I guess we might get to see something happen, then," I said. "Not much usually goes on with outer space law, so maybe they can get on with this a lot faster than with other areas of law."

This was the best café visit ever, as far as I was concerned!

After we said good-bye, I tuned in to NPR on the radio.

My eyes were tired from looking at the screen, but we both still wanted more news.

The topic was, of course, the fallen satellite, but it was just discussion of the legal process, recapping what I had explained in the café.

I grinned as Ileandra looked at me, impressed because she was hearing all over again what I had just explained.

A little while later, as I started to assemble chicken legs and the rest of the ingredients for a curry, Kavi and Ileandra stood in front of the television, staring as the faces of prospective arbiters flashed on the screen.

A Belgian woman in her sixties whose hair and cosmetics resembled that of Madonna in the 1980s was shown. She liked to spend her recreational time as the lead singer in a rock group, the report informed us. She had served on the International Criminal Court in The Hague, Netherlands, for several years.

I loved it.

A Canadian jurist, a cheerful-looking man with thick white hair who had served on the original makeup of the ICC, was next.

Then a Japanese man with salt-and-pepper hair was shown. He had just finished serving as a judge for the International Court of Justice, or ICJ.

Kavi and Ileandra looked up at me, waiting for more, when the list was finished.

"Those are both arms of the United Nations, and both based in The Hague, which is the capital city of the Netherlands," I told them. "It's your money or your life in The Hague, meaning that the ICJ handles civil matters, and awards financial compensation to successful plaintiffs, while the ICC locks up war criminals for life. The ICJ is in the Peace Palace, which was built in 1913, a cathedral-style building with wood panels, elegant chandeliers, and stained-glass windows. The ICC is in a huge, box-like, modern complex designed by a Scandinavian architectural firm. My guess is that the proceeding could take place at either of those venues."

They had listened to me explain this with rapt attention, and then both of their faces swung in unison back to face the TV screen.

It was almost comical.

I went back to the kitchen and checked on the basmati rice, stirred the pan of okra, and blended the mango lassi.

We ate Indian food almost every day, it seemed.

That's it, I thought.

Tomorrow, I would be making coq au vin blanc.

And a raspberry-blackberry smoothie.

My raspberries were ripe at last.

I loved Indian food, but I kept thinking about this recipe.

Kavi didn't object when I announced my plan.

He just came over, kissed me, and helped stir the curries.

Ileandra got a spoon and ate some sauce from the okra.

Not the Most Inconspicuous Person…

Kavi was watching both his wife and the alien.

They had taken a drive out to a reservoir to walk around.

There were other people doing the same thing, but everyone, or every group, was keep at least six feet away from one another.

They had paused to sit on a bench and look at the birds.

It was a beautiful place.

The deciduous trees were fully covered with green leaves for the summer. The fir trees, of course, were also beautiful, but they were covered with needles all year, Ileandra reflected. This was the best time to see them all, and from the ground, in broad daylight. Well…evening light. It was late July.

The birds were fascinating to see, too: Canada geese, Mallard ducks, herons, and even a couple of swans.

"Those mate for life," Arielle told her. "I love swans, even though up close, they are nasty to humans. They're just afraid of us, and it's better for them that way. We humans are, after all, the top predator on the planet. We can fly higher – even into space – and dive deeper than any other species."

An older couple who was walking by heard that and turned to take a second look at the human woman.

Arielle just smiled at them.

Arielle certainly wasn't the most inconspicuous human she could have found to seek shelter with, Ileandra supposed.

"You would never have been taken in by an ordinary, inconspicuous person. They're not as accepting as the unusual ones, nor as intelligent. You got very lucky," Kavi told her.

Ileandra turned to look at him. "I know. And I really appreciate it all. Are you sure you're not a telepath?" she asked.

Kavi grinned. "Yeah, I'm sure. What you don't realize about us is, most humans – the neurotypicals, who comprise the majority of us – can read facial expressions. And you're not as inscrutable as you'd like to think you are."

She stared into space, startled.

"You're right. I'm learning much more by being here than I ever did before."

Kavi smiled. "That's what all the anthropologists say."

She grinned. "I can study that along with botany."

He quipped, "Clearly, we're not going to live out a real-life *Star Trek* and meet the Vulcans first."

They all laughed at that.

"Arielle, who were you quoting or paraphrasing just now?" Kavi asked. "That sounded familiar. I'm sure you've talked to me about that before."

He turned to Ileandra and said, "She always talks to me about whatever she's studying or reading, because so many things fascinate her and it's fun to share. I love it."

Then he looked back at his wife.

"I was quoting Paul R. Ehrlich, the author of many books on human overpopulation."

"Oh, yeah…" Kavi nodded. "He wrote to you once. He sent you an autographed copy of a book that he and his wife wrote, didn't he?"

Arielle smiled. "Yes, he did. And he bought one of mine. It's the kind of compliment an author can live on forever."

"I've heard of him," Ileandra said. "He's right. He isn't accorded the respect he ought to have, but he's right about overshoot and overpopulation. Humans have taken action based on his warnings that have postponed the timing of his predictions, but that won't work indefinitely."

Arielle looked at her.

"You sound like you have been reading my blog."

Ileandra said, "I'm glad you have been writing such things, but no – I'm just saying what I know from what happened with my own planet's ecosystem. We went into overshoot," and, glancing at Kavi, she clarified, "we became overpopulated beyond the carrying capacity of our planet's ecosystem, and we crashed it. Now we have to live with the consequences, and it isn't pretty. Not anymore. Not like your planet still is."

Kavi gaped at her.

Then he looked at me. "I'm glad we didn't have kids."

Superstorm Season

It was hurricane season again.

The weather reports had been tracking them for a month or so, but the first several letters of the alphabet had already been used up without a huge one that left expensive property damage.

"It's still early," I commented, to no one in particular.

Ileandra looked at me. "Early?"

It was nine o'clock at night, and we were watching television. A commercial break had just given us a preview of the weather map, showing that a huge storm was headed our way, in from the southern Atlantic Ocean, curving up the eastern seaboard of the United States.

"I mean, early in hurricane season. We have them, but it's usually a month before we get a big enough one to cause major problems."

"Oh. I see."

"Here – you can read *Isaac's Storm* by Erik Larson if you want to know about the worst one ever, and look up Hurricanes Andrew, Katrina, and Harvey on the internet to follow up."

I laughed as the alien's face lit up with enthusiasm.

"See?" I said. "I didn't show you all of my books at once! I saved a few for later on in the summer."

She laughed, and looked at the synopsis on the back of the book. "1900, Galveston, Texas…120 years ago." She looked at it some more. "Naming hurricanes is done now, but wasn't done then? Why name them at all?"

Kavi grinned. "It's easier for us humans to remember them with names then with a bunch of numbers or a date."

I chimed in, "And in recent years, it occurred to meteorologists that it was sexist to give them all female names, so they switch genders with each hurricane now."

The alien looked nonplussed, but recovered, shaking her gaze away from us and back to the book.

"Why would humans build a settlement so close to a storm zone?" she asked, mystified.

"Because delusional, wishful thinking clouds judgment." Kavi laughed mirthlessly.

"I don't understand." Ileandra wasn't going to get it quickly, and that didn't surprise either of us.

"Humans settle in an unoccupied area to find space of their own. Once people get to like where they are, they make a home that they get emotionally attached to. If they stay long enough to reproduce and make a lot of friends, they will be even less willing to relocate, no matter what. So, if they are flooded out, or a tornado wipes out their home – and a hurricane can achieve both at once – they will just rebuild."

"It is not logical to rebuild in the same spot."

"That is another way of stating the definition of insanity," Kavi said, and he reached over to pet Bagheera.

The cat opened one eye, purred, shifted, and snuggled against my hip again.

I took out another book, *1491* by Charles C. Mann. "You'll like this one, too. The author talks about how logical the humans were who occupied this continent before Europeans were showed up the year after this book's title."

Two pairs of eyes locked onto me.

I continued, "The Native Americans – who call themselves Indians, though that causes some confusion in this house – numbered around 80 million on both American continents combined. They only lived in the central plains of this continent when it wasn't tornado season. They had summer and winter encampments. Then the stupid white people showed up and thought, 'Hurray for us – a whole area that we can lay claim to!' That's Tornado Alley. I wouldn't move there for anything."

The alien's mouth dropped open.

"Have fun reading it after that spoiler alert," Kavi said.

I cracked up. "I give a lot of spoiler alerts, don't I?"

"It's just a teaser of a synopsis. Now she really wants to read it. But which one first…" he grinned at her.

What the Small Gray Visitor Said

It was late July.

The next day, a Sunday, I decided to get the house as ready as possible for storms.

Kavi helped me drag all of the outdoor furniture in from the patio. We stacked it neatly into the foyer: chairs, umbrella, table. I lined up all of the gardening tools and hoped for the best for my garden.

"Don't worry, Arielle," my husband told me. "You tend to have pretty good luck with storms not ruining your garden. That's the benefit of living in a cul-de-sac.

In fact, he had suggested that for precisely that reason.

I smiled and gave him a kiss.

At least I had enjoyed the peonies and irises – my favorites. But would the raspberries make it?

We would soon find out.

Ileandra looked around the living room, and out at the darkening sky.

It was a Tuesday morning, and the hurricane was on its way. It was very windy, and rain was coming down in curtains.

Kavi was staying home with us, and sat in the breakfast nook with his laptop, writing up his notes from the lab.

We had checked every battery in every device we had: flashlights, computers, laptops, etc. The surge protector was working on my desktop computer, and on the televisions.

I filled a few bottles with water from the sink.

The house was clean – bathrooms, kitchen, etc.

So were all of us. I had suggested showers in case we lost electricity and water service.

Ileandra had found that advice odd, but she had gone along with it.

Kavi glanced up. "The power cables are underground in this neighborhood, so unless Nod Road gets its wires knocked out, we should be okay.

What the Small Gray Visitor Said

He had gone out to the grocery store last night for more orange juice, milk, and other items to stock us up, just in case.

When he got back, we had made 3 different smoothies for Ileandra and put them in the fridge.

She had watched us making these preparations in fascinated amazement.

"Don't you have storms in the Owl Nebula?" I asked.

"Not like what you are anticipating."

I felt really curious about her planet's ecosystem.

Meanwhile, she finished reading those books.

The morning dragged on.

I sat on the sofa with the cat, having finished editing the vampire novel, and having begun an outline for one of my own. It was something that I was purposely not drafting yet, though – not until the alien went home, and I knew the story from beginning to end.

I didn't like inactivity. It made me nervous.

Ileandra looked up at me.

"You could read one of your books. I know you have a small stockpile of them to read, not just books that you have already read."

I grinned. "Yeah…" I was in the middle of one about Hedy Lamarr, the Austrian actress whose work on modulating radio frequencies had been used against the Nazis, as she had wished. That work had later been the basis of cell phone technology.

But I couldn't get into it right now.

Ileandra sensed this, and dropped the subject.

I leaned back on the sofa and stared at the walls.

"No more painting to do, even…"

She looked up at me. "Painting? Oh…"

She saw in my mind that I had painted the entire house – every wall – when we had first moved in.

"You don't like gray?" she asked, with a mischievously arched eyebrow.

I glanced at her. "Yes, Small Gray, I don't want any of the walls of my house to be decorated in that color. It reminds me of a storm. I called it 'Imminent Hurricane Gray'. I tend to get nasty headaches just before a huge rainstorm. I'm a human barometer."

"Fascinating."

"Yes, Spock, fascinating," I said, with heavy sarcasm.

She laughed, silently, and said, "Your blue hues are beautiful. I agree with you."

She could see the old dark gray, and me painting the walls an eggshell blue, a French blue, a periwinkle blue…

…but the house didn't need any more work.

I hoped it would stay that way.

I took nothing for granted as the climate changed.

The day went on with the television tuned in to the weather channel. No one went anywhere.

I called my parents and found that they were staying in and doing the same thing.

"One year, we got an ice storm in late October that knocked out power on Hallowe'en. We all went out for Chinese food, and the power wasn't restored until eleven days later, which sucked. We had a generator, thanks to my father. But that meant that we could only have power for a few hours a day, while it was running. And those have to be run outside, not in, and watched carefully, because they emit carbon monoxide fumes. So, no internet except for a few hours, and then it was isolation like we had in the pre-Industrial Age. That was a strange experience for us, of course. We're so used to being constantly connected now, even if it's only in a virtual sense, online."

The alien listened to this, considering it.

"That would be a strange experience for me, too."

"At last! Something in common with an alien," Kavi said, grinning as he continued to type.

I grinned back, and found that Ileandra was doing it too.

Then I had another memory to share.

252

What the Small Gray Visitor Said

"There was one other aspect of that time that I really hated: no showers. I felt so dirty. At least the local health club opened its showers up to the general public. We went there three times once we found out about that."

"Cleaning yourselves with water is very important to humans, isn't it?"

I looked at her.

"Well, yeah! That's one aspect of *Star Trek* that I can never wrap my mind around: sonic showers. Water is just better, and even Captain Kirk admits that."

"Will the health club let you take showers there again?"

"Probably not. Not during a pandemic. Too risky."

Kavi glanced up. "If I can't take a shower, at least no one will care at the laboratory with us all going there one at a time. Social isolation means that we won't have to smell each other while we...smell."

"IF you smell," I said. "Let's not get too negative while we still have power. Maybe we'll get lucky, and it won't go out, and then our biggest problem will be blocked roads on the way to the lab, the grocery store, and wherever else."

The rain suddenly came down harder.

We had curried spinach soup – which I was happily able to heat up – and grilled cheese sandwiches and smoothies for lunch.

So far, so good.

I kept watching the garden.

It seemed okay.

Small branches from the fir trees in the woods, and few from deciduous ones as well, blew around the area, though.

The yard was littered with them.

That seemed to be the worst of it.

It was just a very dark, rainy day for us.

Around dinnertime, I called my best friend from college, Isabelle.

She wanted to buy some face masks from me.

I wrote down the fabric choices and face measurements for her and her daughter, and laid out the outer space masks that she had ordered for her husband and son.

"Do you have power there?" I asked.

"It just went out before you called. I'm going to have to get the grill going for our dinner."

Isabelle was a gourmet cook, like me.

"What will you make?" I had to ask.

"Oh, I don't know yet…I have some vegetables I can roast on skewers, and I can grill some chicken. And we'll eat some ice cream so that it doesn't melt."

"Maybe it'll come back on before the rest of it does," I said. "You can't eat it all tonight anyway, can you?"

"No."

"Well…here's hoping that it comes on soon."

"Thank you. I hope yours stays on."

We rang off.

They got the power restored later that evening, I found out the next time I called.

We ended up being lucky this time.

The power stayed on, and even the garden was fine.

I went out there the next day and collected all of the branches, which I tossed into the woods.

Ileandra helped me as best she could.

"Your garden is still in good condition," she said happily.

"Yes – which means that my offer of botanical samples is still intact, and my season of raspberries is not cancelled."

I was happy, too.

But…my poor friend Elise had no power, and no place to take a shower.

A total of 800,000 households in the state were without power, in fact. That meant no running water, and no electricity.

It was the definition of misery as far as I was concerned.

What the Small Gray Visitor Said

Elise parked in her vehicle outside of Barnes & Noble day and night, bored and frustrated, using the store's wi-fi signal to do her writing and to use the internet.

I felt bad. Here I was, sitting pretty, and I couldn't offer her a place to take a shower due to the pandemic. I would have done so, otherwise.

But, as expected, not even the health club was offering showers to the public.

It sucked.

There hadn't been any deaths in the area, at least.

Just major inconvenience, and a lot of business for tree surgeons.

The power company was under heavy criticism for not getting people back onto the grid faster.

It dragged out for over a week before the job was done.

I did my best to offer sympathy to Elise.

"It's like the current government is running the power company, it's in such disarray!" I typed into the Facebook chat box.

"Exactly!" Elise typed back, when she was able to do so.

Souvenirs

It was early August.

I had made significant progress with my editing projects, to the point that I was almost finished with them all.

Soon, I would have to find more.

I would also have to find more customers for face masks.

There were forty-six of them in my "stock" bag.

Today was a Tuesday, and Kavi was home again.

He spent the time on his laptop, catching up on correspondence and enjoying smoothies and time with me and the cat...and our alien visitor.

The raspberries were thick on the bushes in the back yard.

It was my favorite time of the year for fruit.

I grabbed a bowl and went outside, determined to pick as many raspberries as possible.

I had three different varieties out there: Jewel, which was a black raspberry; Double Gold, which was, as the name implied, a golden one; and Caroline, a red raspberry.

That last one had also bloomed in late June, so I was able to make raspberry tarts earlier in the summer.

Now I was about to do it again, but with all three varieties. Life was good.

No wonder alien botanists snooped around Earth, looking for samples of our plants.

They were wonderful, and not just the ones that I grew.

I picked roughly equal amounts of each kind and came in.

An hour earlier, I had made a sweet buttery tart crust with some cinnamon added (not required by the recipe, but I liked to add it, and Kavi was always pleased to have more spices in the mix).

I had also made some tart filling out of one 8-ounce brick of Neufchatel cheese, a little honey, a little confectioner's sugar, and a teaspoon of pure vanilla extract. That was whipped in the KitchenAid mixer.

Each year, I made jam out of my berries, so now I took out some of last year's batch for the glaze. Adding a couple of tablespoons of rosewater to quarter cup of jam, I whisked it on the stove on low heat.

I washed the berries, laid out the tart shell on a beautiful serving plate, and spread the tart filling in carefully.

Next the raspberries went in.

Finally, the glaze was poured…drizzled…on top.

"Beautiful!" Kavi said, coming over to look at it.

"Thank you," I said, and carried it to the table to photograph it.

He grinned at Ileandra. "She doesn't care if it's cut up once it's been photographed."

Bagheera leaped up to see what was going on, saw, and moved just as rapidly to leap onto the kitchen counter where he could watch from high up without causing any problems.

Smart cat.

I took the photographs.

"Done!" I said, feeling very pleased with the world.

My viewers laughed.

The cat smiled, and settled into a crouch to watch as I put the tart in the fridge.

On to the computer to save the images, post, etc.

"That's a ritual with her," Kavi told the alien.

"I can see that."

I looked up. "We all have our rituals – don't kid yourselves."

I put the camera away and said, "And now for another one. Kavi, take off your extra shirt." I was referring to the long-sleeved, open one that he wore over his tee shirt. "Time for another haircut."

He had just been about to pick up his computer, but he said, touching his head, "Okay."

I pulled a kitchen chair away from the table, into the middle of the room, and put a large towel around his shoulders.

Next, I sprayed his head with a water bottle, combed it, and brandished the scissors over him, considering my moves carefully before cutting any hair. I wanted to keep him looking nice. Then I went for it.

Clip, clip, snip, snip. Comb, snip, fuss, fuss.

He sat still through it all.

Half an hour later, it was over.

I didn't have a hand mirror, so he jumped up to go look at himself in the mirror in the half-bathroom.

He came back in a moment, happy with the results.

Not bad for someone who had figured this out using a tutorial from the internet.

"Thank you!" he said, giving me a kiss. "I don't have to tough out the pandemic looking unkept." He hugged me.

I grinned, kissed him back, and swept up the hair.

Ileandra watched all this.

"You are always busy," she remarked, "and usefully so. He looks good, like he could go on television and do an interview...or something."

Kavi laughed and said, "Yes, unlike Stephen Colbert, I don't have to wait and watch my hair grow out."

"Stephen Colbert looks okay despite that," I said. "He's attractive, and combing his hair into its usual style is helping him get away with not having his hair cut."

Ileandra was looking at the hair clippings on the floor.

I looked at her. "You don't actually want to save Kavi's hair, do you?! I thought you only saved plants."

She looked up at me, startled. "No. I don't."

I wasn't entirely sure that I believed her.

"Wouldn't some other Small Gray with a different profession – not a botanist – want to study the molecular composition of the dead hair of a well-nourished human?" Kavi asked with a devilish grin.

Ileandra looked cornered. "Okay, one might. But I didn't want to ask."

We both cracked up.

Kavi grabbed a chunk out of the pile and handed it to her. "Do what you will with it."

She took it, looking doubtfully at it.

"Thank you."

"So, Ileandra," I said, segueing into a topic that had been on my mind, "it is late in the summer, that bridge reinforcement is progressing, and I wonder: are your people monitoring its progress with a view toward figuring out when they can pick you up?"

She looked up at me.

"They are," she replied.

"And...?"

"A few more weeks, and it should be done."

"Do they intend to pick you up at that same crop field?"

"Yes, they do."

"And can I help you with some souvenirs? I ask because, if so, now is a good time – now that so many plants in my garden are producing fruits and other items – to prepare them. I want to send you home with as many samples of as many things that you might otherwise not be able to get as possible."

The little alien's large almond-shaped blue eyes lit up like a kid's at Christmas or Diwali (the Hindu festival of lights).

"I know you have been saving a few already. I saw you save a peony blossom, an iris bulb, a strawberry plant from that crop field, another from my yard, and a nasturtium. That's a good start, but let's get going on expending your repertoire of souvenirs. I want your people to be glad you were able to maximize your time here, and not be upset with you for not being able to just get over to the ship and beam out with the others."

"You are still worried about that?"

"Well, yeah!"

"Thank you. But they are not angry with me. It was an accident."

"Shit happens, huh?" Kavi said.

"Yes, indeed it does," Ileandra said with a rueful look.

We had just watched the movie *Forrest Gump* last night.

She got the reference from that.

"How will you tote around so much stuff, though?" I had to ask her.

"I shrink it and pack it. It is dehydrated, frozen, and fits neatly in my kit."

"And it stays frozen in something in your kit?"

"Yes."

I didn't ask for more details.

"Well, you can do that too, but I'm also going to give you big bag to carry un-shrunk ones in. You can save time growing them when you get them home that way."

The alien looked delighted.

"Everything is easier without subterfuge, isn't it?" I said.

"It is indeed," she replied. "Thank you very much!"

It was time to get going on those souvenirs.

Kavi abandoned his e-mail chores and came outside with us to watch the process.

But first, Ileandra went upstairs, got her kit bag, and took something out of it.

"I have already made dehydrated, frozen samples from the plants that grew in your garden earlier this summer," she informed me.

"Good!" I said. "I thought it had missed out on some while we were busy with other events, and was upset that you had lost them. You could have told me about that! I was feeling sorry for you about it."

She stared at me.

I could feel a little guilt trip through our link.

Good.

She ought to trust me by now.

"I'm sorry…" she said.

"It's okay. Let's get to work. This ought to be fun, sharing my plants with you. It took me a long time to collect them and get them to grow back every year. Gardening is not something that comes easily to me. I had to work at it, experiment, and ask Sylvia a lot of questions. I don't like to bother her too much with it – she's very busy – but she was very nice."

The alien nodded. "I could tell that about her."

"I bet you could!" Kavi teased.

Another telepathy teasing…one of many.

What the Small Gray Visitor Said

We gathered bits of just about everything that was growing in the garden: rosemary, lavender, basil, chives, every color of nasturtium, each variety of raspberry on a bit of branch (the bushes had plenty to spare), a purple and an orange carrot, a zucchini squash, several different heirloom tomatoes plus a plum tomato, pea shoots, a pumpkin root, a few bell peppers – one red, one orange, and one purple – and a striped eggplant.

"Don't you have a few more weeks here?" Kavi asked, watching all of this packing and preparation.

We looked up at him, startled out of our joint project.

"Yes, she does, don't you, Ileandra?"

"Yes, I do."

"So why all this activity now?"

"Better than waiting until the last minute," I said. "Did you study that way in school, or did you study right along, keeping up with the reading, so that you wouldn't have to rush frantically to learn everything and research a paper when it was time to actually write it?"

He nodded his head in comprehension.

"Got it. You're not procrastinating."

We grinned.

"Exactly."

Earth Overshoot Day

It was August 21st, 2020 – the evening before Earth Overshoot Day. August 22nd, 2020 was it – and I intended to be ready with my yearly essay about it.

"Time to blog," I said. "This absolutely must be posted just after midnight tonight, so that it will be up on my website all day on Earth Overshoot Day, plus posted to every venue I have access to: Facebook, Twitter, tumblr, Pinterest, LinkedIn, and perhaps Instagram, if I can figure out a suitable way to show it there. A good graphic with the link to the post ought to do it," I summed up, settling down to work.

Ileandra looked from me to Kavi.

"This sounds important."

He nodded. "She does this every year. I stay out of her way when she gets going on a blog post, but the ones for World Population Day and Earth Overshoot Day are particularly significant."

The alien came over to see what I was doing on the computer.

I was gathering graphics from the Global Footprint Network and relevant news stories about resource depletion and human overpopulation.

"Unhappy Earth Overshoot Day 2020 – A Year's Worth of Resources, Used Up by Humans by August 22nd!" I wrote for a post title.

It was annoyingly long, but it couldn't be shortened.

It was the same silent complaint I made to myself each year, but then I just kept going.

I paused.

"Ileandra," I invited the alien to sit next to me, "let me show you something. It's depressing, but it's important."

I went to the page for the Global Footprint Calculator.

It was a cartoon program that invited each person to input their own personal use data of space, energy, food, trash data, housing, transportation, and whatever other resources they consumed within a year.

"Watch this: I will enter the data for myself and Kavi."

I did that, and when it was finished, it said that if everyone lived as we did, we would need two and a half Earths to accommodate that.

"I wonder about some of this, because of the way the data is gathered from each person, such as the trash generation and transportation data. I would like to fine-tune it further, but it doesn't let me do that. Even so, I doubt I could shave off much more resource depletion with more flexibility in this program."

She looked at me. "How much less could you get it down to if you could?"

"I don't know – I'm not that great at math, to tell you the truth. My aunt and I have a little case of numbers dyslexia – we mentally reverse them without meaning or wanting to. So this is just a guesstimate, but perhaps it could shrink to two Earths. That's still way too much, though!"

"What could you do to reduce further, then?"

"Live without our own space, perhaps, pressed tightly into a city, close among many more humans, but not if I can avoid it! I don't want to be near many people. So, you see the problem with human overpopulation…we don't want that much togetherness, even if it helps the ecosystem. We are each only willing to do so much to mitigate our collective and personal impact on the planet."

She listened to me with obvious consternation.

"So…you feel guilty, but not very guilty."

"Pretty much," Kavi and I chorused.

"But you aren't adding to your species' population numbers. That is the best thing you can do."

We smiled. "Yes, there is that."

"What about electricity?"

"I hate camping. I want running water. I want to be clean!" I said, frustrated at the amount of resources required to continue life as comfortably as necessary to have healthful sanitation.

"I see." She seemed lost in thought.

Then she added, "It will take fewer humans in existence and some technological advances to enable all of the humans in existence to have enough, and to live in comfort."

"Thank you, Ileandra. You have just outlined my yearly blog post. I feel as though I am repeating myself each year, but to not bother seems like giving up, and that's even more demoralizing, so I will go ahead and say it all again."

Kavi came over to me after a while and rubbed my shoulders.

It took me over an hour, but at last I was satisfied.

I posted, shared, tweeted, and otherwise amplified the essay...and then sat back, disgusted with the world but satisfied that I had made this effort.

All the while, the late-night talk show hosts were background sounds.

They each had three children.

They didn't seem to understand – and perhaps didn't wish to – that having the choice to reproduce meant that far too many people would exercise it, and that would mean a more constrained quality of life for the next generation, and the next, and the next.

And we were already there.

I decided to sew a couple of face masks.

It made me feel better while we were still waiting for the scientists to find a vaccine for coronavirus.

Kavi and other scientists all over the planet were still at it.

Meanwhile, the present generation of young people had missed proms, graduations, theater and sporting events, concerts, weddings, and other gatherings that made life worth living...and they were upset. I didn't blame them.

The impact of human resource use, caused by getting too close to the wild parts of nature and killing and eating creatures from those areas – creatures that we should not have contact with – had caused this zoonotic pandemic.

Unhappy Earth Overshoot Day, humans.

We did this to ourselves, and we still needed to learn to stop doing it.

Firestorms

Ileandra had gotten the signal at last.

The construction crew was packing up to go.

The bridge was reinforced, and the work finished.

She was going home – soon.

How soon was just a matter of details.

"How can we help?" I asked. "Will we be able to go with you to meet your ship? And will they just take you, and leave us here? I don't want to get abducted."

We were eating breakfast in the nook at the back of the kitchen, watching the hummingbirds in their feeder. Bees were working on the flowers in the garden.

It was hard to believe that we had such an unusual conundrum, namely, how to safely get an alien home while not having our own lives disrupted.

We had to come home!

Ileandra gulped her mango coconut cardamom smoothie.

'This was a particularly good one,' she thought…and I heard that!

What would become of our telepathic link?

Would it just break, abruptly and painlessly?

"Yes, it will just break," the little alien said out loud. "And you will not be forced to come with me. My people won't do that. They just want me back, so that all traces of me will be removed. Humans must not have proof of my visit."

Kavi breathed an audible sigh of relief.

Ileandra smiled. "You're glad, aren't you? You want to solve this pandemic and stay here with your wife, and keep her here with you."

He looked at her. "Yes, I do." He drank his coffee.

"When do you leave?" I asked.

"Saturday night, late in the evening."

"Not at 2 a.m.?" I had to ask.

"No. That was too big an imposition on you, and all for nothing. It should be quick. They'll just time it so that no motor vehicles are coming down the road, and make sure that the police are not using their shooting range. The weekend seems like a good idea."

It did.

August was almost over.

Colleges were starting their semesters – online.

Traffic should be light to nonexistent.

I went over to my computer and checked the weather report for Saturday night. Cloudy, with a chance of thunder. Another damned hurricane was coming through, though we would only get the outer edge of it here.

"Will that be a problem?"

The alien said, "Fewer vehicles. I can just get out of your car at the side of the road and go."

Okay…but you know what they say: the best-laid plans…

Saturday came.

It was gray and overcast.

All day, we were on edge, worrying about the drop-off and how it would go.

Worrying was pointless, but we couldn't help it.

And why wouldn't we be pacing around, worrying?! It was not a typical situation to be in, plotting to drop an alien guest off at an agricultural field and watch for a huge hovering craft to just beam her up, or whatever it would do!

We tried to sleep late, but gave up.

To begin with, the cat got us up, leaping onto the bed and nudging us, pushing us, and nipping us. He wanted to be fed.

By nine-thirty, we were all downstairs, making breakfast.

Kavi's colleague from the lab, another scientist who specialized in zoonotic diseases, called, and they talked for an hour. At least it kept his mind off of the impending drop-off.

I sewed a few face masks just to have something to do.

I was too wound up to write or edit.

Bagheera seemed to sense that something was up.

He was in his basket, watching us more than sleeping.

Ileandra sat there, watching us all.

Would she miss being here, and us?

What the Small Gray Visitor Said

She must have been homesick a lot at first.
But that had been almost three months ago.
By now, she had adjusted and enjoyed our food.
She smiled, listening in on my thoughts.
I had given up on objecting to it.
I smiled at that realization.
"Yes, I will miss all of this. But it will be good to go home.
Thank you very much for the plants." She had a big bag of
them to take with her.
"Home is what we need and want, no matter how
interesting a time elsewhere is – usually," I added, thinking of
the expatriates who had moved to other countries and
remained there permanently.
"I could happily continue here," Ileandra confessed, "but
I want to go home. It will be very helpful to share the plants
that you helped me to gather, and I have gained many insights
into both your people and mine that need to be shared."
So: she did lean more toward going than staying.
Good to know.

We ate dinner quickly, because we didn't eat much.
Salads, bread, smoothies, and done.
The smoothies were a feast – a send-off.
We had a carrot-tomato-hot-pepper one with dinner, and
a coconut-almond-raspberry one for dessert.
Kavi and I were too keyed up for a big meal.
Ileandra sensed that and made no comment.

Another few hours passed as we waited for eleven o'clock.
Ileandra was dressed in the clothing that she had arrived
in, with her Small Gray suit, in a perfect state of repair, slung
over her arm, just as I had found her.
In her bag were the many plant samples she had gathered,
all micro-sized, waiting for her to unpack them when she got
back to her ship and its laboratory…and greenhouse.
It had a greenhouse of sorts!
Well, of course it did.

She had also packed, rolled up in her small kit bag, the strawberry-patterned dress I had given her and the two face masks I had sewn for her. She had not shrunk those down.

And...she would carry a large, recycled-plastic bag full of fresh, live plants that I had helped her uproot from my garden.

At a quarter to eleven, the alien took out a small metal device. It looked hilariously similar to what Captain Kirk had used in the classic *Star Trek* episodes, but smaller and sleeker.

She did not, however, say "Ileandra to *Enterprise*," or anything else like it.

She didn't say anything at all, in fact.

She just tapped it a couple of times, and said that it was time to go.

We immediately got up and went into the garage.

Kavi and I had our face masks tucked into our pockets.

Ileandra looked at us for a moment, then took one of hers out and kept it in her lap.

Better prepared than not. Cops could be out driving.

Kavi backed the car out of the garage, turned around, and drove us out onto Tiger Lily Lane and down the street.

No one was out and about.

Thunder rumbled in the distance.

I didn't see the stars. It was just gray up there.

Taking a Small Gray out to meet her ship on a gray, overcast night...

...would it work?

Only one way to find out.

We were out on Nod Road in no time, it seemed.

That's what I got for thinking too much.

Time to pay attention to the world around me!

We pulled over by the field, and looked.

The sky above it didn't look any different.

But the field did. Corn was high in it – twice as high as our alien visitor.

The only light was provided by street lights.

We all got out.

None of us was masked, but that didn't matter.

What the Small Gray Visitor Said

No one was around.

Suddenly, overhead, clouds gathered.

They moved and swirled.

It looked like a huge thundercloud building up, fast.

Ileandra looked up, and began to move away from us.

"Thank you for everything," she said, and stepped into the field.

A couple of paces, and we couldn't see her.

But we could see the rustling of the crops.

The swirl looked bigger and bigger.

And then a huge bolt of lightning, unrelated to that swirl, hit the cloud.

A firestorm lit inside the cloud.

Kavi and I looked at each other in shock, and grabbed each other, scared. We smelled ozone.

I glanced at the corn stalks, and noticed something else.

The rustling was reversing!

Ileandra came running out of there, back toward us.

The cloud flamed, and then dissipated abruptly.

Thunder clapped overhead.

"They're gone, aren't they?" I said.

She looked like she was in shock.

Had she gotten hurt in there?

'I'm not injured,' I heard in my mind.

"Yes," she said aloud. "They're gone."

Kavi opened the back door of the car. "I knew picking you up in a thundercloud was a mistake."

"Come on, Ileandra. We'll figure something else out. Let's go home."

We all got back into the car and drove back to the house.

"You know, Ileandra…" I was thinking of 1947. "Aliens phased into the desert over New Mexico in the summer of 1947 and their ship broke up, and they got killed. See if you can get them to pick you up in nice weather."

She was looking at me in the sideview mirror. "I will."

We pulled into the garage, got out of the car, and went back in, exhausted and stunned by the night's events.

The Small Grays Travel Agency

Helping our guest get a flight home was proving more difficult that we had expected.

But we were determined.

And we were completely on our own in this effort.

She was open to our advice now, at least.

"Your travel will be arranged by the Small Grays Travel Agency," I told her when we got home. "I will be working on your travel plan and itinerary. As soon as I have thought that out, we'll discuss it again."

She had nodded, thanked me, and we all went to bed.

The cat was very confused.

Who goes out for fifteen minutes in a storm?!

And then comes right back?!

I picked him up and cuddled him, and carried him upstairs with me. He was all tensed up, like he knew something different – something out of the ordinary – was afoot.

Kavi and I lay there, staring up at the ceiling.

It wasn't easy to unwind after such a tense day, followed by an anti-climactic moment of terror.

At least no one was hurt.

"I'm glad we waited and didn't leave her out there," Kavi said.

"Me too. I had no intention of going unless and until I saw that ship and a flash of light…something to indicate that she was, in fact, picked up."

Bagheera leaped onto our bed and curled up, staring at us.

We rolled to face each other and petted him.

After several minutes, the cat settled down and relaxed.

So did we; we were tired from a long day and night.

Finally, Kavi and I were able to go to sleep.

The cat fell asleep too, purring against my side.

Re-Booked

The next evening was Sunday – the end of August.

I was thinking.

I had been thinking all day.

We were watching a rerun of *Real Time with Bill Maher*.

He was off for the summer, as usual, probably enjoying some pot and doing stand-up comedy acts in Hawaii.

Watching it was better than worrying.

Maher was saying that it was nonsense that if any of us had lived at an earlier time, we would not have made the same misjudgments about social and political issues that people as a whole made in those past times.

"Of course you would have!" he roared at the camera.

"I wouldn't have," I said resentfully. "How else does he explain the people who risked arrest by operating stops on the Underground Railroad?!"

Ileandra looked at me. "Wasn't that the escape system for fugitive slaves?"

"Yes, it was. Lots of white people who didn't have to do anything to help helped anyway, removing shackles and hiding them. One time, we got to hear about a stop on that railroad – an archaeologist in upstate New York found some at an early 19th-century house that he excavated the yard of. We attended a lecture he gave about that when we visited my cousins."

"Fascinating. There is hope for humans," the alien said.

I could tell that she was trying to sound optimistic.

I was feeling less so, and frustrated at not having thought of a way home for her yet.

"Yes, but overall, there are always very few who are 'ahead of their time' and who see what is wrong and act to counteract it. I don't need a spaceship or a time machine to see that."

"True. But you are a scholar. Your brain is your spaceship and time machine. There are far too few of you to save your species in time, unfortunately."

Damn! She had swung the opposite way…to morbid.

Kavi just watched us, looking dejected.

But then Maher moved on to his *New Rules* segment, and he and I suddenly cheered up. His high-I.Q. comedic commentary always boosted our morale.

The alien visitor observed, but she kept her thoughts to herself.

The laughs had apparently cleared my mind, because I suddenly jumped up, moved over to my computer, and clicked on the week's weather report.

Then I did a Google search: "Moonlight calendar."

Perfect!

"Clear skies and moonlight for tomorrow night," I said.

Both my husband and our guest looked at me.

"Call them back and arrange to get picked up at 1 a.m."

Ileandra looked at me, almost shrugged (not a natural mannerism to her, so she didn't), and took out her signalling device. She did something almost imperceptible with it, paused, and then touched it one more time.

"They have agreed to your plan."

She looked stunned.

She was really, finally, going home…on a clear night.

Hopefully, no one would see her go.

Transference

Kavi took Monday off.

He had called a colleague and traded shifts.

Their experiments would allow for this, fortunately.

The colleague had sounded concerned, Kavi told us, until he had added that he needed to go over some literature online before he would be ready for the next phase of his experiment.

That took care of that.

It was a perfectly plausible excuse.

Kavi did that often, and so did other scientists.

The pandemic shutdown meant a lot of theoretical preparation and virtual research, not to be done in the lab, when only one person could be there at any one time.

This time, exhausted from both the anticipation and the letdown of a deed postponed, we had slept until ten a.m.

Bagheera allowed it.

But that was his limit; he nudged us awake at that point.

It was to have been another meal much like the one we had eaten on Saturday morning, but now we were hungrier.

I made black raspberry pancakes and Georgia pecan coffee, and Kavi squeezed some oranges for juice.

Ileandra ate an eighth of a pancake with maple syrup, plus a few berries, and drank a small glass of juice. No coffee.

I caught her looking at my coffee cup and laughed.

So did she.

After dinner, we sat in the gathering darkness.

The cat wondered what was the matter with all of us.

Sitting in silence was odd behavior for us, at least to him.

We sat there, wondering what to say.

Ileandra was really leaving us this time.

"I'm going to miss you," we suddenly said, both at once.

Kavi watched us, surprised and sympathetic.

He didn't say anything.

We wanted him with us, but this was our connection.

273

And it was really going to break tonight.
Ileandra reached out to me.
She was sitting on the sofa about a foot away from me.
I had just moved from my desk chair.
The alien visitor had never reached for me like that before.
She wanted my hand in hers.
I gave it to her.

Telepathic transference was not something that I could have understood from any science fiction book. Yes, I had read about it in story after story, but this was not that.

In this hand-to-hand-touch, I found that Ileandra's was cold. I thought of Mr. Spock's fingertips at they touched people's faces in mind-melds, but her hand wasn't icy.

I realized that I was simply feeling her standard body temperature while she felt mine.

We knew each other's thoughts in full detail.
No more sneaking glimpses of my thoughts.
She was sharing hers with me.
I caught glimpses of the inside of her ship.
I saw the laboratory, and the greenhouse.

It looked like a brightly-lit counter, full of soil, which I now knew contained microbes from Earth, worms, and other decaying matter that fertilized plants. The aliens were very thorough botanists.

I saw her planet.
Her planet scared me.
It was barely green, and mostly beige.
It had some water, but that wasn't healthy, either.
She showed it to me, seen from space, and on the surface.
It was even scarier up close.

It was what would happen to my planet soon, if humans didn't change any of our habits.

But the oceans and other waters were the concern of scientists with other specialties; Ileandra focused on botany.

What the Small Gray Visitor Said

Was I judging it correctly, or was my impression of what she was showing me based upon my own planet's ecosystems, and what was and was not healthy for them?

Both, came the answer.

She thanked me through our link for all of my help.

She really would miss me.

I would miss her.

I felt a twinge of something – guilt, worry – and knew that the alien had overheard from Kavi's call with his parents during the visit from his sister and her family.

Ileandra had worried about me, and been relieved that I missed that. But now, in our link, she could not hide that.

Now I knew what my mother-in-law had said about us not having kids, her wish that Kavi leave me for a younger woman who would reproduce, and my father-in-law's disapproval of his wife's attitude.

But that was not all. I saw that Kavi had sought to shield me from all that.

Suddenly, Kavi was there in our link.

Ileandra had taken his hand, and he had taken my free hand with his other one.

Kavi knew what we knew. He said, through the link, that he didn't want what he was told to want, and never had.

He wanted me.

I loved him for that. I was the same way.

A moment after we had thought that to each other, the transference stopped.

Ileandra had let go of our hands.

But something of the link lingered between me and Kavi.

It was something that helped us to communicate without so many words.

I liked it.

We still had our own thoughts, but we felt each other there, as company in each other's minds.

I wondered how long that would last.

"As long as you want it to," Ileandra said.

Beamed Up at Last

We got into Kavi's car at 1 a.m. and drove off.

As before, we had our face masks tucked into our pockets, and Ileandra kept one ready in her lap.

A full moon lit up the sky.

The aliens were living dangerously to pick her up.

It was the least they could do, I thought. They should take her back – back home, back among them.

We pulled up to the crop field, got out, and waited.

The corn stalks looked the same.

We looked up, and the sky was empty, except for the stars.

"Where are they?" I asked.

"They are waiting for me to walk out into the field."

"We won't leave until we know that they have picked you up. We're not going to leave you stranded, only to have to walk back to our house – which, of course, you must come back to if they don't come."

"They will come this time. Don't worry."

I believed her.

The alien turned toward the corn stalks, and then back.

"Are you sure you don't want to come with me?"

Ileandra felt that she had to offer this unusual human this chance. It was a chance to evade the coming collapse on her home planet, which wouldn't be easy to endure, let alone survive. But it would also mean seeing a collapsed alien world.

Arielle just smiled, and glanced back at Kavi.

"No, thank you. I realize that my planet is going to have collapsed ecosystems, famines, droughts, floods, too-high too-fast temperatures for current species to adapt, and other disasters, but I would rather be home for that, in a familiar place, seeing the changes and being with my family for as long as possible, than to leave and come back later and see the change with a shock." She paused. "Or to never come back."

Ileandra nodded. She understood.

What the Small Gray Visitor Said

After all, she had thought of nothing but getting home all summer, from the moment she had been stranded on Earth up until now, when she could finally leave it and return to her people, her ship, her planet in the Owl Nebula, and all that was familiar to her.

It would be hypocritical to view the matter otherwise.

But she would miss her new friend.

Echoing that sentiment, Arielle was suddenly crying, though not audibly, not in huge sobs, but quietly. Her eyes were tearing, and the tears were running down her face.

"I knew I would miss you when you were finally, really leaving," she said.

Ileandra couldn't help it.

She didn't care that her colleagues, waiting in the ship above them, could see them.

She hugged her friend good-bye.

Kavi and I stood there by the corn stalks, and watched as our visitor walked into them.

In a moment, we couldn't see her.

But we could see the stalks rustling as she moved through the plants, walking out to the center of the field.

The plants stopped moving when she got to the center.

We looked up quickly, and there it was – an alien craft.

It hovered over the field, motionless.

It had abruptly appeared, seeming to have uncloaked, but I knew it had done no such thing. It had phased into our part of the universe, into this exact spot.

There was a flash of light under it, and then it was gone.

No rainbows, no more light from it, nothing.

It was just gone.

So was the feeling that I had had all along, while the little alien visitor was with us, of her presence in my mind.

She was gone.

I felt sad, but only for a moment.

Kavi was here.

We hugged, and then got into the car and drove home.

How Was I Going to Share This Story?!

With Ileandra gone, I was left to wonder what was next.

I mean, how was I going to share this story?!

Telling anyone about it was bound to get me in a straightjacket, carted away by the proverbial whitecoats, unable to ever control my own life again.

That was not going to happen. I had made my mind up about that long ago.

So…what would I do?!

Ileandra had had some really important things to say.

She had had some things to tell humans that we really ought to hear, take seriously, and act upon.

Granted, I was the sort of human who was open-minded enough that she could not only say them to me, but actually have them taken in and taken seriously.

That wouldn't have happened with all of us.

She hadn't been manipulating me, either. We had both had our say about the world.

I thought it over the next morning as I drank coffee, ate breakfast, went through e-mails, news articles, and the rest of my routine.

And I knew what to do.

I would do what I normally did after completing all of those standard tasks.

I would, as planned, write it all down…as fiction.

Doing that would probably get me a lot more readers anyway, without the risk of being committed to anything against my will…such as a mental hospital, or professional mockery.

I created a new folder in the "Arielle's Writings" one on my computer and started it. "What the Small Gray Visitor Said" would be my way of telling the world about my now-absent friend.

After a bit more software set-up, I began the story.

"Something in the night had woken me up…"

What the Small Gray Visitor Said

Acknowledgements

I have several people to thank for help with this story.

One of them is my father, Paul W. Fox, for sharing his knowledge and expertise about road construction projects with me. He explained that a structural reinforcement on a small, steel bridge would take an entire summer, and that an encampment of construction equipment would be set up on a real strip of land right across from the site of the crop field where my alien gets stranded.

Another person who deserves mention is a librarian who probably would not like to be named, so I shall withhold it here. She described something to me in 1992, an incident that took place on New Year's Eve in 1981. She and her sister, returning from a party – absolutely sober, I must add – went up Nod Road in Simsbury, Connecticut, and saw an alien craft hovering over that agricultural field. They stopped the car and stared at it, looked at each other, said, "This is too weird," and drove away immediately.

It was from that short story that the idea grew in my mind for this novel, and for that, I thank them.

I agree with their decision to keep driving.

Meanwhile, I decided to have some fun.

To me, "fun" is research. I found and read everything I could about U.F.O.s and aliens shortly thereafter, and watched movies and documentaries about them.

I decided that it is absurd and arrogant to assume that we humans are alone in our galaxy, let alone in our universe.

Have we in fact been visited? Probably.

I have not personally seen evidence, in the form of a close encounter. I don't want to experience one of the fourth kind, which is abduction. But I will not discount someone else's story of a close encounter. That would be rude.

While in law school, which was the next chapter of my life, I decided to write my thesis on provable outer space data, specifically, human activities in space. The topic was a United

Nations treaty governing orbital debris, which I discuss in this story.

The title of my law thesis, which my professor enjoyed, was *International Toxic Torts Caused by I.F.O.s (Identified Flying Objects)*. He specialized in environmental law, and was teaching a seminar, for which I wrote this paper, in international environmental law.

At graduation, he told my parents that I had convinced him that outer space was part of the ecosystem, and therefore part of environmental law.

That was a great moment for me…and it came a year after I had done that work.

This novel combines provable reality and what is alternately called conspiracy theory and science fiction.

I think that aliens are real, but that is confined to individual perception and opinion.

Therefore, it must be presented as science fiction.

Either way, it is all food for thought.

There is one more acknowledgement that I wish to make: Bagheera is inspired by Phantom, my real-life black cat.

He really does find missing jigsaw puzzle pieces.

About the Author

Stephanie C. Fox, J.D. is a historian, writer, and editor. She is a graduate of William Smith College and of the University of Connecticut School of Law.

She runs an editing service called *QueenBeeEdit*, which caters to politicians, scientists, and others, which can be accessed at https://www.queenbeeedit.com.

Stephanie lives in Connecticut, and has written books about other topics, including Asperger's, the global financial meltdown, honeybee colony collapse disorder, travelogues of a trips to Kuwait and Hawai'i, the effects of human overpopulation on the environment, and cats.

About the Illustrator

William John Studenc is a graduate of Southwestern Community College for Advertising & Graphic Design. His skills include graphic design, print shop engraving, editorial cartoon, video editing, and sound design. His portfolio may be viewed at https://williamstudenc.myportfolio.com/.

William's work focuses on science fiction, ufology, and fantasy art. He lives in North Carolina, where he works as a freelance illustrator.